Praise for Carla Cassidy

"Small towns, dangerous secrets and painful pasts are expertly conveyed in Cassidy's clever hands, speeding readers toward surprising revelations."
—*RT Book Reviews* on *Scene of the Crime: Widow Creek*

"Cassidy crafts sympathetic characters...along with a strong, well-developed plot. A charmingly sweet and ruggedly strong hero is the icing on the cake...."
—*RT Book Reviews* on *Cowboy with a Cause*

"A sweet story filled with strong tension and endless conflict. The intricate plot and strong suspense will keep you turning the pages."
—*RT Book Reviews* on *The Colton Bride*

Praise for Cathy McDavid

"*Her Cowboy's Christmas Wish* was the perfect Christmas gift. Cathy McDavid has done a magnificent job in creating two wounded characters that are so deserving of love's healing balm."
—*Romance Junkie Reviews*

"McDavid's characters are stubborn and entertaining and they have a supporting cast that will leave readers laughing out loud."
—*RT Book Reviews* on *First Homecoming*

Praise for Marin Thomas

"A delight to read. Watching the hero be won over by two rambunctious boys and their intelligent and tenderhearted mother makes for a charming tale."
—*RT Book Reviews* on *Twins Under the Christmas Tree*

"*For the Children*...will have readers laughing out loud and glued to the pages thanks to the author's zany characters. Ms. Thomas manages to keep the romance center stage in this wonderful story...."
—*RT Book Reviews*

CARLA CASSIDY

is a *New York Times* bestselling and award-winning author who has written more than one hundred books for Harlequin. Before settling into her true love— writing—she was a professional cheerleader, an actress and a singer/dancer in a show band.

Carla believes the only thing better than curling up with a good book to read is sitting down at the computer to write her next story. She's looking forward to writing many more books and bringing hours of pleasure to readers. Visit her website at www.carlacassidy.com.

CATHY McDAVID

New York Times bestselling author Cathy McDavid lives in Scottsdale, Arizona, near the breathtaking McDowell Mountains, where hawks fly overhead and mountain lions occasionally come calling. Horses and ranch animals have also been a part of Cathy's life since she moved to Arizona as a child and asked her mother for riding lessons. Little wonder she loves ranch stories and often incorporates her own experiences into her books for Harlequin American Romance. Cathy and her family enjoy spending time at their nearby cabin. Of course, she takes her laptop with her on the chance inspiration strikes. You can visit her website at www.cathymcdavid.com.

MARIN THOMAS

Marin grew up in Janesville, Wisconsin. She left the Midwest to attend college at the University of Arizona in Tucson, where she played basketball for the Lady Wildcats and earned a BA in radio-TV. Following graduation she married her college sweetheart in a five-minute ceremony at the historical Little Chapel of the West in Las Vegas, Nevada. Over the years she and her family have lived in seven different states but now make their home in Arizona. The rugged desert and breathtaking sunsets provide inspiration for Marin's popular cowboy books for Harlequin American Romance. Visit her website at www.marinthomas.com.

A
Mistletoe
CHRISTMAS

New York Times Bestselling Authors
CARLA CASSIDY
and
CATHY McDAVID

MARIN THOMAS

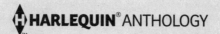 **HARLEQUIN**® ANTHOLOGY

ISBN-13: 978-0-373-83805-9

A Mistletoe Christmas

Copyright © 2014 by Harlequin Books S.A.

Recycling programs for this product may not exist in your area.

The publisher acknowledges the copyright holders of the individual works as follows:

Santa's Mistletoe Mistake
Copyright © 2014 by Carla Bracale

A Merry Little Wedding
Copyright © 2014 by Cathy McDavid

Mistletoe Magic
Copyright © 2014 by Brenda Smith-Beagley

This edition published by arrangement with Harlequin Books S.A.

For questions and comments about the quality of this book, please contact us at CustomerService@Harlequin.com.

® and TM are trademarks of Harlequin Enterprises Limited or its corporate affiliates. Trademarks indicated with ® are registered in the United States Patent and Trademark Office, the Canadian Intellectual Property Office and in other countries.

HARLEQUIN®
www.Harlequin.com

Printed in U.S.A.

CONTENTS

SANTA'S MISTLETOE MISTAKE   7
Carla Cassidy

A MERRY LITTLE WEDDING   105
Cathy McDavid

MISTLETOE MAGIC   217
Marin Thomas

SANTA'S
MISTLETOE MISTAKE

Carla Cassidy

To everyone who believes in the spirit of giving, of children's laughter and open hearts, may you have a magical Christmas filled with miracles!

Happy holidays.

CHAPTER ONE

JAKE HANSON HATED Christmas. Every year he swore that when the holiday approached he'd get on a plane, leap on a train and leave the small town of Mistletoe, Texas, where everyone went just a little more than crazy at Christmas.

The madness started just after Thanksgiving, when colorful lights were strung and the gazebo in the town square was draped with ribbons and candy canes and the ever-present mistletoe.

It was a week before Christmas, and the mistletoe madness had nearly reached its peak as he parked his truck in front of the Mistletoe Café.

He got out of his truck and hurried toward the café door, eager to get out of the cold and get some dinner before heading back to his silent, empty two-story ranch house.

The heavenly scent of warm muffins and hot coffee greeted him, along with the clink of silverware and the laughter of friends dining together, which shot a surprisingly sharp pang of loneliness through him.

"Jake!" Suzie Walker, the red-haired owner of the establishment, met him at the door, a sprig of mistletoe in her hand. She raised her hand as high as it would go, which thankfully didn't reach near the top of his head.

"Are you going to bend down so that we can share

a kiss under the mistletoe?" she asked. Her bright blue eyes sparkled with merriment.

"Not a chance, Suzie. Roger would beat the living heck out of me if he saw me kissing his wife."

She dropped her plump arm down and gave him a look of mock disappointment. "I haven't managed to snag a single kiss because of that big fat old man of mine."

Jake smiled. Roger was a big fat older man, who made a perfect Santa each year for the children of Mistletoe. "How about you snag me a booth so I can get some dinner?" He pulled his Stetson off his head.

Suzie sighed. "Follow me, cowboy."

As she led him toward a booth in the back, he raised his hand and nodded to nearly everyone he passed. He'd grown up with most everyone in the café. The town's total population was only between 1,800 and 2,000 people, small enough that practically everyone knew everyone else. However, at this time of year there were always tourists drifting in and out of town.

As he passed the booth in front of the one Suzie was leading him to, he saw his neighbor, Melody Martin, seated alone. On impulse he stopped at her booth. "Melody, mind if I join you?" He slid into the seat across from her before she could reply. He smiled at her and set his hat next to him. "I hate to eat alone."

"Oh…I… Sure," she stuttered in surprise.

"Well, then," Suzie said, looking at Jake and then at Melody. "I've already taken Melody's order. What can I get for you?" She looked back at Jake.

"Whatever the special is—that should do it," he replied, slightly shocked at his own forwardness now that he was seated across from the first woman who had captured his attention in years.

"Meat loaf, mashed potatoes and a Mistletoe muffin," Suzie replied.

"And coffee," Jake added.

As Suzie left to head to the kitchen, Jake looked across the table and noted the bright red coat and the shopping bags that took up most of the booth beside Melody.

"Where's your daughter?" he asked. He didn't know a lot about Melody, but he knew she was a widow and had a six-year-old daughter.

"She's spending the evening with a friend. It gave me the opportunity to do some Santa shopping for her." She wrapped her hands around a cup that he saw held the famous Mistletoe Toddy, a mulled-cider drink with all kinds of secret ingredients assured to bring happiness.

Bah humbug, he thought. He looked around the busy café and then back at her, feeling slightly ill at ease. "I really didn't give you a chance to say no before I sat down. If you'd prefer that I sit someplace else, I'll move."

"You're fine," she replied with an easy smile that shot a touch of warmth through him. "I was just thinking that it isn't much fun to eat alone. I'm so used to Libby filling every silence."

"How's the dance business going?" he asked as he worked his way out of his leather coat and set it next to his hat beside him.

"Good. We had our Christmas recital last night, so classes are officially finished until after the New Year."

Melody had bought the house nearest his ranch eight months before and had immediately built on a dance studio in the back. According to local gossip, half the kids in town now took lessons from her.

Suzie arrived with his coffee, and after she left, Jake took a drink, wondering what the heck he was doing sitting across from a woman he found ridiculously attractive when he had no intention of ever having any kind of serious relationship with a woman again.

Melody wore a blue sweater that perfectly matched her eyes. She had the elegant features of classic beauty but didn't appear to be wearing any makeup except for a touch of mascara.

"So this is your first Christmas here in Mistletoe," he said as he set his cup back on the table. "What do you think?"

Her blue eyes sparkled as she shoved an errant long dark strand of hair that had escaped the low ponytail behind her shoulders. "I think it's all wonderful. There's such joy in the air, and it's amazing how the whole town comes together to create Mistletoe magic. What about you? Don't you love it?"

"Ms. Christmas…meet the Grinch," he replied.

She raised a perfect dark brow. "Really? You don't like Christmas?"

"A far as I'm concerned, I'd be happy if we all just skipped this holiday."

"But from what I've learned, mistletoe and Christmas is important to the town. It's what made the town, and the mistletoe has become a profitable cottage industry."

The conversation halted as Suzie arrived with their orders. Meat loaf, mashed potatoes and one of the muffins the café was known for, and for Melody, rabbit food—a salad with grilled-chicken strips.

"What brought you and your daughter here?" he asked once they were alone again. "I heard through the grapevine that you were from the Dallas area."

She picked up her fork and smiled once again. She had a beautiful smile, and he felt as if he'd just swallowed a shot of scotch that warmed him from head to toe.

"I've learned that the grapevine is pretty healthy here in Mistletoe."

He grinned. "By morning, everyone will know that you and I had dinner together, and trust me, there will be embellishments."

"At least neither of us is married, so there can't be too much of a scandal," she replied in amusement. "Anyway, to answer your question, it's true we're from Dallas. My husband passed away two years ago, and it wasn't long before I realized Libby and I needed a change, a place to start over. We'd visited Mistletoe a couple of years ago and I decided it was a good place to make a new beginning."

"Have you always been a dancer?" he asked. She looked like a dancer, tall and lithe and graceful, the exact opposite of what he'd always thought to be his type.

"Always. I had a studio in Dallas, so it was only natural that I'd open one here. Not only does it pay the bills, but I love it. Do you dance?"

He laughed, the sound a bit rusty to his ears, making him realize that he couldn't remember the last time he'd laughed out loud. "I can manage a Mistletoe two-step if I'm forced, but that's about it."

For the next few minutes they fell silent as they focused on their meals, and once again Jake found himself questioning the impulse that had made him jump into the seat opposite her.

He hadn't looked twice at a woman for over five years, but the first time he'd encountered his new neighbor, a spark of something had lit inside him.

Lust, he told himself. It had been so long since he'd been with a woman he'd forgotten what lust felt like, and he certainly didn't understand why the dark-haired, blue-eyed beauty across the table from him seemed to stir it up inside him.

"Tell me about your daughter," he said, certain that a discussion about a little girl would squelch any inappropriate thoughts he might entertain.

Again she flashed him that wide, beautiful smile. "Libby is the love of my life. She's bright and giving and makes me laugh. She's also precocious and willful and occasionally throws a temper tantrum when she doesn't get her way."

"Sounds as though you've got your hands full."

"In a good way," she replied easily.

He relaxed a bit. Not only was he not interested in any kind of a long-term relationship with a woman, he especially wasn't interested in kids.

They both turned to look as bursts of laughter came from the front of the café. Suzie had managed to get her mistletoe over the head of old George McKnight, and as the two shared a kiss, the crowd clapped its approval.

"That's a tradition I don't particularly like," he said as he focused his attention back to Melody. "I also don't like New Year's Eve kisses. I think kisses should mean something and should only be shared between people who love each other."

He felt the flames that filled his cheeks. What was

he doing sharing that with a woman who was a virtual stranger? The madness of Mistletoe had obviously made him truly crazy.

"That's a nice sentiment," she replied softly.

"Thanks," he replied, and motioned for a check from Suzie. He felt the sudden need to escape. He needed to get back to his ranch, where there were no Christmas decorations and no mistletoe anywhere in sight.

Suzie arrived at the table with the check, and Jake looked at Melody. "Since I invited myself to your meal, I'd like to buy your dinner."

"That's not necessary," she protested.

"Consider it a Christmas gift," he replied as he stood and grabbed his coat and hat from the booth next to him. With a murmured goodbye, he left the booth and hurried to the cashier. He paid the bill and then put his hat on his head and left the café.

As he drove home, he knew he'd mentally gone around the bend. He hated the tradition of a kiss under a sprig of mistletoe, and yet he couldn't get the vision of Melody Martin in his arms beneath the shiny green leaves with their waxy white berries.

MELODY RELEASED A deep breath as Jake left the table. Once again she curled her hands around her cup of warm Mistletoe Toddy.

The man was sin on legs, she thought. His slightly shaggy dark hair begged for female fingers to thread through it. His eyes were an interesting shade of silvery-gray, and his rugged features came together in a way that radiated both strength and handsomeness.

His pasture came very close to her yard, and she had spent far too much time over the past several months standing at her kitchen sink and watching him ride his fence line.

Long-legged, broad-shouldered and with a slender waist... The man could have been a pinup model in a Cowboy of the Month calendar.

Town gossip had let her know that he was a loner who came in the café often to eat but didn't do much socializing. Not that it mattered to her; the very last thing she'd ever want in her life again was a cowboy.

Been there, done that and had the heartache that would last a lifetime. Her marriage had been a happy one, and at least she had Libby to fill some of the space that had been emptied in her heart when Seth died.

Moving to this little town with its community closeness and aura of joy had been a good decision. Libby was thriving, as was the dance studio, and it was only occasionally after Libby went to bed that the ache of loneliness unexpectedly gripped Melody.

Tonight there would be no time for loneliness. Once Libby was asleep, Melody would creep out to the car to retrieve the gifts she'd bought, and then wrap them and hide them back in the trunk of the car.

There would be no time for loneliness in the next week. There was so much going on in the town, events and fun that she and Libby intended to immerse themselves in. There were sing-alongs and tours of the local mistletoe ranches, a night of caroling and of course a visit with Santa.

She glanced at her watch and realized it was time for her to load her packages into the car and head out to pick up Libby. She took a last drink of the yummy hot toddy and then pulled on her coat, grabbed her shopping bags and hurried toward her car, which was parked in front of Carrie's Christmas Shop.

Within minutes she was on her way to Laura and Jack McKinny's house on Mistletoe Lane. Their daughter, Megan, not only took dance lessons at the studio, but she and Libby had become best friends.

Mistletoe Lane was decked out for the season with bunches of mistletoe hanging from every streetlamp, along with trailing red ribbons. White sparkling lights created a lovely shimmer on the whole street.

Laura greeted her at her front door with a warm hug. "Did you get finished with what you needed?" she asked.

"Santa shopping all done," Melody replied. "I can't thank you enough for keeping Libby busy so I could get out alone."

"No problem. Want to stick around for a cup of coffee?" Laura asked.

"Rain check?" Melody replied. "To be honest, I'm exhausted and ready to get home and settled in."

"Then, next time," Laura replied with a friendly smile. She was one of the first women Melody had made friends with when they'd moved here. Laura was a teacher at the grade school and her husband worked at the bank.

She took a couple of steps down the hallway. "Libby, your mom is here." Girlie groans filled the air.

"That sounds like her 'not so happy to see me' noise," Melody said.

Laura laughed. "They're at that age." She rolled her eyes.

Libby came running up the hall, her long dark pigtails bouncing with each step. "Mom, my princess doll was just about to meet her prince." Blond-haired Megan ran just behind Libby.

"I guess she'll have to wait until another time to meet her prince. It's time for us to head home. Now, what do you say to Ms. Laura and Megan?"

"Thank you for having me over. I had a super time," Libby said. "And maybe Megan can come over real soon and we can play at my house."

"That sounds like a plan," Laura said as she handed Libby her coat.

"Thanks again," Melody said, and then she and Libby headed to their car.

"I had such fun," Libby said as she buckled her seat belt. "We played games and then got out all of Megan's fashion doll stuff. She has a ton of it."

"I'm glad you had a good time. Did you eat dinner?"

"We had mac and cheese and hot dogs. Megan is my best friend ever. We've decided we're going to get married on the same day and we'll buy houses next to each other and our husbands will be best friends, too."

As Libby continued to chatter, Melody found her thoughts drifting back to the unexpected dinner with Jake. Why had he decided to join her?

She hadn't been averse to his company, and he certainly hadn't been hard to look at from across the table, but it seemed out of character from what she'd heard about him.

She had to confess that she'd entertained a silly crush on him since the moment she'd first seen him. But she'd decided when Seth died that there would be no more cowboys in her life. If she ever decided to marry again it would be to a lawyer or a banker who didn't work with horses that could kick them in the head and kill them.

Libby was still talking about her time with Megan when they arrived home. Home was a nice little ranch house with three bedrooms, an airy kitchen and a living room.

She'd used most of Seth's life-insurance money to build the dance studio on the back of the house, knowing that teaching dancing was what she knew and was what would put food on the table and keep the lights on.

There was also a small barn complete with running water and several hay bales that Melody had bought a month ago when Libby had decided she'd like to have rabbits. By the time Melody had bought a cage and the hay, Libby had changed her mind.

It was after seven, and she pointed her daughter toward the bathroom. "Bath time," she said. "And then I'll read you a story before you go to bed."

It had been a long day for both of them, and Melody was hoping to get her daughter to sleep early so she could take a little time to unwind and dance a bit in the studio and wrap the presents she'd bought that day.

With the Santa shopping done, she had nothing to worry about for the rest of the week except enjoying the town activities and immersing herself in the Christmas spirit.

It was close to eight-thirty by the time she finally got Libby into bed. She sat down next to her daughter and pulled the blanket up around her neck, then kissed her strawberry-scented cheek.

Libby slammed her hand against her cheek to keep the kiss there for the remainder of the night. It was a routine that had begun when she was little more than a baby.

It was also a routine that Melody read to Libby each

night before the lights went out. She wanted her daughter to love reading, to know that by reading you could explore all kinds of new worlds.

Although she knew eventually Libby would be asking for electronic readers and computers that played games and whatever, for now Melody was glad that the toys on Libby's Christmas list had been of the nonelectronic type. Time enough for all that later.

When she had finished reading for the night, Libby reached up and placed her palm against Melody's face. "I can't wait for Santa Claus to come," she said drowsily. "He's gonna have a big surprise for you."

"For me?" Melody smiled at her sleepy daughter. "I already have the best present in the world, and that's you."

Libby's hand fell to the bed and she smiled with sleepy secretiveness. "You just wait. I wrote a note to Santa to tell him what we want, but I didn't give it to you to mail. I mailed it all by myself so you wouldn't know the secret."

"Enough talk of Santa and secrets," Melody said. "Now it's time to sleep."

Libby nodded and closed her eyes, and before Melody left the side of her bed, Libby fell asleep.

Whatever Libby had asked Santa for Christmas, she hoped she had it in the trunk of her car, because there was nothing worse than a disappointed six-year-old at Christmas time.

It was just after eleven when she'd wrapped the final present and tucked it back into the trunk of her car. Still wide-awake, she sat down on the sofa and stared at the Christmas tree that had yet to be decorated.

Christmas Eve she and Libby would pull out the ornaments and tinsel, the twinkling lights and the angel to dress the tree. The past two Christmases had been bittersweet, as they'd pulled out ornaments that Seth had bought to make the perfect cowboy Christmas tree.

There were hats and boots, saddles and horses, and each and every one of them reminded both Libby and Melody of what it had been like to be a real, complete family.

Maybe this year she wouldn't use those particular ornaments. Instead they'd string popcorn and use ribbon and mistletoe and make aluminum-foil stars and do an old-fashioned tree.

Why continue reminding themselves of what they'd lost? New beginnings and new decorations, she thought drowsily. The impromptu meal with Jake had been nice, but she would never seriously entertain a relationship with a cowboy again.

Still, as she fell asleep, it wasn't visions of sugar-plums that danced in her head; rather, it was the hot, handsome Jake who invaded her dreams.

CHAPTER TWO

"LIBBY, YOU CAN'T wear your tap shoes to town," Melody told her daughter for the third time.

"But I like the way they sound on the sidewalks," Libby replied.

Melody gathered her coat around her and sat on the sofa. "You have two choices. You can either change your shoes and we'll go to town, or you can keep your tap shoes on and we'll just stay home. It's your decision."

Libby frowned thoughtfully. "I think I'll go change my shoes." She quickly disappeared down the hallway to her bedroom.

Melody had learned long ago that Libby responded best when given the option to make her own decision, and usually Libby made the right decision when faced with choices and consequences.

Melody was looking forward to spending the day wandering in and out of the shops. There was nothing particular she wanted or needed to buy, but if something caught her or Libby's eye she had a little mad money tucked into her purse.

Libby returned, this time wearing a pair of black boots that were perfect for the cold weather and a long day of walking. She pulled on her bright blue coat, and together mother and daughter left the house.

"Do you think it will snow before Christmas?" Libby asked as she looked out the passenger window of the car.

"According to the weatherman, we're supposed to have a white Christmas."

Libby clapped her hands together. "Then on Christmas Day we can make a snowman with a carrot nose and red gumdrops for a mouth and some of my blue sequins for eyes."

Melody laughed. "Sounds like you've put a lot of thought into this snowman."

"Everything is going to be just perfect this Christmas," Libby replied with a smug smile. "You just wait until you see what Santa Claus brings for us, and then we'll both be so happy."

"Then I can't wait," Melody replied lightly, but she couldn't help but wonder what it was her daughter expected to happen when Santa came.

By the time she found a parking place smack-dab in the middle of Main Street, Libby had already moved on to talking about the different stores she wanted to visit.

It was just after ten and already the sidewalks bustled with people. An energy filled the air, the energy of only seven days left until Christmas Day. While most of the people who shared the sidewalks walked with purpose, as if knowing what needed to be bought and determined to get it done, Libby and Melody walked hand in hand and at a slower pace.

"Carrie's Christmas Shop first," Libby said as they approached the store.

Their entry into the store was announced by the tinkle of bells, and the scent of cinnamon and spices filled the shop. "Mmm, it smells good in here," Libby said, and then raced forward to watch a miniature train making its way around the base of a beautifully decorated tree.

"Isn't it cute, Mom?" Libby said. "And the tree is so pretty."

"It is, but remember that I told you that this year we're having an old-fashioned tree? We'll spend Christmas Eve having so much fun decorating it."

"Hi, Melody," Carrie, the proprietor of the store, greeted her. Carrie's thirteen-year-old daughter took dance lessons at Melody's.

"Hey, Carrie. Libby and I decided to do a little window-shopping today, but I have a feeling I'm not going to get out of here without buying whatever it is that smells so wonderful," Melody replied.

"It's probably the cinnamon candles. Don't they smell lovely?"

Melody cast a quick glance at her daughter, who had drifted off to a display of teddy bears. "Remember, Libby, we don't touch."

"I know." Libby shoved her hands in her coat pockets. "I'm just looking."

"She's so cute," Carrie said, and sidled closer to Melody. "I heard a little tidbit of gossip this morning that was very interesting. It had to do with you and Jake Hanson."

Melody felt her cheeks fill with the warmth of a blush. "It was just an impromptu quick dinner at the café. Goodness, news travels fast around here."

Carrie laughed. "Especially when it involves Jake Hanson and any woman. He's been the town hermit since his wife died five years ago."

"Oh, he's a widower?" Melody hadn't heard about him having had a wife.

"Stacy died in a car accident.... It was just around this time of the year." Carrie frowned. "As I remember, it was a bad winter and we had an ice storm. Stacy had come into town to do some last-minute shopping, and on her way home a semitruck scissored in front of her and she hit it."

"How tragic." Melody's heart squeezed tight as she thought about the man she'd shared her meal with the night before. No wonder he'd said he hated Christmas. She would forever hate rodeos because it had been at one of those events that Seth had died. But it was much easier for her to avoid rodeos than for Jake to avoid Christmas, especially in this town.

Melody was almost grateful when the bell over the door tinkled, announcing new shoppers in the shore. She found Libby looking at a tree-topper angel that turned bright colors like the lights on a Vegas casino.

"Isn't she beautiful, Mom?"

Tacky was closer to the word Melody might have used.

"Wait a minute and she'll turn purple. You know how much I love purple."

Melody thought of the angel that had always topped their tree, a beautiful white one whose feathered wings had become rather bedraggled through the years.

"I'll tell you what. How about I buy one of those scented candles for me and for you we'll get this angel to top our tree from now on?"

"Oh, Mom, thank you!" Libby threw her arms around Melody's waist for a quick hug and then grabbed one of the boxed angels and held it tight against her chest.

So they'd have an old-fashioned Christmas tree with a Vegas stripper on the top, Melody thought as she paid for the two items. Definitely new beginnings, she reminded herself.

She and Libby stepped back outside into the bracing December air, and she tried to put out of her mind the handsome face of Jake Hanson, who she now knew had lost at love just as she had.

JAKE HAD NO idea what he was doing, but when he saw the dark-haired woman in the bright red coat with the little girl by her side, he knew he'd come to town specifically for the possibility of running into Melody again.

He'd been chased out of the house by the silence that for a long time had felt comforting, but in the past few months had grown more and more oppressive.

As he'd driven by Melody's house, he hadn't seen her car parked outside, but he hoped to run into her in town. He had enjoyed his dinner with her and discovered a hunger to see her again.

It had surprised him, the desire to spend more time with her. He'd sworn when he lost Stacy that no woman would ever hold any place in his life again. But wanting to spend a little time with somebody and inviting them fully into his life were two very different things, he reminded himself as he hurried to catch up to Melody and her daughter.

"Hey," he said as he touched her on the shoulder.

Both Melody and her daughter turned, Melody's face lighting with a smile and her daughter's face holding distinct suspicion as she eyed him from the tip of his hat to the toes of his boots. "Who are you?" she asked.

"Libby, this is Mr. Hanson. He lives next door to us," Melody said. "Surely you've seen him on his horse in the pasture next to our house before."

"I don't like him. Come on, Mom, let's go." She grabbed Melody's hand and attempted to drag her away.

Melody looked at her daughter in obvious shock. "Libby, you're being very rude. Now, you apologize to Mr. Hanson."

"Sorry," Libby said, but the mutinous pout of her lower lip indicated otherwise.

"Apology accepted, and you can call me Jake, although I have to say that I've never had anyone not like me before they got to know me." He glanced back at Melody. "So where are you two headed?"

"We are doing a little window-shopping," Melody replied.

He gestured to the shopping bags in her hand. "Looks as if the window got the best of you."

She laughed, and for a moment, in the sound of her laughter, he didn't feel the cold wintry air nor notice the other people who passed them on the sidewalk. He was filled with a warmth he hadn't felt in a very long time—the warmth of pleasure in the simple sound of a woman's laughter.

"Where are you headed now?" he asked.

"I'd like to check out the store in the old Victorian house at the end of Main Street," she replied.

"Mistletoe Magic. It's a new age kind of store, but I happen to know that the owner, Finley McCarthy, is selling a magic potion this year just for kids."

"A magic potion?" Suspicion darkened Libby's blue eyes as she looked up at him.

"You sprinkle it on your pillow on Christmas Eve and it's supposed to bring you dreams of all the toys and things you want for Christmas." He'd actually visited the shop the week before when the silence of his life had driven him out of the house.

"Mom, we need to get some of that potion," Libby said.

"It definitely sounds like a must-have for Christmas," Melody agreed.

"Do you mind if I walk with you?" he asked. There he was again, insinuating himself where he probably didn't belong.

"That would be nice," Melody agreed. Libby huffed in obvious disapproval and walked three steps ahead of them as they continued down the sidewalk. "I apologize for Libby's behavior. I've never seen her act out this way."

"Maybe she just doesn't want to share her mother for a little while," he replied easily.

Melody frowned thoughtfully, her gaze remaining on the little girl just ahead of them. "Maybe. In the past couple of years she hasn't had to share my time or attention with anyone other than my dance students, and she knows my time with them is important."

"She's a cute one," he said.

Melody gazed up at him, her blue eyes shining brightly. "She's much cuter when her lower lip isn't stuck out in a pout."

"She's fine," he replied easily as they moved toward the front door of the three-story Victorian home with its shop on the lower level. "Maybe I can find a little magic potion in here that will make little girls like me just a bit."

He opened the door and the three of them entered the shop, which held herbs and crystals and incense and oils. Finley McCarthy greeted them, her long blond hair held back with a beaded headband and half a dozen bracelets jangling on her wrists.

As she took Libby and Melody to show them all the wares she had to offer, he trailed behind them, admiring the shiny length of Melody's hair. It fell in loose waves below her shoulders, making him wonder what those strands might feel like wrapped around his fingers.

The thought nearly caused him to stumble, and at the same time Libby turned around to give him another wary glance. He had a feeling if he intended to spend any time with Melody he would somehow have to find a way to win over the petite miniature next to her.

He frowned again, trying to recall exactly when he had decided he wanted to spend more time with his lovely neighbor. He watched as she and Libby smelled some of the oils and laughed as both of them turned up their noses at one particular scent.

They left the store with the magic potion for Libby. "It's almost noon. Do you ladies have plans for lunch?" he asked.

"Mom and I are going home for lunch," Libby said firmly. "We're going to eat stuff that cowboys don't like."

"Well, then, I guess that leaves me out," he said smoothly before Melody could reprimand Libby again for bad manners. "I have heard that tonight there's going to be some caroling going on at the gazebo. I was thinking it might be fun to hitch a couple of horses to my wagon and fill it full of hay and take a ride back into town for the evening fun."

Libby's eyes widened with more than a hint of interest. "But I doubt you two would be interested in joining me," he added.

"We could be interested," Libby said. "We like horses and hayrides, don't we, Mom? And maybe we could stop and pick up Megan." She looked up at Jake. "She lives on Mistletoe Lane and she's my best friend in the whole wide world."

Jake rocked back on his heels. "It wouldn't seem right to have a hayride without a best friend included."

Libby's eyes narrowed. "Just because I'd like to go ride in your wagon and go on a hayride doesn't mean I like you, Cowboy Jake."

"Libby!" Melody's cheeks reddened in embarrassment to match the color of her coat.

Jake grinned. "That's okay. I think maybe we can have some fun even if you don't like me. Why don't I plan on picking up the two of you about seven?"

"I can't imagine why you would want to be so nice to a little girl who shows such bad behavior," Melody replied. "But I have to admit the idea of a wagon ride into town to listen to people caroling sounds like fun. We'll be ready, and maybe as we eat our girl-food lunch, we'll talk about a little attitude adjustment." She released a sigh that Jake found charming.

"Don't worry about it. I'll see you two at seven, and I'm sure we're going to have a fine time."

"We'll be ready," Melody replied.

As he walked away from the two females, his heart beat faster than it had in a very long time.

Something about Melody stirred a spark of life inside him that he hadn't even known still existed before sitting down across from her at the café the day before.

He couldn't let his heart be vulnerable ever again, but surely there was no harm in just enjoying some time with Melody and her daughter.

If nothing else, maybe their company would help him get through this holiday, which for the past five years had meant nothing more to him than loss and heartache.

He thought about all the things he needed to take care of in order to get the old wagon out and appropriately bedecked for the night's festivities and hurried toward his truck, a foreign excitement flooding his veins as he thought of the night to come.

CHAPTER THREE

A DOZEN TIMES throughout the afternoon, Jake thought about calling Melody to cancel the wagon ride. The first thought came when he viewed the wagon, which had been stored in a shed for the past five years.

It had been Stacy's idea to buy the wagon with the bench seat and slatted sides specifically to chauffeur friends and neighbors into town for the Christmas festivities. He hadn't realized that the sight of it again would bring a pang as he remembered his late wife.

He hitched up two of his strongest horses and pulled the wagon from the shed, and then spent the next two hours cleaning away the dust and cobwebs that clung to it.

He unhooked the horses to let them graze on some hay, as it was far too early to have them ready for the evening ride, then he grabbed a machete and headed for a large stand of evergreens that stood on his property.

Instantly he was surrounded by the sweet scent of pine. It took him two trips to get enough boughs to tie along the sides of the wagon.

Again, he thought of calling Melody and canceling the whole night when he pulled down from the shed a box of huge bright red bows that Stacy had made specifically to decorate the wagon.

He'd loved going to all this work for her, and now he

was doing it for a woman he hardly knew and a little girl who had taken an instant dislike to him. Still, he tied the bows onto the wagon and didn't make a call to cancel.

In the box with the bows, he found several brand-new packages of battery-operated red-and-white lights, and he knew that Stacy had bought them for the wagon just before her death.

Emotion rose in his throat while he strung the lights and tested each string, vaguely surprised that after all this time they worked.

It was nearly five o'clock by the time he had finished the transformation from an old dusty wagon to a vehicle Santa would be proud of. All he had left to do was lay down fresh hay, put bows on the horses' ears and strap a band of jingle bells across their backs.

He ate a dinner of leftover chili, and thoughts of Stacy filled his head. She'd been a Christmas freak, ready to put up a tree by Thanksgiving, and decorating the house with spinning Santas and dancing reindeer and all the tinsel and baubles the furniture would hold. She'd been so filled with life, and when she died, she'd stolen the very life out of him.

He'd gone through all the stages of grief, denial and anger, isolation and depression, but he realized now that at some point over the past year he'd moved quietly into tenuous acceptance.

He would always mourn what he'd lost, but he was also tired of being angry and depressed, and something about Melody Martin had pulled him out of his shell of isolation.

After dinner he showered and dressed in a pair of jeans and a blue flannel shirt, and as an afterthought sprayed on a bit of cologne.

He grabbed his suede coat, knowing the night would be cold, and headed back outside to finish up the final touches to the wagon and the horses.

NERVES JANGLED THROUGH his veins as the time to leave arrived. Crazy, he told himself. It was crazy to be nervous about a simple jaunt down Main Street. It was even crazier to believe that his nerves had to do with Melody sharing the bench seat with him.

At the last minute he grabbed a thick red blanket and tossed it on the bench next to him. He and Melody would get the brunt of the cold as they traveled. Libby would be warmed by the sweet, scented hay that filled the wagon.

The sound of the jingle bells filled the air with a joyous melody, and the lights twinkled along the sides of the wagon as night fell fast. He pulled up in front of Melody's house at precisely seven o'clock.

It was as if she and her daughter had been standing at the door waiting for him. They burst out of the house, and as he saw Libby's face light up with such excitement, such joy, he knew at that moment why he'd gone to all the trouble.

"Oh, Mom, it's beautiful," she exclaimed.

"It is," Melody agreed. Her gaze met Jake's, and he wanted to fall into the warmth that radiated from those beautiful blue eyes. "You shouldn't have gone to such trouble."

"What are the horses named?" Libby asked. She jumped up and down, looking cute in a red coat that matched her mother's.

"Why, Dasher and Dancer, of course," he replied. "I thought your mother might ride up here next to me, and as you can see, the wagon bed has bales of hay for seats and a nice soft bedding of hay to help keep you warm."

Libby walked to the back of the wagon and looked inside. "Perfect," she announced. "Even though I don't like you much, could you help me up?" she asked him.

He tilted his cowboy hat back just a bit to eye her. "I suppose I could if I heard the magic word."

"Please," Libby replied.

She was as light as a feather and as wiggly as a worm as he lifted her into his arms and placed her in the bed of the wagon. She went to the bale of hay directly behind the bench seat.

"I only have one rule," he said once she was settled. "While we're going into town, you have to stay sitting down. Once we get to town and slow down, then you can stand up and hang on to the top of the sides."

"All my friends can stand up when we are in town?" she asked.

"All of your friends? I thought we were only picking up one."

Libby pulled her coat closer around her and eyed him boldly. "I called some of my other friends this afternoon. Since you want me to like you, I thought you wouldn't mind." She blinked long dark lashes innocently.

She was a pip, that one, he thought as he helped Melody up to the bench and then joined her and took the reins. "I should have told you about the other friends earlier, but I didn't know she'd made the calls until ten minutes before you arrived," Melody said.

"It's all right. Maybe this will get me on her good side," he replied with a smile.

"I asked her this afternoon why she didn't like you, but she refused to give me an answer."

"Maybe she'll warm up to me just a little bit after tonight." With the jingle of bells and the lights on the wagon casting out in the darkness, and the scent of Melody's perfume mingling with the fresh smell of pine, a sense of peace stole over him.

"So tell me what you two window-shoppers bought today," he asked.

As she talked about what stores they'd gone in and what they'd bought, he realized he would gladly listen to her if she were reading a cookbook out loud. Her voice held a joy that he had a feeling was her natural state of mind.

Thankfully he wasn't haunted by visions of Stacy at his side. His attention was divided between the road and Melody. Her cheeks had turned pink with the wind and her hair quickly became a windblown mass of silky strands.

When they went over a bump in the road, Melody's laughter mingled with Libby's, and Jake felt a sense of connection, a wave of utter happiness he hadn't felt for a very long time. It was delightful, and it was equally dangerous.

He didn't mind spending some time with his beautiful neighbor and her daughter, but he would never, ever give his heart away again. Been there, done that, and the pain of loss had left him forever incapable of love.

MELODY SNUGGLED BENEATH the red blanket Jake had provided and listened to the magical sound of childish laughter coming from the bed of the wagon.

It seemed that Libby had invited half the town's children to join them in their ride. She marveled at Jake's patience as he stopped by house after house and lifted little bodies into the back.

Seth had been a good man, a good husband, but patience had never been one of his strong suits. She'd often wished he'd display a little more patience to the little girl who had been so enamored of her daddy.

By the time they finally headed down Main Street toward the center square, the back of the wagon was filled with chattering, laughing children.

"Let's make a real entrance," he yelled back to the kids. "How about we all start singing 'Jingle Bells'?" He started them off, his baritone voice sending an unexpected shiver of pleasure up Melody's spine.

She could smell his cologne, a spicy scent that made her want to find the source. Had he splashed it on his shirt, or was it in the hollow of his throat where she could nuzzle her nose?

Something about Jake Hanson made her feel like a giddy teenager with a crush. Conversation had become impossible between them the moment the children had begun to pile up.

Still, she was happy just sitting next to him, watching the play of emotions on his handsome face. Main Street in Mistletoe was filled with shoppers and people lingering around the beautiful gazebo in the center of the square.

A group of people had begun singing carols, their voices adding to what was already for her a festive night. She wondered how Jake would react if she snuggled closer to him.

The thought flew out of her mind as quickly as it had

come. Not only would Jake probably think her forward and inappropriate, Libby would have a hissy fit.

He brought the wagon to a halt in a parking space in front of the center square. "Sit tight," he said to Melody, and then he got down and went to the back of the wagon to unload the children. "There are ten of you here, and when the wagon gets ready to leave again, there'd better be ten of you back here. You're only allowed to go directly to the gazebo. Ms. Melody and I will be there in a few minutes."

He climbed back on the seat as the children all ran toward the gazebo. "We can see them all from here, and I thought if we waited just a bit we'd have a chance to talk."

"I'd like that," she replied. "For a man who hates Christmas, you sure pulled out all the stops tonight."

"The look on Libby's face was worth it. Besides, Christmas is for kids. Adults don't have to like it, we just have to endure it."

"You're wrong, Jake. Christmas is magic, and it's magic for everyone. It's the one time of year people come together and sing about peace on earth, and even the most curmudgeonly of human beings find something to be joyful about."

"Are you calling me a curmudgeon?" he asked, a teasing twinkle in his eyes.

"If the boot fits…" She laughed as he looked outraged.

"Maybe it has fit over the past couple of years," he finally said thoughtfully.

"I heard about your wife. Trust me, I understand the pain." She touched his gloved hand with her own, wishing she could feel the warmth of his skin. "I was lucky.

I had Libby. I had to get past Seth's death so I could be the mother she needed." She pulled her hand from his and looked toward the gazebo. "Maybe we should get out and make our way to the kids," she said, not wanting the conversation to get too deep. It wasn't the time or the place.

"When it comes time to leave it's going to be like herding cattle," he said as he got down and came around to her side of the wagon to help her. He surprised her by grabbing her around the waist and sliding her to the ground.

For a brief moment he held on to her. Despite all their clothing, warmth filtered through her at his nearness. She fought the impulse to lean into him, to have his arms surround her as she closed her eyes and listened to the childish voices singing, "Santa Claus is Coming to Mistletoe."

Instead she stepped back from him, both appalled and intrigued that the man who had just been a neighbor had squeezed a little bit into her heart.

She grabbed his hand and tugged him to run with her. He groaned aloud, but when she caught a glimpse of his face in the twinkling lights that decorated the gazebo, there was a relaxed happiness that only made him more handsome.

The fact that the loner, the self-proclaimed Christmas Grinch smiled as he tightened his grip on her hand assured her that Mistletoe magic was at work…at least for tonight.

It was an evening of laughter and song and visiting with friends. While the kids expended their energy running races around the gazebo and singing, Melody and Jake found an empty bench nearby.

"Stay here. I'll be right back," he said. He returned a few minutes later with two steaming cups of Mistletoe Toddy.

"If you aren't careful, somebody might think you're actually enjoying all this," she said after she thanked him for the drink. She took off her gloves to hold the warm foam cup and noticed that he was also gloveless.

"Actually, I think it's the company I'm keeping that I'm enjoying, not so much the holiday or the silly mistletoe madness."

Her cheeks warmed. "I'm enjoying the company, too," she replied.

For the next hour they drank their toddies and talked about favorite movies, types of music they enjoyed and all the questions that people asked when getting to know each other better.

It felt like a first date, although Melody reminded herself it was nothing of the sort. It wasn't a date at all. It was simply neighbors getting better acquainted.

At nine o'clock they began to round up the children for the trip home. The parents had been promised that their sons and daughters would be delivered back home safely before ten.

The children were quieter when they piled back into the wagon, but their faces glowed with a tired happiness. By the time they pulled up in front of Melody's house, Libby was curled up on a hay bale and sound asleep.

"I'll get her," Jake offered. He climbed into the bed of the wagon and picked up the sleeping child, who immediately wrapped her legs around his waist, but didn't appear to awaken.

Melody hurried to unlock her front door and guided

Jake through the living room and down the hallway to the purple explosion that was Libby's bedroom.

He placed her gently on her bed. "Night, Daddy," she murmured, but it was obvious they were the words of a sleeping child.

Jake left the bedroom and followed Melody back to the front door. "Thank you so much, Jake. It was such a fun night."

"I enjoyed it," he said, his voice holding a touch of surprise.

He took a step toward her, and her heart skipped a beat. Desire glowed from his eyes, a sweet desire that made her think he intended to kiss her. She found her lips parting slightly in anticipation.

He reached out a hand and shoved back a strand of her hair, and then stepped back once again. "Good night, Melody," he said, and walked out the door.

She watched as he climbed back on the wagon seat and with a jingle of bells, finally disappeared into the darkness. She closed and locked her front door and then leaned her back against it.

She closed her eyes at the memory of his scent, of the drowning depths of his gray eyes. She was slightly appalled by the fact that she'd wanted him to kiss her. It had been a long time since she'd hungered for a man's kiss, a man's touch. It was a reminder to her that her grief had passed and the future held all kinds of exciting possibilities.

She didn't know yet if Jake was simply a friendly neighbor or if he might become something more in her life. She would have to wait and see how things progressed between them and if he could possibly win the heart of a little girl, because if he couldn't do that, then he would never be more than a very hot, very nice neighbor.

CHAPTER FOUR

JAKE AWOKE CRANKY, and he had a feeling it was because he felt guilty that he'd enjoyed the night before with Melody and the kids.

He'd rolled over in his big king-size bed, and the first thing he saw in the early dawn light was the picture of Stacy that had been on his nightstand since the day they had married over seven years ago.

Her chocolate-brown eyes appeared to glare at him accusingly, even though he knew he was imagining it. Her short, curly blond hair set off her pixielike features.

The tormenting pain he'd felt for so long whenever he gazed at the picture or allowed himself to dwell on thoughts of what might have been no longer plagued him. But he would always have a wealth of sadness when he thought of her.

He'd promised to love her through eternity, and while he would always have love in his heart for her, he'd never dreamed that he'd want to spend time with another woman—a woman who made him laugh, a woman who made him feel wonderfully alive for the first time in years.

He got out of bed, grateful that he had morning chores that hopefully would keep the thought of all females out of his head. It took him most of the morning to check on his herd of cattle and ride the fence line looking for breaches or other issues.

It was only as he rode the fence nearest Melody's house that visions of her once again filled his head. She'd looked so beautiful the night before with the wintry breeze whipping color into her cheeks and her beautiful eyes sparkling with merriment.

Night, Daddy. Libby's sleepy words had shot a different kind of pain through him.

Jake had been ready for children the minute he and Stacy had finished their wedding ceremony. But Stacy had wanted to wait. If they'd had a child at the time Jake had wanted, he or she would have been about Libby's age.

Maybe if he'd had a child when Stacy had died, he would have pulled himself together more quickly instead of wallowing in grief and isolation for so many years.

By the time he finished his chores and got back into the house, it was lunchtime. He made himself a couple of sandwiches and listened to the news and weather. He frowned as he heard the forecast for a fast-moving winter storm predicted to move in midevening on Christmas Eve.

He couldn't care less about the storm, because he had no intention of participating in whatever festivities the town might have planned for the night, but he'd hate to see the people of Mistletoe disappointed if special events had to be canceled due to weather.

He finished his meal with a cup of coffee in hand as he stood at the window that gave him a view of Melody's house. He sipped the hot brew and realized he didn't want the day to pass without seeing her and Libby again.

Acting strictly on impulse, he set his coffee cup down and pulled his cell phone from his pocket. It took him only minutes to locate the number for Melody's dance studio, and he punched in the number before he might change his mind.

"Melody speaking." Her voice filled the line.

"Jake speaking," he replied, his heart lifting at the mere sound of her voice. "I was wondering if you and Libby would like to join me tonight for dinner at the Mistletoe Mountain Restaurant."

"Oh, that's one of the places Libby and I had on our list of things to do before Christmas, but had decided we'd do it next year because it's rather expensive."

"If you come with me tonight, then you won't have to worry about the expense. You'd both be my guests."

"Jake, it's too much," she began to protest.

"Don't you worry about anything but putting on your pretty clothes and being ready around six," he replied. "Besides, you'd be doing me a favor. That place has the best steaks in the entire state and I'm hungry for one, but you know I don't like to eat alone."

She laughed, obvious of the fact that he'd turned it around so that they would be doing him a favor rather than the other way around. "Okay, then, we'll be ready at six."

What are you doing, man? he asked himself once he had hung up the phone. Mistletoe Mountain Restaurant was located ten miles outside of the town. It was built on a hill that overlooked one of the mistletoe farms and was a favorite for tourists and townspeople celebrating special occasions.

He and Stacy had talked about going there often but had never actually gone. This would be a new experience for him as well as Melody and Libby.

The afternoon crawled by, and he was grateful when it was time to shower and dress for dinner. He exchanged his jeans for a pair of black dress slacks and his flannel shirt for a long-sleeved blue button-up shirt. Splashing on cologne, he then took a little time to polish up his black cowboy boots, and with his hat on his head, he took off for Melody's place.

He tried to ignore the quickened beat of his heart in anticipation of spending another evening with her, but there was no denying that he felt like a schoolboy headed on a date with a popular cheerleader.

Even his palms were slightly damp by the time he pulled up in front of her house. Dusk had fallen, and night wasn't far behind.

Melody's house looked like an homage to gaudy. Not only did colored lights outline her house and end at a huge, bright white star at the peak of the roof, but each window was also framed by flashing purple lights. Jake had a feeling the purple lights were the idea of the little purple-loving princess.

He got out of his Jeep and walked to the front door. When Melody answered his knock, for a moment he couldn't speak as he took in the vision of her in a royal blue dress cinched at her slender waist with a blue-and-black belt. Her legs beneath the flirty skirt appeared to go on forever and ended in a pair of blue high heels.

"Wow," he finally managed to say. "You look absolutely amazing."

"Thank you, sir. And you clean up pretty well yourself."

Libby came down the hallway in a purple velvet dress and with a tiara on her head. "No tiara," Melody said, and held out a purple coat with white furry cuffs to her daughter.

"But you said it was a fancy restaurant, and I want to wear it," Libby protested.

"How about we compromise?" Jake suggested. "You can wear it on the way to the restaurant, and then when we get there you can take it off."

"Fine," Libby said in a tone that belied her acquiescence.

Melody pulled on a black coat and the three of them left the house.

"I made sure to reserve a window table so you and Libby will be able to see the mistletoe farm," Jake said. "They have lots of lights turned on at this time of year so tourists can see the trees."

He glanced in the rearview mirror to see Libby staring at him, so he continued explaining that there weren't mistletoe trees, but that the plant grew on other types of trees. "Mistletoe is like a baby monkey wrapped around a mama or daddy monkey," he said, hoping he was using a description that she would understand.

"I just like mistletoe because everyone in town likes mistletoe," she replied.

She didn't say another word to him or to her mother for the remainder of the drive. Jake found it hard to divide his attention between the road and the beautiful woman next to him.

He thought he'd never tire of looking at her, and it wasn't just because her features were arranged in delicate beauty, but rather because she radiated such warmth, because her eyes held a wonderment and curiosity about everything. He knew instinctively that she was a woman who embraced all that life had to offer.

When they arrived at the restaurant, built to appear like a rustic mountain resort, Libby reluctantly removed her tiara and the three of them headed for the front door.

Melody released a small gasp of pleasure as they stepped into the restaurant. Although the outside had looked like a well-kept sports lodge, the interior was sleek, with intimate tables lit with candlelight and pictures on the walls that turned photos of mistletoe into works of art.

"It's all so beautiful," Melody said softly as they were led to a table by a large window. Jake pulled out her chair for her and then did the same for Libby. When he was seated, the hostess handed him the wine list with the promise of a waitress arriving quickly.

He'd thought Melody couldn't get lovelier, but as he gazed at her with the candlelight dancing in her eyes and on her features, he'd never seen anyone prettier.

"Any particular kind of wine you like?" he asked. He tore his gaze from her and instead looked blankly at the wine list.

"I wouldn't mind a glass of white wine, but I'm certainly no connoisseur. When I buy wine I always buy whatever is on sale."

Jake turned his attention to Libby. "And what would you like to drink?"

Libby frowned thoughtfully. "Do you think they have root beer?"

At that moment the waitress arrived, and Jake ordered white wine for Melody, red for himself and a tall root beer for Libby. The waitress left behind menus, and for the next several minutes they talked about what they all wanted to order.

Once the orders were placed, Jake directed their attention out the window, where bare trees were lit with white lights, and nestled in the boughs were the green balls of mistletoe plants.

"Cool," Libby said. "I always thought mistletoe grew on mistletoe trees."

"It grows on all kinds of trees," Jake replied. "Oaks and elms, even apple trees can host mistletoe plants."

"I like my apples with cinnamon, not mistletoe," Libby replied.

By the time their meals were delivered, the conversation was light and easy. Even Libby was animated as she explained to Jake the difference between a leotard and a tutu.

Jake was both electrified and surprised that having dinner with Melody and Libby felt so natural, so right. About halfway through the meal, he began to have trouble focusing on the tenderness of his steak and instead began to wonder if Melody's kisses would be just as tender. He wondered if her skin was as soft and silky as it appeared in the candlelight. Somehow, some way, she'd lit a fire of desire in him, one that had caught him by surprise.

"Cowboy Jake?"

Libby's impatient voice pulled him from his thoughts. "Yes, Libby?"

"I asked you twice if we could get dessert," she exclaimed, and then smiled at him brightly. "Dessert might make me like you better."

Jake laughed. Whether Libby liked him or not, he

was growing quite fond of the little minx. "There's no way we can end our meal without dessert."

Libby gave him a little smile. "Then I'd like ice cream with chocolate syrup."

They were a merry group when they finally left Mistletoe Mountain behind. Libby chattered like a magpie about the mistletoe farm and the facts that her spaghetti had been the best she'd ever tasted and her ice cream had been topped with just the right amount of chocolate syrup.

Melody was quieter, but cast him warm gazes that heated every inch of his body. If they were a real family they would now go home, tuck their daughter into bed and climb into their own bed and make love.

He tightened his grip around the steering wheel, forcing his thoughts away from the crazy fantasy. They weren't his family, and he had no desire to make them so. He never again wanted anyone close enough to him that he would feel the way he had when he'd lost Stacy.

He could enjoy Libby, he could lust after Melody, but ultimately the very core of his heart was covered with a shield that he'd never allow anyone to pierce again.

"Would you like to come in for some coffee?" Melody asked when they'd arrived back at her house. She was reluctant for the evening with him to end.

"Coffee sounds good," he agreed, and entered the living room where a tall bare fake tree stood in the corner awaiting ornaments and tinsel. "You've decorated everything for Christmas except your tree."

"It's been tradition that we decorate it Christmas Eve especially for Santa's arrival." She turned to her daughter. "Libby, why don't you go get ready for a bath?"

"Okay, and thank you, Cowboy Jake, for the dinner and stuff." She skipped down the hallway.

"I think I'm making a little headway with her," he said as Melody gestured for him to follow her into the kitchen.

Melody moved to the counter with the coffeepot as he sat in one of the chairs at the round oak table. "I've never seen her act the way she does with you with anyone else." She poured water into the coffeemaker and shook her head. "And she won't give me a clue why she doesn't like you, although she's certainly pleasant enough when she's getting her way with you."

She finished with the coffeemaker, and within seconds the scent of fresh brew filled the air. She had just poured their coffee and joined him at the table when Libby came back in the room. She was clad in a pink tutu and had on tap shoes.

"You were supposed to be getting ready for a bath," Melody said.

"I wanted to show Cowboy Jake my pink tutu and show him my two most important dance steps," Libby replied.

Jake raised a dark eyebrow, making him look like a dashing rake from a romance novel. "I definitely think showing me important dance steps is way more important than getting ready for a bath."

Libby beamed him a smile that pleased Melody. She wanted Libby to like Jake as much as she did. And she so liked Jake. Every minute she spent with him only made her more excited for the possibilities of their relationship.

Somehow in the past two days she'd put aside her reluctance to get involved with another cowboy. She'd managed to rationalize to herself that Jake was a wonderful man who just happened to wear a cowboy hat.

"Okay," Libby said, pulling Melody from her thoughts. "This is the step I do when I'm happy. It's just a flap." She executed the two-tone step around the table.

"That sounds like a happy tap," Jake observed, amusement twinkling in his eyes.

"And this is my mad step. It's a flap ball change." Once again she made her way around the table. The tap of her feet definitely sounded angry as she flapped hard and ball changed even harder.

She came to a halt at Jake's side and leaned into him just a bit. "Now you know without me telling you if I'm happy or mad."

"I think that's a good thing to know," Jake replied.

She leaned closer to him, pulled his head down and then cupped her hand around her mouth and whispered in his ear. When she was finished, she stepped back from him.

"I'll keep that in mind," he said to her.

Libby looked back at Melody. "I know, I know. Bath time." She flapped her way out of the kitchen and back down the hallway.

"What was that all about?" Melody asked Jake the moment Libby was gone.

"Ah, a gentlemen never tells secrets," he replied. "All I can say is that it was nothing for you to worry about."

Melody looked at him dubiously. "With that kid I never know what to expect."

"She's an absolute delight."

Melody laughed. "Most of the time that's true, but she can be as hardheaded as a mule at times."

"A trait she picked up from her mother?"

"Perhaps," Melody agreed with another laugh.

"I'm ready," Libby's voice drifted to the kitchen.

Melody stood. "If you'll excuse me for just a minute, I need to set the water temperature for her bath."

"Take as much time as you need," he replied, looking utterly relaxed and as if he belonged at her table.

She hurried down the hallway to the bathroom, where Libby sat naked on the edge of the tub. "Bath and then bed," Melody said as she turned on the faucets. "And what did you whisper to Jake before you left the kitchen?"

Libby yawned and then shrugged. "I just told him he'd better enjoy spending his time with you now 'cause after Santa comes you won't have time for Cowboy Jake anymore."

"And why is that?" Melody put in the drain stopper and felt the flow of water one last time.

"I can't tell you. It's a secret between me and Santa." Libby crossed her arms over her chest, an indication that no matter how hard Melody pressed, Libby wasn't going to give up her Santa secret.

Libby slid down into the filling tub. "Don't overfill, and call me when you're ready for a tuck in," Melody said.

When she returned to the kitchen, Jake was still in place, his long legs sprawled beneath the table and his cup of coffee nearly gone.

"Sorry about that," she said, and went directly to the coffee carafe and refilled his cup. "She told me what she whispered to you." She rejoined him at the table. "I have no idea what she thinks Santa is bringing to me that will take up all my time."

"Maybe one of those yarn kits where you have to

pull little pieces of yarn through holes to make a rug," he said. "Stacy got one of those at her wedding shower. It was to make a little rug of sunflowers to go in front of the kitchen sink. She worked on it for months and finally packed it up in a box half-finished."

"So she was the crafty type?" Melody asked, curious about the woman who had captured his heart.

He smiled softly. "She never met a Popsicle stick she couldn't turn into a birdhouse or a Christmas ornament."

"I admire people who can make something useful out of everyday things," Melody replied. "The closest I get to anything crafty is bedazzling outfits for my little dancers."

"There's room for both talents in this world."

She took a sip of her coffee and drank in the vision of him. She set her mug back down. "And you—what's your talent, Jake Hanson?"

"I raise quality cattle and I can hammer down a fence post fairly fast. I'm not bad at a two-step and I can cook a mean pot of chili. Stacy used to say I gave the foot massage from heaven."

"Don't underestimate the value of a good foot massage. That's a dancer's dream," she replied.

"Now tell me about your dancing. Were you a little tutu-wearing tap dancer when you were Libby's age?" he asked.

"Absolutely. My parents put me in dance classes when I was three, and in that first lesson I fell in love with it."

"Did you ever dance professionally?"

She shook her head. "As much as I loved dancing, it was always in my plans to become a teacher. I wasn't willing to make the kind of sacrifices professional dancers have to make. I wanted marriage and a family. I love dancing, but it isn't the sum of my life."

"I'm glad I didn't have to go all the way to Broadway to meet you," he said.

She smiled, heated by the look in his eyes. "All you had to do was look out your window." Her insides trembled slightly as she thought about how often she'd watched him from her kitchen window.

Had he noticed her when she'd been out in the yard? Had he been drawn to her as she'd been to him? Did he feel the attraction that crackled in the air at this very moment? Or was she the only one feeling a magnetic pull toward him?

"Mom, come tuck me in," Libby yelled from her bedroom.

"And that sounds like my cue to call it a night," Jake said. He got up from the table as she did, and she wanted to protest and tell him that the night was still young.

Instead she walked with him to the front door, pausing as he grabbed his coat and pulled it on. "It was a lovely evening, Jake."

"Yeah, it was," he agreed. His eyes darkened as his gaze lingered on her face, and then on her lips. "Good night, Melody."

He turned and walked out the door.

She blew out a breath of sheer frustration. Why was it every time she anticipated that he was about to kiss her, she saw the backside of him running out her door?

Maybe he didn't feel the sparks. Maybe he really was just a lonely cowboy passing the painful Christmas season with his neighbor and her daughter.

CHAPTER FIVE

JAKE WAS BEGINNING to feel as if he suffered from some sort of mental illness. Last night he'd desperately wanted to kiss Melody, and he'd known by the smolder of her eyes that she'd wanted him to kiss her.

What had held him back? Guilt? Fear? Maybe a little bit of both. His feelings for Melody and Libby had spiraled out of his control in such a brief period of time, and yet he felt as if he'd known Melody for months.

He awoke to the sun shining brightly despite the forecast for a wintry storm in the next forty-eight hours. He was in the process of stacking wood for the fireplace on the front porch when an old red pickup truck pulled into his driveway.

Bill Johnson owned the ranch next to his on the opposite side from Melody. Bill was in his early seventies and a widower like Jake. He occasionally stopped by just to jaw about local happenings, but it had been a while since he'd visited.

"I see you're getting ready for the storm," Bill said when he'd climbed out of the driver seat.

"From what the forecast is saying, it's supposed to move through fairly quickly, but you can't always trust what the weathermen tell you. Coffee?"

"I wouldn't mind a cup if you've got it."

Jake smiled at the older man. "You should know

after all these years that most mornings I've got it." He took off his gloves and motioned for Bob to follow him inside.

Bob sat at the kitchen table and Jake filled two cups with coffee and then joined him. For the next few minutes the two men talked cattle and crops and everything that had to do with ranching.

"Although you wouldn't know it by looking around here, I've heard a little gossip that you're in the Christmas spirit again," Bob said when they'd exhausted the ranch talk.

"I don't know about that. I've just been showing Melody Martin and her daughter around town. It's their first Christmas here in Mistletoe."

Bob lifted his cup to his mouth and eyed Jake over the rim. He took a drink and then lowered his cup. "If I were a good-looking young man like you I'd be doing more than just showing that pretty lady and her cute kid around town."

"Did you come over here to give me a lesson in romance?" Jake asked drily.

"No, but I did come over to remind you that this afternoon is the day I open up my pond area for the annual ice-skating party. As I recall, there was a time when you cut a fine figure on the ice."

"I haven't skated in years." Not since Stacy's death. His skates had been packed away along with all the Christmas decorations they'd owned and stored in boxes in the barn. He'd intended to donate it all to a local charity but had never actually gotten around to it.

"I wasn't thinking so much about you. I thought maybe you'd like to bring Melody and her girl out, enjoy the festivities for the afternoon."

"I'll think about it," Jake replied. He couldn't help but think how much fun Libby would have. Bob always went all out for his yearly skating parties. There were blow-up Santas and giant reindeer, bushes decorated with the ever-present mistletoe and hot cocoa for the children and Mistletoe Toddies for the adults.

"I'd like to see you out there again." Bob took another drink of his coffee. "In fact, you'd be doing me a favor if you come."

"How's that?" Jake asked dubiously.

"You know there are always more kids than adults out there, and I've got my hands full. If you come and bring Melody and her daughter then that makes two more adults and only one more kid." Bob looked at him innocently.

Jake narrowed his eyes as he stared at the man who had brought him meals after Stacy's death, who had sat with him for hours without speaking, just being there as the worst of Jake's pain had peaked.

"Are you trying to do some sort of matchmaking?" Jake asked.

Bob grinned and raised one of his gray eyebrows. "From the gossip I've heard, the match has already been made. I just stopped by to remind you about the skating party this afternoon, that's all." He finished his coffee and stood. "And now I'd better get back to my place. I've still got plenty to do before this wingding happens."

Jake walked with him back outside and to his truck. Bob stopped at the door and turned to look at Jake. "So can I expect you all at my place later?"

Jake shoved his hands into his pockets. "I don't know. I've got a lot to do around here."

Bob stared at him for a long moment. "Don't close

yourself off anymore, Jake. You've grieved long enough. Stacy wouldn't want you to live the rest of your life all alone."

Jake nodded to acknowledge Bob's words. Intellectually he knew that, but emotionally he wasn't sure he was there yet. "Thanks for stopping by, Bob," he finally replied as Bob got back into his truck. "You've been a good neighbor, a good friend."

"That's been easy. You're a good man, Jake. You've just been lost for the past couple of years. I see a new spark in you, and if Melody and her daughter have put it there, then you should grab on to it." Bob started his truck and pulled away.

Jake stared after him until the vehicle disappeared from view. He returned to stacking the firewood next to the front door and tried not to think about Bob's yearly ice-skating party, tried desperately not to think about Melody and Libby.

He'd spent the first couple of years after Stacy's death thinking only of her, and then he'd reached a place where he'd tried desperately not to think of her or any other woman. Now he was fighting Melody and Libby filling his every thought.

Were they baking cookies this morning? Filling their kitchen with the sweet homey scent of sugar and cinnamon? Or had they gone into town to continue to explore the charm of a Christmas-bedecked, mistletoe-laden little town?

At noon he moved to the window that gave him a view of Melody's house, half hoping her car wouldn't be parked in front of the garage, indicating that she was home.

It was there, and before he realized what he was

doing his cell phone was in his hand. She answered on the second ring, her voice warm and with that musical lilt of life.

"Melody, it's me."

"Hi, Jake. I was just thinking about you."

"Oh?" Warmth suffused him. When was the last time any woman had entertained any thoughts of him at all? "Good thoughts, I hope."

"Great thoughts," she replied. "I was thinking about our dinner last night and how much I enjoyed it."

"I enjoyed it, too. Do you and Libby ice-skate?"

"Libby used to skate a little, but it's been a long time. She's probably quite rusty. Why? What's up?"

He told her about the yearly skating event at Bob's pond. "I thought maybe the two of you would enjoy the circus and might be interested in going with me."

"Do you skate?" she asked.

"I used to cut a great figure eight on the ice, but like Libby, I'm probably rusty."

"I don't skate, but we'd love to go, and I'll cheerlead from the sidelines."

Arrangements were made for him to pick them up around three, and when he hung up he headed out to the barn to find his old ice skates.

He didn't think about Stacy as he pulled down box after box of Christmas decorations in the hunt for the skates. He didn't even think about Melody and Libby. He didn't want to dwell in the past any longer, but he was also reluctant to look toward any future.

JAKE PULLED UP in front of the house at precisely three. It had been a busy couple of hours for Melody as she realized Libby's skates were too small, requiring a fast trip into town to get a new pair.

Libby had been slightly disappointed that the sporting-goods store didn't sell purple skates, but her spirit had only been dampened for a few minutes.

She raced ahead of Melody to the car before Jake could even get out of the driver's-side door or Melody could close the door to the house.

"Cowboy Jake, I colored you a picture," Libby said as she slid into the backseat and Melody got into the passenger seat. Libby handed her work of art over the seat to Jake. "And here, I even brought a baggie with two purple butterfly magnets in it so you can hang the picture on your refrigerator. That's where Mom always puts my art stuff."

Jake looked at the coloring of a Christmas tree, a fireplace with a blazing flame and three people. The man figure wore jeans, a shirt and a cowboy hat, the woman had on a red coat and the little girl was clad in purple. Melody had watched her daughter labor over the drawing and had been pleased that she wanted to give it to Jake.

"I'd be proud to hang this on my refrigerator door, Libby. You did such a good job."

Libby beamed with pleasure, and Jake placed the picture and the baggie of magnets in his glove box and then smiled a greeting to Melody.

"I found out that my best friend, Megan, is coming later to the pond party with her parents," Libby said.

"I imagine half the town will be there," he replied. "You both look ready for a little outdoor activity."

Melody had dressed for a cold afternoon with black leggings and a long pink sweater beneath her black coat. Pink gloves adored her hands and pink earmuffs covered her ears. Libby had prepared for a cold day as well, clad in blue jeans, a purple sweater, her coat, a hat and gloves. "I've got on long underwear," she told Jake. "Mom is hoping it will protect my bottom when I fall, but I'm not going to fall, right, Cowboy Jake?"

Jake laughed. "I'm not sure that I'm not going to fall. It's been a long time since I skated. I might do a cowboy slide clear across the pond on my bottom."

LIBBY GIGGLED AND Melody smiled warmly at Jake. It was going to be another wonderful day, and she loved that Libby seemed to be opening herself up to Jake.

As am I, she thought. Despite the shortness of the time they'd known each other, Melody was precariously close to being heart and soul in love with Jake. It both scared her a little bit and excited her a lot.

By the time they reached Bob's ranch, cars were parked not only in front of his house but also in the grassy area next to the house.

"Looks like there's already a crowd here," Melody said.

"Bob's party usually brings out a crowd. The Mistletoe Bakery donates cookies, and the café donates Mistletoe Toddies and hot cocoa," Jake explained.

They got out of his Jeep, and Jake grabbed his skates and a blanket and then pointed toward a pasture gate. "We've got a little walk from here. The pond is just over the hill."

Libby skipped ahead of them, barely containing her excitement, and as she crested the hill ahead of them she stopped and gasped with obvious awe.

"Mom, hurry. You have to see everything," she said as she clapped her hands together and jumped up and down.

Melody reached the top of the hill and her breath caught as she took in the view. The large frozen pond glittered in the afternoon sunshine. Benches were interspersed with barrels that radiated a fire source obviously intended for warmth.

But she knew that what had captured her daughter's excitement was the path lined with candy-cane lights, the huge yard ornaments in the shape of everything Christmas and the reindeer that appeared to dance down the hillside. She guessed that they were constructed of wire forms and then covered with mistletoe.

"Bob has gone plumb Christmas crazy," Jake said as they followed Libby down the candy-cane path. "Last time I was here he only had a couple of those yard blow-ups."

"How long ago has that been?"

She didn't miss the slight darkening of his eyes. "A little over five years ago," he replied.

She realized that this was the first time he'd been here since his wife's death, and the fact that he'd invited them here meant even more than it had before.

She wrapped her arm with his and smiled up at him. "Let's go have some fun."

"That's the plan." He smiled down at her, the darkness in his eyes gone.

They found an empty bench and sat. Immediately Libby and Jake began to put on their skates. When he had on his, he turned to look at her. "And why don't you skate?"

"To be honest, because of my dancing I've always been a little afraid. I feel the same about skiing. The last thing I want is a broken bone that interferes with my livelihood. But I do make a great sideline cheerleader."

By that time Libby had her skates on, but as Jake got up and stepped out on the ice, Libby remained seated next to Melody. "I'm afraid," she said in a small voice. She grabbed hold of Melody's arm. "I haven't skated for a long, long time."

Jake bent down in front of her. "It's kind of like riding a bike, Libby. You never really forget how. It's been a long, long time for me, too."

He stood and took off across the ice, zigging and zagging around colorful-clad children and other adults. He looked amazing, both athletic yet graceful. Melody loved the way he wore his worn jeans tight and topped them with the suede jacket with the white wool lining, which made his shoulders appear even broader.

He made any other man on the pond look a bit smaller and insubstantial, a bit clumsy and so ordinary. Jake was definitely hot on ice.

He skated back to them and then once again squatted down in front of Libby and held out his hand. "Come on, Libby, come skate with me."

She looked at his hand and then gazed up at her mother. Melody remained silent. She didn't want to force Libby to do anything she didn't want to do.

"Libby, you can trust me. As long as you hold my hand I promise you that I won't let you fall," Jake said.

Libby held his gaze for a long moment and then slipped her little hand into his and stood. Melody didn't realize she'd been holding her breath until it released on a sigh of relief.

Her heart expanded as she saw Jake and her daughter venture out onto the ice hand in hand. She'd not only grieved her own loss of Seth as a husband, but also grieved for Libby no longer having a daddy or a strong male presence in her life.

Melody knew the statistics of the failure of young girls to thrive without a positive male role model in their lives, and seeing the happiness on Libby's face as she skated with Jake she was grateful for his presence as a neighbor…as a friend…and she was beginning to hope as something much more.

As Jake and Libby skated, several women who had children taking lessons at her studio stopped by to say hello to Melody. She chatted with people, cuddled under the blanket Jake had provided, and raised her hand to wave at the couple on the ice who held her heart.

After twenty minutes or so, Libby was on the other side of the pond with friends and Jake was skating back toward Melody and the bench. "She's a natural," he said, sitting down next to her. "By the time she met up with her friends, she was pretty much skating without me."

"Thanks for helping her over her stage fright," Melody replied. "Are you warm enough? I'll be glad to share the blanket."

He blew on his bare hands. "Thanks, I'd welcome it. I forgot to bring my gloves."

She moved closer to him and arranged the blanket over the two of them, then grabbed one of his hands and grasped it firmly in her gloved hands. "Silly man to forget your gloves," she said teasingly.

"Smart woman to share the blanket," he replied with a twinkle in his eyes.

She settled against the back of the bench, acutely aware of every place their bodies touched beneath the blanket. Although she hadn't been overly warm before, with his thigh and hip against hers, a flaming heat burned inside her.

He finally pulled his hand from hers and for a few minutes they watched the skaters on the ice. Melody kept an eye on her daughter, who had found Megan, and the two were on the ice together, barely moving around the edges of the pond.

"Tell me about your husband," he said. "I've told you a little about Stacy, but you haven't told me much about the man you were married to."

She gazed at him and then looked back at the skaters. "Seth and I were high school sweethearts. We started going steady in seventh grade and never dated others. I had just graduated from college when my parents were killed in a small plane crash while they were on vacation. Seth was my rock through that horrible time, and after I'd grieved, he asked me to marry him."

"So you were young when you married."

"I suppose in this day and age twenty-two is considered young, but I didn't feel young. I had no desire to sow any wild oats. All I really wanted was to be a wife and eventually a mother and own a dance studio."

"It was a happy marriage?"

She paused a moment before replying, thinking back over her marriage. "Yes, for the most part it was a happy one. We only had one topic that we fought about. Seth was a rodeo cowboy. He rode bulls and broncs. I hated it. He followed the circuit so he was gone a lot and I was always afraid." She shrugged. "And then my worst fear came true. He was at a rodeo riding a bronc and fell. The horse's hooves came down on his head and he died instantly."

"I'm sorry," Jake replied, and the emotion behind

the words let her know he wasn't just saying an empty platitude.

"I tell myself that at least he died loving what he did. Seth lived for those adrenaline-filled moments on the back of a wild beast. I'll always have a special place in my heart for Seth, but life goes on."

For the next few minutes the two of them sat silently, watching the skaters. It was a comfortable silence. Melody was not warmed just by the blanket, but also by the very presence of the man seated next to her and her daughter's laughter drifting across the pond.

She wanted to take this moment and wrap a bright red ribbon around it, top it with a sprig of mistletoe and hold it in her heart. It was a wonderful new memory that she would carry with her from this day forward.

Her gaze lingered on Libby and she frowned. "I'm a little bit worried about this Santa secret thing that Libby has," she said. She turned and looked at Jake. "I've bought her nearly everything she asked for, but I don't have any idea what special gift she's expecting from Santa."

"She hasn't given you any clues?"

"None, and trust me, I've tried to get her to tell me. I just wish I knew so that I could see if I could get it for her. I don't want her to lose her innocent belief and trust in Santa."

"And what is it you want for Christmas, Melody?" Jake asked, his eyes glittering more silver than gray in the twilight of approaching night. She loved the way her name sounded falling from his lips.

She smiled and snuggled a little closer to him. "I already have what I wanted—happiness. Oh, I bought myself a bottle of perfume and a new sweater to wrap and put under the tree so that Libby wouldn't think that Santa forgot me, but all I hoped for this Christmas was peace and happiness, and I've already found that here in Mistletoe."

With you, she wanted to add. She wanted to tell him that he had become part of her happiness equation, but he hadn't even kissed her yet. He might never kiss her the way she wanted him to, she told herself, although she was certain she'd seen desire for her in his eyes more than once.

It was after eight when they finally left the pond and headed back home. Jake was unusually quiet on the way to her house. Melody chalked it up to tiredness. He'd skated several more times throughout the evening and had also helped Bob carry more cookies and drinks from the house to the pond. Libby was quiet as well, obviously happy and exhausted.

They arrived at the house and Melody thanked him for yet another wonderful day. Libby got out of the backseat and ran to the front door to await Melody.

"I'm cooking a big roast and potatoes tomorrow," she said, and unbuckled her seat belt. "Why don't you come to dinner? I'd love to cook a nice meal for you."

"Thanks for the offer," he replied, a distance she'd never seen before in his eyes. "But I've got a lot of chores to take care of around the ranch, so I have to say no."

"Oh, of course." Melody's heart plummeted, both with disappointment and with guilt. "We've been taking up too much of your time."

"By my choice," he said.

Melody opened the car door and stepped out. "The

dinner invitation is a standing one. Just let me know when you're available."

He nodded. She began to walk toward the house but stopped as he rolled down the window and called out her name. "I hope you and Libby have a merry Christmas."

Before she could reply he rolled up the window and drove away. She hurried toward the front porch where Libby waited for her to unlock the door. Her mind whirled with his words…words that indicated he didn't intend to see or talk to them again before Christmas.

She unlocked the front door and Libby ran down the hall to her bedroom to get out of her extra clothes, while Melody closed the door and sank down on the sofa, Jake's parting words still playing in her mind.

She hadn't realized until now that the picture she'd had of Christmas Eve had been the three of them decorating the tree together. In her visions of the holiday, it had been three at the table eating a Christmas Day feast.

It felt as if something had ended before it really had a chance to begin. She felt as if she'd lost something she'd never really had, and she'd forgotten until now what the pain of loss felt like.

CHAPTER SIX

"I'M CALLING TO invite you and Libby to lunch today," Laura McKinny said when she called at ten o'clock the morning after the skating party. "I figured the girls could play for a little while and you and I can enjoy lunch before the snow moves in tomorrow."

"We'd love to come. What can I bring?" Melody welcomed the opportunity to spend some time away from her continuous thoughts of Jake Hanson.

"Nothing. Don't expect anything fancy. I've got homemade chicken-noodle soup and sandwich fixings."

"Sounds perfect to me," Melody replied. With plans made for eleven-thirty, she hung up the phone and told Libby about the lunch date.

"Awesome," Libby exclaimed. "Today if we play dolls again, then it's time for the prince to propose to the princess and then we'll have a wedding."

"Sounds like serious happily ever after," Melody replied.

"It is. I've got to go get my princess doll ready to go." She raced back to her bedroom, where Melody knew she'd sort through her fashion doll items until she found a wedding dress and shoes and everything a princess would need for a magical wedding.

Melody sat at the kitchen table with a fresh cup of

coffee before her and stared out in the distance, where she could see Jake's place.

Had she snuggled a little too close to him last night? Talked too much? Too little? Had the silence that she'd felt was so comfortable actually been uncomfortable for him?

What surprised her most was the pang that shot through her as she tried to figure out what had happened. Was he truly being neighborly, and she had just misread him?

With frustration she got up and moved to the chair that placed her back to the window. She and Libby had had a wonderful time with Jake over the past week, and he'd made the lead up to their first Christmas here in Mistletoe wonderful.

Despite her overwhelming and fast feelings for him, she shouldn't have expected any more from him. But that didn't halt the shard of pain that pierced her heart, letting her know she'd gotten too close, allowed him to get too deep into her heart.

By the time she and Libby left the house to head to Laura's place, Melody had forced thoughts of her neighbor right out of her mind. Besides, it was difficult to concentrate on anything as Libby chattered about the wedding of the holiday between the prince and the princess.

Melody parked in Laura's driveway, and Libby was out of the car with her doll carrying case clutched tight against her chest before Melody could unfasten her seat belt.

Megan greeted them at the front door. She and Libby squealed and exchanged girlfriend hugs and then quickly disappeared down the hallway to Megan's room.

Thankfully, Laura greeted Melody slightly less en-thusiastically. She raised an eyebrow and rolled her eyes. "It's the wedding of the century, don't you know?"

Melody laughed and followed her friend into the kitchen, where the table was set for two and the scent of chicken soup filled the air. "I thought we'd let them play while we enjoyed our lunch, and then I'll feed them and they can pretend chicken-noodle soup and sand-wiches were on the menu at the wedding reception." Laura gestured her into a chair.

"Sounds perfect to me," Melody replied. "I saw you on the ice last night at the pond. You and Jack skate well together."

"Thanks. And I noticed you didn't move your butt from your bench all night." Melody pulled a tray of cold cuts from the refrigerator and placed it and a loaf of bread on the table, then went back to get two bowls of the yummy-scented soup.

"Of course, I don't blame you," she continued, sit-ting across from Melody. "If I had a handsome hunk like Jake cuddled under my blanket, I wouldn't have been inclined to move, either."

"It's not like that," Melody replied as warmth filled her cheeks.

"What do you mean? The two of you looked quite cozy last night, and from what I've heard, the three of you have been spending a lot of time together."

Melody should have known she wouldn't get through this lunch without talking about Jake. She had a feeling she and the handsome cowboy had definitely been fod-der for the local gossip mill for the past several days.

"We had a nice few days together, but that's all there

was to it. After last night I doubt that we'll be hanging out together anymore."

"What happened last night?" Laura asked.

"Nothing. I mean, we had a wonderful time together, but when he took us home I got the feeling that our time together was finished." Melody placed her spoon in her soup, but her appetite had fled.

"And you didn't want it to be finished," Laura said softly.

Melody sighed and looked at her friend with a slow shake of her head. "I've been foolish. I allowed myself to get caught up with him too quickly, too deeply." She released a dry laugh. "I had even started to see him as my forever-after man, the one who would spend the rest of his life with us."

"He looked so happy with you and Libby," Laura said.

"He seemed happy. He actively sought us out. I could have sworn I saw things in his eyes when he looked at me that made me feel as if we were both on the same page."

"Did you sleep together?" Laura asked.

"Heavens no. We didn't even kiss, although there were several times I thought he wanted to kiss me. I wanted him to kiss me. I'm just not sure what happened between us. I thought we were on our way to building something special, and then last night he told me to have a merry Christmas. I knew what he really meant was goodbye."

"I'm sorry, Melody. I thought the three of you looked so happy together last night, and I'd heard that you all had been seen around town together. I had hope that you'd found the man who could be a father for Libby and a loving husband to you. You deserve that, and Jake is a good man who also deserves to have a family."

"I don't think Libby will mind much whether Jake is around or not. Initially she didn't like him, and she was only beginning to really warm up to him."

"Maybe what happened was Jake got scared by his feelings for you and Libby. He's been alone for a long time. Or maybe you're reading too much into his parting words. I mean, with the storm forecast to hit tomorrow, early evening, maybe he figured he wouldn't be able to see you again until after Christmas."

"Maybe," Melody replied, but she didn't believe it. "I invited him to dinner tonight before the storm and he declined. In any case, enough talk about me and my tragic foray into romance. Libby and I are going to have a wonderful Christmas whether Jake is with us or not."

For the next half hour the two ate and talked about the magic of Mistletoe. They laughed about Suzie Walker's attempt to kiss every man who walked into the café and how terrific her husband, Roger, was in playing the role of Santa Claus for the children of the town.

They lowered their voices and talked about gifts they'd bought for their daughters and an ugly Christmas sweater contest that was scheduled to take place later that afternoon at the community center.

"I've never understood the ugly Christmas sweater thing. I mean, if it's ugly, I don't buy it," Laura said.

Melody laughed. "I'm afraid that I'm probably guilty of owning some sweaters that I didn't think were ugly at the time I bought them, but they're definitely gaudy under normal circumstances."

By that time the two girls had drifted into the kitchen, ready for their lunch. The four sat together,

Melody and Laura sipping hot tea while Libby and Megan ate and talked about the wedding that had just taken place in Megan's bedroom.

"It was wonderful," Libby said between bites. "The prince promised to love and take care of the princess and any children she might have for the rest of their lives."

"And then they kissed," Megan said, and the two giggled while Laura rolled her eyes once again. Melody smiled, but she couldn't help but wish she'd shared just a single kiss with Jake.

Now she'd never know what his lips tasted like; she'd never know what might have been. She'd sworn at one time she wouldn't let a cowboy back in her life, and it was ironic that another cowboy had pierced a tiny hole through her heart.

LIBBY'S ARTWORK, WHICH he'd hung on his refrigerator the night before, haunted Jake throughout the day. Morning chores kept him out of the house, but each time he came into the kitchen, the Christmas drawing caught his attention.

He'd realized last night at the skating party that he was in over his head with Melody and Libby, that his heart had gotten far more involved than he'd ever thought possible.

He'd never meant for his time with them to really mean anything. He'd been happy to spend time with them as they enjoyed their first Christmas in Mistletoe.

What he hadn't expected was desire. What he hadn't been prepared for was his heart to have an opening wide enough for both Melody and her daughter to crawl in.

It had scared him. Things had moved too fast, and he'd suddenly become overwhelmed by it all.

Still, when he sat at his table to eat lunch, his attention was once again caught by the picture stuck to his refrigerator door by purple butterflies.

He remembered the moment Libby had slipped her little hand into his to venture out onto the ice, and his heart constricted tight in his chest.

There was a part of him that wanted to be in the picture she'd colored for him. He wanted to be in the room with the blazing fire and the purple-and-pink decorated Christmas tree.

Then there was the part of him that wanted to run and hide from Melody and Libby, a little piece of him that wanted to protect himself from any more pain than he'd already experienced in his life.

As he kept himself busy outside during the afternoon hours, he told himself that he'd done the right thing in turning down her dinner invitation, that it was time to put some distance between himself and the two females who threatened him on an emotional level.

He'd been fine alone for the past five years, and he'd be fine for the next five. When the silence in the house grew too great, when the loneliness became too vast, he could always drive into town and have dinner at the café.

Maybe he'd start inviting Bob over occasionally for dinner, or renew some of his friendships with other people in town. He could run from the loneliness without putting his heart on the line once again.

By the time he sat down for dinner, he'd taken down the drawing and placed it in a kitchen drawer, unable to stand looking at it any longer.

Of course, he'd see Melody and Libby around town, or maybe exchange pleasantries across the fence that separated their properties, but there would be no more dinners together, no more special moments shared, or cuddling together beneath a blanket.

He believed this was the right choice for him, and as much as he hated to admit it, he also believed his decision made him a coward.

CHAPTER SEVEN

IT WAS CHRISTMAS Eve day. Libby and Melody spent much of the morning popping popcorn and stringing it with a needle and thread to make garland for the tree.

Melody was determined not to think about Jake. They'd spent wonderful times together, and although she'd hoped for something more, she was also a realist. She couldn't change the decisions he made.

If what Laura had said the day before about him perhaps being afraid to love again was true, then Melody felt sorry for him.

Clutching grief and fear so tightly would ensure that he would always be alone, and that was just too sad for her to think about.

Libby flapped from the table to the microwave and took out the package of popcorn that had popped a few minutes before. Her tap shoes had made happy sounds since the moment she'd put them on. And this was important to Melody, that Libby have one of the best Christmases of her life.

Knowing a snowstorm was due to hit later in the day, late last night after Libby was asleep Melody had sneaked out of the house to the trunk of her car to retrieve all the presents that would arrive overnight, special delivery from Santa.

She'd taken them to the dance studio and hidden

them in the closet, knowing that Libby would have no reason to go where only costumes hung and spare tap and ballet shoes lived.

After storing the wrapped presents, she'd changed into a leotard and a gauzy blue dance skirt and danced for half an hour. Most nights, she spent time in the studio dancing when Libby was in bed.

"I can't wait," Libby said, and strung another piece of popcorn. "I just can't wait until tomorrow morning. I don't think I'll ever sleep tonight."

"You have to sleep. Santa only comes when children are sleeping and dreaming of sugarplums and mistletoe," Melody replied with a smile at her daughter.

"We have to remember to use the magic potion we bought on my pillow tonight," Libby said. "Then I'll dream of everything Santa is going to bring me." She giggled. "You're going to be so surprised."

Melody looked at her daughter worriedly. "You do know that Santa doesn't always bring every single thing you ask for."

"I know," Libby replied. "But he knows how important this thing is." She threw two pieces of popcorn into her mouth.

"Hey, you're supposed to be stringing them, not eating them," Melody said, and Libby laughed.

Although Melody was concerned about whatever secret Libby believed Santa would bring, she hoped that Libby's disappointment when it didn't show up would be overridden by the presents Melody had bought.

The morning passed quickly, and they finished the popcorn strands and carefully placed them on the floor in front of the Christmas tree. Melody had strung white lights on the tree earlier, but they wouldn't officially decorate until after dark.

They ate lunch, and then Melody brought out several rolls of aluminum foil. "Now we can make beautiful silver stars to go on the tree," Melody said.

"Cool. This was a good idea, to do a tree with stuff we make. Is Cowboy Jake coming over later?"

"No, I'm sure he's got things to do at his own house to prepare for the snow that's supposed to come."

Libby flapped to the window and peered outside. "No snow yet," she said, and then returned to the table, where Melody showed her how to fashion stars from foil wrap.

The two worked on the stars for the next two hours, and then when they decided they had enough, Libby decided to work on construction-paper ornaments.

As she worked at the kitchen table, Melody made a cup of hot tea and found herself standing at the window that gave her a view of Jake's place.

What was he doing? What would he be doing tonight and tomorrow in his house alone while all over town families would share the holidays?

Her heart ached not only for herself, but also for him. She blew on her tea and then took a sip as her gaze went to the dark, gloomy sky overhead. It appeared low and heavy, as if ready to let loose fat snowflakes at any moment. The wind had picked up, coming from the north and portending a frigid night. Thankfully, she was prepared with enough wood stacked by their fireplace to help warm their living room for the next couple of days.

The town had plenty of activities planned both tonight and tomorrow, but she had a feeling no matter how much it snowed the streets and sidewalks would be quickly cleared to accommodate the festivities.

She gazed back at Jake's place one last time, and then moved away from the window. Although things hadn't gone as she'd hoped they would with Jake, she had a lot to be grateful for this year.

She and Libby had truly found their home here in the small town where mistletoe was honored and joy seemed to abound. Her dance business was thriving, as was her daughter, who was now humming "Frosty the Snowman" as she cut out a variety of circles that would become decorations for their tree.

The town had welcomed them as their own. Both she and Libby had forged friendships and moved on from the loss of Seth. It was healthy for them to let go of their grief and to embrace all that life had to offer them.

She was blessed with or without Jake in her life, and although her heart ached with a new loss, she knew that she wouldn't close herself off, refused to be anything but open to whoever might walk into her and Libby's life in the future.

They were seated at the kitchen table for dinner when it began to snow, small little glittery flakes that shimmered in the illumination from their outside Christmas lights.

"Oh, Mom, isn't it beautiful?" Libby exclaimed as she danced in front of the window.

Melody moved to stand just behind her daughter and peered out into the darkness that had fallen unusually early due to the storm. "Breathtaking," she replied. "The storm moved in a little earlier than the weatherman said it would."

She couldn't see Jake's house in the darkness and

with the snow swirling in front of the window. *Let it go,* she told herself.

She patted Libby's shoulder. "How about we finish up our dinner, and then I'll build a fire in the fireplace and we'll decorate our tree for Santa?"

"Okay." Libby hurried back to the table, her face animated with excitement as she chattered about the imminent arrival of Santa and how nice it would be that his sleigh would have a bed of snow to land in.

Melody smiled at her daughter. Maybe Jake was right after all: Christmas was for children, and adults just got through it. She hadn't realized until now that she'd somehow hoped for a Christmas kind of miracle between her and Jake.

But there would be no miracle of love for her this year. Even though she'd felt love in her heart for Jake, even though she had thought his feelings for her were the same, it hadn't been a miracle. It had simply been a mirage.

IT HAD BEEN one of the longest days in Jake's life. He'd puttered around the house for most of the morning, replacing a sticking doorknob on a bedroom door and repairing a faucet in the bathroom that had an irritating drip, anything to keep his mind off his neighbor and her precocious child.

He spent the early afternoon stacking more firewood both inside the house and outside on the porch, and then checked the barn to make sure there was plenty of hay for the horses.

It was after four when he saddled up a horse to head to the pasture, his goal to herd the cattle closer to a shed and a stand of trees where they could shelter through the worst of the weather.

He tried not to glance at his neighbor's place, but his eyes and his brain seemed to have different ideas. Their outside lights were turned on, shining merry illumination across the darkening and gloomy day. The scent of a wood fireplace lingered in the air, and he knew that Melody had probably built a fire.

He focused his attention away from the house that looked so inviting and instead pulled his collar up closer around his neck to ward off the frigid air. Not only did the air hold the fragrance of woodsmoke but also the scent of snow.

The forecast had been for the storm to move in around seven that evening, but it felt as if it was already upon them. He located the herd at the far end of the pasture, quite some distance from the sheltered area where he wanted them.

He'd just started moving them when the first snow began to fall. Tiny crystals quickly covered the shoulders of his coat. He pulled his hat down lower on his forehead as the wind began to blow and visibility became more difficult.

"Come, bossy," he yelled at the cows, his usual term that got them moving. He circled around to the back of the herd, his horse, Hercules, dancing his feet to get the cows surging forward.

He had them almost to the shed area when the wind once again picked up and the icy snow drove straight into his face, stinging his cheeks and frosting his eyebrows.

The snow flew sideways with the treacherous wind, and it didn't take long for Jake to realize the cows would have to be okay where they were. He needed to get out of the elements.

The visibility was now at zero, and his face felt frozen in place. He headed in what he thought was the direction of his barn, and after a few minutes stopped Hercules and gazed around.

The world was white, with no sign of the barn or his house. He realized his sense of direction was gone, and he no longer even knew for sure which way to go.

His face was numb and an inner chill stole through him. He needed to get back to the house…but which way should he go? For the first time in his life as a rancher, he was afraid.

He should have been out here earlier in the day to move the cattle. The moment it had started to snow he should have headed home. Instead of working, he should have sought shelter.

Too late now, he told himself. He needed to get to shelter, both for himself and for Hercules. The horse moved restlessly beneath him, as if eager to move, to at least work up some body heat.

Once again Jake gazed around frantically as he attempted to get his bearings. There, not so very far away, he saw through the storm a shimmer of a star.

Melody's place.

He was far closer to her house than he was to his own. Allowing the star to guide him, he nudged Hercules in that direction.

At least there was a small barn where Hercules could ride out the storm. And heat…there would be heat in Melody's house. He felt more than half-frozen and needed some warmth.

He drew closer and more Christmas lights shone,

outlining her house and the windows. He reached her property and the small barn, grateful to see that it not only held a couple of bales of hay but also a water trough and a faucet to fill it.

Shivering uncontrollably, he made Hercules comfortable. He considered remaining in the barn with the horse for the night, but knew that would be foolish. There was no telling how long the storm would rage, and he needed to get warm before hypothermia set in.

Whether he desired it or not, it looked as though he would be spending Christmas Eve with Melody and Libby.

CHAPTER EIGHT

MELODY AND LIBBY had just finished making sugar cookies for Santa's treat and had moved into the living room to begin decorating the tree when a knock came from her front door.

"Maybe it's Santa bringing my special present a little early," Libby exclaimed as she flapped her tap shoes toward the door.

"Only Santa would be out on a night like this," Melody replied as she walked to the door and pulled it open. "Jake," she gasped.

He stood on the porch as if unable to move. His eyebrows were hidden beneath a cover of ice, his face was pale and his lips held a faint blue hue.

"Get in here." She grabbed him by the arm and pulled him inside, and then quickly closed the door behind him. "What are you doing here?"

"It's a long story," he said. He shivered and took off his snow-covered hat and coat and hung them on the coatrack near the door.

"Come on." Melody once again took him by the hand and pulled him down the hallway to the spare bedroom. "Get out of all of those wet clothes and I'll give you a blanket to wrap around you."

She grabbed a throw stored on a top shelf in the

closet and tossed it on the bed. "Let me know when you have those clothes off and I'll get them into the dryer."

She stepped out of the room and closed the door, wondering what had happened to him. She didn't want to entertain any hope that he'd suddenly realized he was falling in love with her and had forged his way through a blizzard because he couldn't wait another moment to tell her.

He opened the bedroom door, jeans and shirt in hand while the other hand clutched the beige blanket around his chest. He still looked frighteningly cold. "Go lie down on the sofa. I'll be right there," she commanded.

She raced into the laundry room off the kitchen and threw the clothes into the dryer, then poured chicken broth into a cup and popped it into the microwave.

Libby came into the kitchen. "What's he doing here?"

"I guess Santa dropped off an early Christmas gift," Melody said lightly.

"Cowboy Jake is not from Santa and he shouldn't be here," Libby said. To Melody's surprise, she stomped out of the room and into the living room.

Melody grabbed the warm broth from the microwave and hurried after her daughter, afraid that Libby might tap-dance on his head.

Jake was on the sofa with the blanket pulled up to his chin. He took the cup of broth she offered and between sips told her that he'd gotten lost in the storm and only the star on top of her house had saved him.

Libby stood in front of him, her arms crossed over her chest as she stared at him. "All I can say is it's gonna get crowded in here after Santa comes." Her tap shoes made unhappy sounds as she walked to the tree.

"And we were going to decorate our tree before you showed up."

"I'd love to watch you decorate your tree," he replied.

"Are you warm enough?" Melody asked worriedly. At least some of his natural color had returned to his face.

"I'm fine. Thanks." He handed her the now-empty cup. "I hope you don't mind that I put my horse in your barn. I'll probably owe you a bale of hay."

"Nonsense. You don't owe me anything," she replied and took the cup back into the kitchen, oddly disappointed that he was here only because he'd gotten lost in the snowstorm.

She returned to the living room and tuned the television to a station that was playing all Christmas music. She'd like to just go about her evening plans with Libby, but it was difficult to ignore him when he half sat up and the blanket fell to expose his broad bare shoulders and his magnificent chest.

She moved to the window and peered outside. "You'll be here for the night," she said. "It looks like a blizzard out there."

"Mom...the tree," Libby said with a touch of impatience.

Melody turned and smiled. "Yes, it's time for us to make our beautiful tree."

They began by stringing the popcorn strands around the tree, Melody acutely conscious of Jake's dark gaze following her every movement. There was also the problem of his wide expanse of bare chest, which kept her more than a little distracted from the task at hand.

By the time they had strung the popcorn garland and

had begun to hang the construction-paper ornaments Libby had made, the dryer buzzed.

Melody excused herself and hurried to the machine, hoping his clothes were dry enough to put back on. The thought of a near-naked Jake on her sofa spun all kinds of ridiculous fantasies in her mind.

Thankfully, the clothes were ready and by the time he redressed in the bedroom and returned to the living room, Melody and Libby were hanging aluminum-foil stars.

"Libby, if you want to hang them up high, then I could lift you up," he offered.

"Okay," she agreed with a happy smile, her earlier bad mood when he'd first shown up at the door apparently forgotten. "And maybe you could reach to put the new angel on the very top."

"I think I could manage that," he agreed.

Melody's heart squeezed with emotion as she watched Jake pick up her daughter and help her place the stars in the upper branches of the tree. She'd envisioned this picture in her mind, but in her fantasy he'd been here with them because he wanted to be, not because he had been stranded there.

Still, he appeared to be making the best of a bad situation, and she intended to do the same. No matter what the circumstances were, he was a guest in her home.

Once he had placed the angel atop the tree, they all stepped back. Melody placed her hand on the switch that would turn on both the twinkling little white lights and the colorful angel on top.

Libby giggled when Jake insisted they all do a countdown to the lighting event. They counted backward from five, and when they got to one, Melody flipped the switch.

"Oh," Libby said breathlessly as the tree lit up the dark corner and the angel on top turned green, and then pink and then purple. "It's so beautiful." She raced to Melody and hugged her around the waist. Then, to Melody's surprise, she ran to Jake.

"Cowboy Jake, isn't it the most wonderful tree ever?" She threw her arms around his waist. "Thank you for helping."

Jake appeared stunned by Libby's affectionate behavior.

"How about cookies and milk before bedtime?" Melody said in an effort to rescue him. It worked. Libby immediately released him and tap-danced her way to the kitchen.

Melody hurried after her daughter and Jake trailed behind. Within minutes the three of them were at the kitchen table with four saucers of cookies and four glasses of milk set out.

"This one is for Santa," Libby explained as she pointed to the extra plate. "He loves Mom's sugar cookies."

"I can understand why," Jake replied, and popped the last of a cookie into his mouth. For the next thirty minutes he entertained them with memories of Christmases from his youth.

Melody knew he was exaggerating facts and throwing in fiction for Libby's benefit, who giggled again and again at his outrageous stories.

It all would have been perfect had he chosen to be here with them instead of being forced by circumstances out of his control. She'd dreamed of him being here for

Christmas, sharing laughter and building on the foundation of a relationship she'd believed was magical.

By eight-thirty, Melody announced bedtime for Libby and reminded her daughter that the faster she fell asleep, the more quickly Santa would arrive.

When Libby was clad in her pajamas, she returned to the kitchen to announce she was ready for her tuck-in. "You can tuck me in, too, Cowboy Jake."

The three of them returned to Libby's room. Before she climbed into bed, she got the can of magic potion they'd bought from the Mistletoe Magic store and liberally sprayed her pillow.

She got into bed, and Melody leaned down and kissed her on the forehead. "Sweet dreams, Libby," she said, then stepped back and watched as Jake approached the bed.

He leaned over and tucked the blanket around Libby's shoulders. "Good night, princess."

"You could kiss me on the cheek," Libby said to him.

Jake leaned over and gave her a gentle kiss. Libby instantly slammed her hand over the place he'd kissed. "This is how I keep good kisses," she explained.

Jake straightened, cleared his throat and left the bedroom.

"I can't wait for morning to come," Libby said. "But I feel bad for Cowboy Jake 'cause after Santa comes you won't have any more time for him."

"I think Cowboy Jake has more important things to do than spend any more time with us," Melody replied, and tried to shove aside her heartache. "He's just here now because he got lost in the snow and saw our big star. Now close those peepers and get to sleep and dream of all the magic and wonder of Santa."

Libby dutifully closed her eyes, and Melody left the bedroom, dreading the next hour or so before she could gracefully escape to her own bedroom.

Jake had returned to the table and remained silent as she cleaned up their cookie dishes and glasses. She looked at him in surprise as she saw one Santa cookie missing, the second cookie on the plate with a distinct bite taken out of it and half the milk gone.

He shrugged sheepishly. "I just figured I'd make sure she knew Santa enjoyed his treat.

She nodded, silently cursing the man for being everything she wanted and yet knowing she obviously wasn't what he wanted. "I'll make up the spare bedroom for you," she said.

"That's not necessary. I can just bunk on the sofa for the night."

"Are you sure? I have a nice guest bedroom," she replied.

"The couch is fine. I can keep the fire burning through the night so that Santa is nice and warm when he arrives."

"I need to get out the presents that Santa brought and put them under the tree." They were so formal with each other, and she welcomed the distance as a shield against any emotions that might stir once again inside her for him.

He got up from the table and moved to the window. "I think it's stopped snowing. I should be able to get back home first thing in the morning." He turned to look at her. "Need help with those presents?"

"Sure," she agreed. With two of them they should manage to get all the presents in a couple of trips. By herself it would take much longer to empty out the closet in the studio.

She led him through the kitchen and into the large room where she made her living. She flipped on a light, illuminating the large expanse of wooden dance floor, the mirrored walls with the ballet bars and, hanging from the center light, a long red ribbon with sprigs of mistletoe tied to the end.

Her students had loved the mistletoe accent, although there had been no kisses shared beneath it. Instead if students found themselves standing beneath the mistletoe, they had to perform an impromptu dance to entertain the other students. It had been fun for the students and a tradition she had decided to continue each year.

Jake followed her to the closet and she began to load him down with gaily wrapped presents. Once his arms were filled, she filled her own. They went back to the living room and carefully arranged the gifts beneath the tree.

It took them two trips to and from the closet to finish up. Everything was ready for Libby's Christmas morning. Santa's snack had been consumed, the gifts were under the tree, and although she had a feeling the special gift Libby was expecting wasn't under the tree, she hoped her daughter would be thrilled with all the other presents.

"I think I'm going to call it a night," she said. "Libby will be up early and she'll be exploding with energy. I'll just get you a pillow for the sofa if you're sure you don't want to sleep in the spare room."

"A pillow would be great," he replied.

She went into the spare bedroom and grabbed a pillow from the bed. She hugged it to her chest for a long moment, feeling like a heartbroken child who had just been told there was no Santa Claus.

A solemn distance radiated from Jake, reminding her that there would be no happily ever after for them.

She'd believed she'd found the man who would complete her family, fulfill her dreams, but Mistletoe magic had fooled her.

FROM THE MOMENT he had shown up on her doorstep, it was as if he'd stepped into Libby's drawing. The fire had blazed, the air had smelled of cinnamon and spice and he'd somehow felt as if he'd finally come home.

The desire to belong here had been a physical ache inside him while they'd decorated the tree, shared cookies and milk and finally kissed Libby good-night on her sweet little cheek.

He'd felt Melody's loving concern as she'd pulled him off the porch, placed him beneath the blanket and given him the broth to warm him. He'd watched her interaction with her daughter and his heart had grown even warmer.

Now he tossed and turned on the sofa, fighting what he knew to be true. The only light in the room was the flames from the fire that burned, not enough illumination to keep him from sleep. Only the burn of his heart and his racing thoughts kept sleep at bay.

He finally sat up on the edge of the sofa, and that was when he heard the faint music drifting softly in the air. He didn't recognize the instrumental but knew it was coming from the dance studio.

Quiet as a mouse, he crept through the kitchen and paused at the studio door. The lights in the room were dim, but Melody was like a bright beacon, dancing with obvious emotion.

Dressed in a short gauzy blue skirt and a loose-fitting tank, she moved on ballet shoes as if floating just above the surface of the floor.

Jake's breath caught in his throat at her graceful beauty. She leaped, she turned, and her movements were liquid and flowing from step to step.

She turned and gasped as she saw him. "Sorry." Her cheeks dusted with obvious embarrassment. "Is the music too loud?"

"No, it's just right." He stepped out on the dance floor, wanting more than anything to take her into his arms. "Actually, I was wondering if I could have the next dance?"

He didn't give her a chance to deny him. He took her in his arms in a traditional dance position and began to move them across the floor.

Her body was warm and she smelled like heaven, but her eyes were wary as she gazed up at him. "I thought you only danced the two-step," she said.

"I found myself inspired by watching you," he replied, tightening his arm around her waist. "You dance beautifully."

Once again the wariness was back in her eyes. "What are you doing, Jake?"

He spun her beneath the mistletoe and stopped moving, his gaze drinking in her loveliness. "I'm giving up the battle with fear," he confessed. "You scare me, Melody. You scare me because I'm in love with you."

She caught her breath and froze in his arms, her gaze searching his features. "Say it again," she whispered.

"I'm in love with you, Melody, and I want to belong with you and Libby. I want you both to be in my life forever."

"Oh, Jake, I want the same thing. I'm in love with you and I want you in our lives forever and always."

His heart filled with all the emotions he'd tried so hard to keep in check. "You know we're standing under the mistletoe."

"I also know that you don't believe in the tradition, that for you kisses are supposed to mean something," she replied, her lips tormenting him with need.

"Trust me, this means something," he said just before he lowered his mouth to hers. She tasted just as he'd always imagined she would—sweet and hot, giving and filled with love that washed over him, rushed through him and nearly stole his breath away.

His blood heated through his veins with the desire to take more from her, to give more to her, but reluctantly he broke the kiss, knowing now was not the time or place to make love to her.

Her eyes were misty as she once again gazed up at him. "Don't ever be afraid, Jake. I knew Mistletoe would be a magical place for me, and I know in my heart that fate and a shining star brought us together for a reason, and that reason is love."

"I thought I was dead inside, but you and Libby breathed life back into me, filled the past week with a joy I'd forgotten existed in the world." He stroked a hand down the length of her hair. "I want you to be mine, and I want to be yours and I want Libby to be ours. I want it all, Melody, everything you'll give to me."

She stepped back from him, her features lit with the joy that had first drawn him to her. "Everything, Jake. You have my everything, but not tonight. We need to get some sleep, and we'll have lots of time going forward."

It was the most difficult thing he'd ever done to return to the sofa for the rest of the night, but he knew she was right. They could build on what they had, and for the first time in years, he couldn't wait for his future.

He awakened the next morning to the scent of fresh coffee, soft Christmas music playing through the house and the tree in the corner already lit.

Sounds from the kitchen got him up and off the sofa. He found Melody there putting a turkey into the oven. She looked like a young, sexy Mrs. Claus in her red robe with a furry white collar.

As she closed the oven door, he stepped behind her and wrapped her in his arms. She turned to face him, her features glowing with happiness. "I thought last night in the studio was a dream," she said.

"It was the beginning of the Mistletoe magic we're going to share for years to come."

She smiled. "I thought you didn't believe in Mistletoe magic."

"I met a beautiful woman and a sassy little girl who stole my heart and made me a true believer." He kissed her on the cheek and then released her. "You've already been busy this morning."

He poured himself a cup of coffee, and she did the same and joined him at the table. "I like to have things ready for the day before Libby wakes up, which should be any time now. Once she's up, it's impossible to focus on anything but her and Santa."

"I'm sorry both you and Libby have nothing under the tree from me."

"You gave me the best gift I could have gotten last night, and Libby will be so overwhelmed she won't care. Besides, Santa didn't drop off anything for you here, either."

He reached across the table and she stretched her hand out to meet his. "I'm sorry, Melody. I'm sorry that I got scared, that I dropped you off here after the skating party and pretended that you meant nothing to me."

She squeezed his hand. "All's well that ends well."

At that moment the sound of flying tap shoes came down the hallway. Libby slid to a halt in the kitchen. "Come on, it's Santa time!"

She waited for them to get up, and then the three of them walked into the living room, where Libby danced and clapped her hands at all the presents that awaited her. She looked as cute as a bug wearing a pair of Christmas pajamas that were red and had white, dancing reindeer all over them.

As Melody gestured Jake to the sofa next to her, Libby looked around the room as if expecting to see something. She walked to the window and peered out. She frowned, but only for a moment, and then returned to the tree and sat down for the gift opening.

The first gift was a hit. She exclaimed in excitement as she opened a box containing a purple tutu. She promptly pulled it on over her pajamas and then continued with other gifts.

Each present brought a new squeal of joy and another trip to the window to look outside. Melody exchanged a worried glance with Jake each time Libby peered outside.

Finally all the gifts had been opened. "I love everything that Santa brought me," Libby said, even as her lower lip began to tremble. "But he didn't bring my special present and it was the most important of all."

"What was it, honey?" Melody asked.

"It was supposed to be the man who'd be my forever

daddy, and I think he brought stupid Cowboy Jake instead." She whirled on her heels, sobbing as she ran for her bedroom.

"I need to go talk to her," Melody said, and hurried down the hallway. When she'd disappeared into Libby's room, Jake got up and crept down the hallway and stood just outside the door.

He knew he was eavesdropping on a private conversation, but it was a conversation that could potentially complicate his future with Melody and Libby.

"Libby, honey, talk to me," Melody said.

"Santa was supposed to bring us a prince, not a cowboy. Santa made a big, stupid mistake. Daddy was a cowboy and he died. I don't want to love another cowboy and just have him die."

Libby's sobs shot pain for the little girl through Jake's heart and brought clarity to her reluctance to accept him.

He quietly crept back down the hallway and into the kitchen, wondering if this was really going to be a happily ever after or not.

CHAPTER NINE

MELODY PULLED HER daughter into her arms as she continued to cry, knowing that a coherent conversation would be impossible until Libby was finished crying and ready to listen.

She stroked her daughter's hair, grieving over the fact that she hadn't recognized Libby's feelings toward "Cowboy Jake," that she hadn't realized that Libby equated Seth's death with the fact that he'd been a cowboy.

The sobs slowly halted, but still Libby clung to her mother, her face buried in the crook of Melody's neck. "I thought a prince would be nice for you to marry and to be my daddy," she finally said.

"A prince might be nice, but I think Jake might be better," Melody said, unsurprised when Libby stiffened in her arms. "Libby, your daddy wasn't just an ordinary cowboy, he was a rodeo cowboy. He did dangerous things that Jake would never do."

Libby raised her head and looked at Melody. "So maybe Santa didn't make a mistake after all?"

Melody smiled. "I think Santa brought a snowstorm and Jake got lost in it. Then he saw the star on top of our house and followed it to be here with us for Christmas. I don't know about you, but I don't think Santa makes mistakes."

Libby sat up and looked at Melody for a long moment. "Cowboy Jake won't ride wild horses and bulls?"

"Never," Melody replied. "And maybe you should just call him Jake instead of Cowboy Jake. Libby, he's a really nice man who cares about us a lot, and he just happens to wear a cowboy hat and boots."

Libby tilted her head, her gaze quizzical. "Do you think he could love me like a real daddy?"

"Could you love him as a real daddy?" Melody asked.

"I think maybe I already do, but I've been scared," Libby replied. "I didn't want to love another cowboy who would die on us."

"Sometimes you just have to open your heart and not be afraid."

Libby scrambled off her mother's lap. "I gotta go talk to him. I called him a stupid cowboy and maybe he doesn't like me anymore."

Melody followed her daughter out of the bedroom. They found Jake seated in the living room with an aluminum-foil crown on his head. In that moment Melody knew he was the man she would love forever.

JAKE FELT RIDICULOUS, but he would go to any lengths to win the heart of the little girl he wanted as part of his life. Melody and Libby stopped short at the sight of him, Melody's gaze filled with love and Libby staring at him as if he'd grown a horn out of the center of his forehead.

He'd had a speech all prepared in hopes of winning Libby over with the idea that he could be the prince of a father she'd asked for from Santa.

Before a word fell from his mouth, Libby began to giggle. "You look like a total dork," she exclaimed.

He reached up and pulled the makeshift crown from his head. "I was supposed to look like a prince."

Libby sidled up next to him where he sat on the edge of the sofa and leaned into him. "I'm sorry I called you a stupid cowboy."

"That's okay. I know you didn't mean it."

She leaned closer against him, bringing with her the sweet scents of innocence, of strawberry shampoo and the hint of a burgeoning trust. "Do you think you'd make a good daddy?"

"I don't know a lot about being a daddy. I've never been one before. But I'm a fast learner, and all I need you to do is to teach me."

Melody sat down on the opposite side of him as Libby crawled up in his lap. "Do you love my mom?" she asked.

"Very much," he replied, and felt the warmth of Melody as she leaned closer against him.

Libby placed her palms on either side of his face. "Silly man, then it's easy to be a dad. All you have to do is love me."

She kissed him on his cheek and then slapped her palm against it. "That's to keep my kiss there," she explained.

A rush of emotion buoyed up in his chest, and tears of happiness misted in his eyes. "I already do love you, Libby."

"That's good, because I was scared before, but now I can tell you that I love you, too." She hugged him around the neck and then climbed off his lap. "And now I'm going to do a happy Christmas dance for you and Mom."

Jake's chest felt as if it might explode with joy when

Melody's hand found his. He watched as a purple-tutu-and-pajama-clad dancer kicked away the remnants of wrapping paper to make room for her dance.

Libby began to make joyful noises with her tap shoes, and Melody's hand tightened around his. As the angel on top of the tree turned from green to purple, Jake saw a vision of Stacy's face. She was smiling down on him with happiness and approval.

While he knew the vision was only in his mind, it was confirmation that he was where he belonged, in a home filled with joy and love and the magic of Christmas and Mistletoe.

* * * * *

A MERRY LITTLE WEDDING

Cathy McDavid

To Kathleen Scheibling, editor extraordinaire.
Thank you for always being in my corner
and for opening so very many doors for me.

CHAPTER ONE

EMMA STURLACKY APPROACHED the gazebo in the center of town square, feeling as though she'd entered a storybook Christmas village. Six years away and nothing had changed. With each step she took, the sense of déjà vu increased until the chilly air became too thick to breathe.

Her gaze traveled the length of Main Street, each image almost identical to the many in her memory. Multicolored lights illuminated storefront windows. Wreaths adorned every door. A gaily decorated Christmas tree, easily twelve feet tall, had been erected on the lawn in front of the utility company offices. Various versions of Santa and his sleigh with eight tiny reindeer sat atop roofs. Rows of candy canes lined the sidewalks.

And, of course, sprigs of mistletoe hung in all the doorways, arches and entryways and even from the street signs, including the one pointing to the North Pole. No one could fault the people of Mistletoe, Texas, for not doing right by their favorite holiday.

The only thing missing was soft, glittery flakes falling from the sky. Not for long, however. According to the weather report Emma had listened to on her car radio, snow was in the forecast. The town would soon be a winter wonderland. With luck, the storm would hold off until after her mother's Christmas Eve wedding five days from now.

She'd delayed this trip home as long as possible. Her duties as maid of honor required her to stay in Mistletoe for at least a week. Much longer than her typical semiannual hit-and-miss visits when she holed up in her mother's house for twenty-four hours at most, then sneaked out either at nightfall or the crack of dawn. Emma much preferred it when her mother visited her, wherever Emma might be living at the moment. These days, it was outside Austin. Next month? Who knew?

"Oh, sweet heaven! Is that you, Emma Sturlacky?"

The loud, scratchy voice could belong to only one person. Mrs. Merrick.

Emma was immediately enveloped in a fierce hug and the familiar scent of evergreen. Served her right for not paying attention. Despite her low profile in recent years and her change of hairstyle, someone was bound to recognize her.

"Mrs. Merrick. Good to see you." The greeting was literally squeezed out of her as the older woman compressed Emma's lungs to half their normal size. The gift she'd tucked beneath her arm took a beating.

"You were always so polite." Mrs. Merrick finally released Emma, only to pat her cheek as if she were a child and not twenty-seven. "I think it's long past time you called me Karen. Don't you?"

"All right…Karen." The name sounded odd on Emma's lips. It wasn't the only thing. This whole returning to her former hometown in order to attend a wedding had left Emma off balance. She fought the urge to run back to her car and tear out of town, tires squealing.

"Too bad you didn't get here earlier." Mrs. Merrick—

Karen—made an exaggerated sad face. "You missed the pageant last week."

"Oh, darn. Maybe next year." *Not likely.*

In addition to owning and operating the area's largest mistletoe farm with her husband, Mrs. Merrick directed the town's annual holiday pageant—a source of great personal pride and joy for her. As children, Emma and her brother, Cole, had participated. In Cole's case, against his will.

"Are you heading for the bridal shower?" Mrs. Merrick asked.

"On my way now." Emma forced a smile.

Any talk of weddings, especially in Mistletoe, never failed to make Emma uncomfortable. Sooner or later, someone was bound to bring up Emma's own thwarted nuptials.

"Why in the world did you park here?" Mrs. Merrick glared at the nearby pubic parking lot as if it had committed an unforgivable offense. "The library closed this afternoon for your mother's shower. You could have parked there."

"I wanted to leave spaces available for the guests."

And buy herself another ten minutes, the amount of time it took to walk from the town square to the library where her mother worked as head librarian. Now that Emma had run into Mrs. Merrick, she realized the error in her thinking. Out in the open like this, she was a moving target. Within an hour, the whole of Mistletoe would learn she'd returned, including Nick Hayes. The man she'd quite literally left at the altar.

"You do know we're supplying the floral arrangements at the church and for the reception." The fuzzy tassel atop Mrs. Merrick's stocking cap bobbled as she talked.

"Mom mentioned it."

"I still remember when you worked for us."

"Best job I ever had." Emma gave credit where credit was due. She'd learned a lot from the older woman during her four years as a clerk, then assistant manager, in the Merricks' farm store.

"My goodness! Whatever is wrong with me?" Mrs. Merrick pressed a mittened hand to her throat. "We have an opening. Office manager. You'd be perfect."

Emma was indeed looking for a new job. Wasn't she always? Returning to Mistletoe, however? Not an option. "Thanks, but I like my current job."

"Aw. Too bad." Another sad face. "Well, I won't hold you up."

"Take care."

Mrs. Merrick's attention was suddenly diverted to a place behind Emma, and a huge grin blossomed on her face. "Seems to me your escort has arrived."

"Escort?" Emma glanced over her shoulder.

Amazing, really, how her heart could just stop like that. Literally freeze inside her chest.

Nick Hayes stood not ten feet away, staring at her with an expression like granite. She remembered a time when he'd looked at her with love and devotion. All that had changed when she'd called off their wedding.

"What are you doing here?" she blurted, immediately regretting her outburst. Mrs. Merrick had yet to leave, which meant every second of this awkward reunion was going to be noted and relayed. Emma infused lightness into her tone. "I wasn't expecting you."

He kept his reply succinct. "Your mom sent me."

Oh, those eyes. Still the same vivid blue. Still the same ability to turn the bones in her knees to mush.

Be strong, she told herself.

"Did she think I was going to bail?"

His brows rose. "The idea occurred to her."

Ow! The dig hit its intended mark. And was completely uncalled for. She might have left him at the altar, but he'd given her a heck of a reason.

Emma straightened her spine. "I assure you, I'm on my way to the shower right this second." She held out the squashed gift as proof, then faced Mrs. Merrick. "Nice seeing you again."

"It won't be the last time." She patted Emma's cheek again.

Right. Decorations. The church and reception.

A moment later, Emma and Nick were alone. Unlike before, she was suddenly in a huge hurry to reach the library.

"You don't have to escort me. I promise not to flee."

Without saying a word, he fell into step beside her. Fine, they didn't have to talk. In fact, she preferred they exchange as few words as possible. But five minutes into the walk, the silence was killing her.

"Why did my mother send *you* to find me?"

"I was handy."

"Because she's marrying your boss?"

"Something like that."

"I heard you were promoted to livestock foreman." And that he and his boss were close.

"Two years ago."

"Belated congratulations."

She was glad for him. Truly. Nick loved his job at the Yule Tide Ranch. They'd met soon after he was hired on as a cowhand. He'd been twenty-two. She, twenty-one and three days. It had been love at first sight, if there was such a thing. Emma had believed it. Then. Nowadays, she blamed her head-over-heels fall on youthful hormones.

And his incredible good looks, which he still possessed. The two-day scruff on his strong, square jaw and his wavy black hair in need of a trim only enhanced his appeal. His tan Stetson was pulled low on his brow, and the Carhartt jacket he wore smelled of ranch and outdoors. A very attractive and potent combination.

Emma had always been drawn to working men. Wait, who was she kidding? She'd only ever been drawn to *one* working man, and he was right beside her.

"Don't you usually work during the day?" she asked.

"I'm off this afternoon."

"To hunt me down and make sure I attend the shower?"

"Among other reasons."

As they passed a four-foot Santa outside the Four Seasons Real Estate Office, the statue came suddenly to life. Waving an arm, it sang out, "Ho, ho, ho. Merry Christmas."

Startled, Emma jerked and bumped into Nick. He grabbed her arm to steady her.

"Sorry," she muttered. "I should have expected that."

He didn't let go.

"I'm okay, Nick." She raised her gaze to his. Big mistake. Looking away was impossible.

"You sure?"

No. She wasn't sure of anything anymore, except that coming home to Mistletoe might be the worst mistake she'd made in a long while.

"Yes. Thank you."

He released her, and not a moment too soon. Next door to the real estate office was the library. Only a wide circular courtyard separated them from the main entrance. The next second, the door flew open. Gladys Givens, her mother's best friend and another bridesmaid, appeared on the stoop.

"There she is!" Gladys waved. "Hurry up, you two."

Despite the fact that Gladys's invitation had included Nick, Emma didn't expect him to accompany her across the courtyard and up the steps. But he did. At the entrance, Gladys gave Emma a hug of equal proportions to the one from Mrs. Merrick.

"Here." She snatched the gift from Emma. "I'll take that."

"I guess this is goodbye," Emma said to Nick the second Gladys scurried away.

"Not yet." His hand holding open the heavy door, he gestured her inside. "I'm going to the shower."

"Seriously?" She gaped at him before pivoting on her booted heel and marching through the door.

This could not be happening. Nick escorting her to the shower was bad enough. Now he was insisting on following her into the library—the same place where their ill-fated romance had begun.

NICK STOOD OFF to the side, leaning against a bookshelf. The home and gardening section, to be exact. The study area in the center of the three-room building had been cleared and the table and chairs arranged for Candy Sturlacky's bridal shower.

As head librarian and Mistletoe's unofficial expert on both the town *and* the plant, Candy had a lot of friends. Nick among them. He'd always liked Emma's mother. She had been especially kind to him after Emma's departure.

That was how Candy referred to her daughter's abandoning Nick at the church an hour before their wedding and then leaving town two days later. A *departure*. As if softening the word would soften the blow. It hadn't.

He swirled the fruit punch in his plastic cup, watched the blob of green sherbet dissolve, then took a healthy swig. A beer would go down a lot better. Maybe later. His glance inadvertently connected with Emma's, who sat next to her mother amid a veritable mountain of gifts.

Same large, soulful brown eyes he remembered. Different hair—eight inches shorter and blonder. From what he could tell, she didn't smile much anymore. A shame, really.

Their staring contest continued for several more seconds. She looked away first.

Man up, he told himself, and guzzled the rest of the punch. He'd anticipated this day for the past two months, ever since his boss had announced he'd be marrying Emma's mother on Christmas Eve. Nick had thought he was ready to see Emma again. That he was prepared.

A stupid miscalculation on his part. The jolt he'd received when he'd first seen her standing by the gazebo had knocked him harder than any kick to the gut by a flying hoof. Kind of like when he'd first met her. Only then, he'd been hit by an entirely different feeling. One that had had him walking on air.

Nick crushed the empty plastic cup in his fist, then stared at it. How could he still be so angry after all these

years? It was asinine. He was made of stronger stuff.
So she'd dumped him. It happened to guys all the time.
Hadn't he picked himself up by the bootstraps? Gone on
to become one of Mistletoe's most eligible bachelors? At
least, that was what the Valentine feature in last Febru-
ary's edition of the *Mistletoe Herald* had dubbed him.

The article had garnered him a ton of dates. None of
the woman had interested him enough to see them past
a third date. Par for the course. His current relationship record, post-Emma, was a whopping four months.

So besides being one of the town's most eligible
bachelors, he was also the town's most notorious se-
rial dater. He didn't like the term, but he supposed if
the shoe fit…

A chorus of high-pitched laughter erupted, bouncing off the walls of the small room. The women were
playing some sort of game having to do with how well
the bride and groom knew each other. The answers
were apparently hilarious, and everyone was in stitches.
Well, not everyone.

Emma would rather be doing anything else, judging
by the fake smile she wore. Same for Holly, the groom's
youngest daughter. Then again, she'd made no secret of
the fact that she didn't approve of her father's upcom-
ing marriage.

"Quite a hen party." Leonard had sauntered over
while Nick was preoccupied. The older man wore a grin
so bright, it might have leaped off his face.

"They're having fun."

"I'll say." Leonard had eyes only for his bride-to-be.
"Isn't she just the prettiest thing?"

"You're a lucky man."

"Who knew when I went to that cookout last summer I'd meet the love of my life? And to think I almost didn't go."

With a population of around two thousand, Mistletoe wasn't so small that everyone knew everybody. Leonard's and Candy's paths hadn't really crossed until the day of the cookout. When they did cross, however, it was magic. Kind of like when Nick and Emma had first met.

He'd been looking for a book on auto mechanics—the ancient piece of junk he'd driven had broken down again. She'd been studying for an online college class in business administration. Rather than leave with his book, he'd sat down at the table across from her.

Was she also remembering? Nick cursed himself for even wondering.

"It means a lot to me, you being here." Leonard reached over and clamped a beefy hand on Nick's shoulder. "I know it can't be easy."

"Piece of cake. Speaking of which, I hear they're serving red velvet."

"Don't change the subject," Leonard admonished. "You and Emma have a history. If you feel the need to cut out, don't be—"

"I'm not cutting out. Today or any day."

Leonard wasn't just Nick's boss or even his friend. He also wasn't just Nick's mentor or role model. He was the man who'd replaced the father Nick had lost in a senseless hit-and-run accident when he was fifteen. And Nick knew he was the son this father of two grown women never had.

"Good. Glad to hear it." Leonard's brilliant grin was replaced with a fond smile.

The next hour dragged, but Nick toughed it out, aided

by a second helping of red-velvet cake. In place of the mountain of wrapped gifts, there was now an assortment of housewares, picture frames, linens and a few articles of rather sexy lingerie that had Leonard guffawing and Candy blushing. One by one, guests were starting to leave.

Nick supposed he could go, too, and no one would think anything of it. He'd put in an appearance. Even hung around for a while. Instead he stayed, telling himself he was keeping Leonard company. Right. Then why was he constantly seeking out Emma?

Deciding to make himself useful, he took out the trash and helped return the tables and chairs to their original positions.

"Can you carry these to the car for me?" Candy asked. Without waiting for an answer, she passed Nick an unwieldy stack of presents.

"Sure." He grabbed his jacket on the way out.

Too late, he realized he should have refused Candy's request. Emma stood at the rear of her mother's sedan, loading more presents into the trunk. It occurred to Nick he'd been set up.

She didn't notice him, not right away. She was busy trying to cram a too-big box into a too-small space. The silly little paper veil she wore—they'd been distributed to all the women as part of some activity—sat crookedly on her short blond hair. The bulky cardigan she wore had slid off one shoulder, and the tails of the long belt hung at her sides. Somehow, she still managed to look cute.

"Here." He set his stack on the ground. "Let me."

She retreated a step, either to give him room to maneuver or to put some distance between them.

"Leonard seems nice." She observed him closely as he filled the trunk with the remaining presents. Did she not trust him?

Dumb question. Not trusting him was the reason for her *departure*.

"He's a great guy," Nick said. "None better."

"They haven't known each other long."

Quick to the point. He hadn't expected that from her. He could get to the point, too.

"Sometimes it doesn't take long."

"You're talking about us."

"I'm talking about them."

"We were also getting married six months after we met."

"Don't make this about you, Emma. It's your mother's wedding. Be happy for her. She and Leonard aren't like us."

Her eyes widened, then narrowed. "Meaning he's been completely honest with her from the start?"

Nick supposed he deserved that. Nonetheless, he couldn't keep the bite from his voice. "Let's just try to get along for their sakes, okay?"

"No problem." She swiped her hands together as if done with an unpleasant task, then tugged her sweater into place. "The good news is, we won't have to see each other until the wedding. I'm assuming you'll be there."

"I'll be there. And at the Walk of Lights tomorrow night. Also the rehearsal and rehearsal dinner. Leonard asked me to pick your brother up at the airport." He sent her a pointed look. "You can't avoid me that easily."

Frowning, she drew back. "Why in the world would you do all that?"

Candy Sturlacky materialized beside them, her eyes

aglow with happiness. Putting one arm around Emma and the other around Nick, she gushed, "Because he's one of Leonard's groomsmen. Isn't that wonderful?"

Emma made a low, strangled sound.

Nick chuckled. He was half enjoying this.

CHAPTER TWO

"SORRY FOR PUTTING you on the spot yesterday. I was afraid if I told you about Nick being a groomsman, you wouldn't be my maid of honor."

"Of course I'd be your maid of honor." Emma chewed on a thumbnail and studied the passing scenery through the passenger-side window.

They were on their way to the Yule Tide Ranch for lunch. Afterward, they'd tackle the ginormous list of tasks her mother carried around with her and constantly consulted. There was a lot to be done at the ranch house, readying it for the reception.

Their morning had been spent at her mother's, packing and organizing. Emma noticed a number of things were missing. Pictures from the wall. Her mother's favorite chair. The cedar chest from the foot of her bed. Half the clothes and shoes in her closet.

Emma suspected her mother was already staying at the ranch with Leonard and had been for some weeks. Not that it mattered to her.

"I was speaking to Karen Merrick this morning. We decided on gold-and-silver ribbons for the centerpieces rather than red plaid." After a pause, her mother added, "You didn't tell me you ran into her yesterday."

"With all the excitement of the shower, I forgot."

"She said she offered you a position."

"Mom," Emma warned.

"Won't you at least think about it?"

"I'm not moving back to Mistletoe."

"Why? It's been six years. You're over it. Nick's over it."

"I like Austin."

"You hate Austin. And you're looking for another job."

"I am not."

"Don't lie, Emma. Karen told me she's getting reference calls again."

That would teach Emma to list Mrs. Merrick on her résumé. "I'm just putting out feelers."

"You're always putting out feelers. How many jobs have you had since you left here? Four, by my count. In two different cities."

"I'm searching for my niche."

"You had your niche. When you lived here and worked part-time for the Merricks."

Her mother tapped the brakes as they left the pavement for the bumpy dirt road leading to the outskirts of town. Tall trees dotted the rolling landscape, lush in summer but barren now in winter. With no grass to graze on, cattle gathered around bales of alfalfa left out by the ranchers. Such a stark contrast to the town, with its myriad holiday decorations, quaint, crowded storefronts and country charm.

Up ahead, after the bend, they would take the left fork. Emma could navigate the way to the Yule Tide Ranch in her sleep. She must have driven there a hundred times to see Nick when they were dating.

Would he be there now? Probably. Would she do her best to avoid him? Absolutely.

"I just want you to be happy," her mother continued, giving Emma a tender smile.

"I am." At least, she wasn't unhappy. That counted, didn't it? "Tell me about Holly," Emma said. She didn't want to argue with her mother. Not about moving home and not days before the wedding. "What's with her?"

Her mother sighed. "She's not entirely in favor of Leonard and me."

"She doesn't like you?" Emma was aghast. Everyone adored her mother.

"What can I say? Leonard's first wife died a couple years ago. Cancer. Holly thinks it's too soon for him to date, much less marry. That no one can replace her mother."

"You're not trying, are you? To replace her mother?"

"Not at all. I would like to be her friend, if she'd let me."

"She doesn't strike me as the friendly type." Emma thought her soon-to-be stepsister had all the personality of a crybaby.

"I asked her to be a bridesmaid."

"I take it she refused."

Emma's mother shrugged one shoulder. "I'm hoping she'll warm up to me eventually. It might be easier if she didn't live at the ranch. So many memories of her mother."

"Wow. She still lives at home? Isn't she around thirty?" Holly had been a senior in high school when Emma was a freshman. Their paths had seldom crossed.

"Leonard could hardly ask her to move. Besides, she manages the ranch office. Pretty good at her job, I'm told."

Emma didn't envy her mother. She had her work cut

out for her with Holly. "What about his other daughter? Megan, isn't it?"

"Oh, my gosh! She's an absolute doll. Lives in town. Married, with two of the cutest kids you ever saw. They're going to be our ring bearer and flower girl."

"Do you think if you and Leonard postponed the wedding, Holly would be more receptive?"

"Possibly, but we're not waiting." Her mother let out a bright laugh. "At our age, we need to make hay while the sun shines. Besides, we're in love."

In love. Right. Emma had said those exact same words once about Nick. Felt the exact same way. She'd loved him to the point of distraction. And because of that, they'd rushed headlong to the altar after a mere six months of dating. How different things might have gone if they'd waited. Even a few months.

She turned her car onto the long drive leading to the sprawling ranch house. Like everything else in town, it hadn't changed a bit. A small herd of horses ran along the pasture fence parallel to the car, their tails arched and heads held high. Leonard obviously still raised the finest quarter horses in the area.

Parking behind a shiny black pickup truck, they unpacked the car. Emma took charge of the portable ice chest containing their contribution to the meal: macaroni salad, homemade sugar cookies and the Sturlacky-special-recipe eggnog.

"Hi, we're here!" Emma's mother entered the house without knocking.

Emma thought that interesting but refrained from commenting.

"There's my bride," Leonard's booming voice called

to them from the kitchen. "Get in here and give your man a kiss."

Emma's mother sparkled like a string of shiny new Christmas lights as she hurried across the spacious living room with its leather couches and striking Western decor. Emma followed her into the large and comfortable eat-in kitchen. In the center of a table that easily accommodated eight sat a huge bowl of tortilla chips and guacamole. Emma's weakness. Her mother must have told Leonard.

She'd barely set the cooler on the counter when her mother propelled her across room. "Emma is so excited to be here today."

"Been a long time." Leonard swept her up in a bear hug. "I didn't have a chance to tell you yesterday how pretty you are."

"Thank you for having me over, Mr. O'Donnell," Emma said once he released her.

"Call me Leonard. And you're welcome anytime. You're family now."

At that moment, the back door flew open, and Nick stepped inside, bringing a gust of cold air with him. His glance went straight to Emma. Without breaking eye contact, he removed his jacket and cowboy hat, hanging both on the back of a chair. Going to the sink, he washed his hands.

"Can I help with anything?" he asked Leonard.

"Got it under control. Hope you're hungry."

"Always."

Nick's easy conversation with his boss and familiarity with the kitchen's layout gave Emma reason to think he frequently ate with the family. That was new.

Back when they'd dated and he was just a cowhand, he'd rarely set foot inside the house.

"Hey, Nick." Leonard's daughter Holly appeared and sauntered past Emma to where her father stood at the counter, loading a mountain of French-dip sandwiches onto a serving platter. "Daddy." She kissed his cheek, then inspected the sandwiches. "Yum."

"How's my girl?"

"Tired." She expelled a long breath. "The office was crazy this morning, phone ringing off the hook. I was lucky to get away for lunch." Only then did she acknowledge Emma and her mother. "Hi, Candy. Emma." If her smile grew any tighter, it would snap in two.

"Don't you look nice today, Holly." Emma's mother busied herself helping Leonard with the meal. She, too, exhibited a familiarity with the kitchen's layout, reinforcing Emma's belief that her mother spent a lot of time here. Emma, feeling awkward and useless, waited by the cooler, arms crossed over her chest.

Nick plunked down at the table and dug into the chips and dip. Swallowing a large bite, he glanced around the room. "Was I supposed to wait?"

"It's all right." Emma's mother set the macaroni salad on the table and patted his shoulder. "You go right ahead. You've been working hard this morning. Too," she added, her glance including Holly.

"How's the roundup coming?" Leonard delivered the sandwiches to the table, along with a soup tureen of beef broth.

"Sections twelve through fourteen are clear."

"Nick and the hands are moving cattle from the leased grazing ranges to the home pastures." Emma's mother began pouring eggnog into cups. "In preparation for the blizzard."

That had to be quite a task. If Emma's memory served, the Yule Tide ran about twenty thousand head.

Deciding to pick her seat while there were plenty of empty ones to choose from, she sat kitty-corner from Nick. Not too close and not in his direct line of vision. Holly also sat. Right next to him. Interesting. Perhaps they were friends. They did work together.

The smallest flicker of displeasure crossed Nick's face before vanishing. If Emma wasn't so familiar with his expressions, she might not have noticed. Even more interesting.

The meal progressed quickly, if not always comfortably. Leonard doted on her mother, touching her hand or arm with affection and singing her praises. Her mother reciprocated.

It was sweet, really, and Emma was glad for her mother. She'd been single since Emma was ten. The divorce had been amicable, and Emma enjoyed a close relationship with her father, who'd moved to Dallas fourteen years ago and married a nice lady. It was past time her mother found someone.

Leonard did seem to care for her. Emma, however, couldn't dispel her doubts. Her mother and Leonard hadn't known each other long. It was always wonderful in the beginning. But that phase didn't last, as Emma knew firsthand. Reality, when it came crashing down, was a bitch.

Leonard smiled at Emma's mother. "So what are you girls up to this afternoon?"

"Back to the office," Holly said. "I have a ton of papers to push."

"What about you and Emma?"

"We're working on getting the house ready for the reception." Emma's mother displayed not the tiniest reaction to Holly answering a question intended for her, though she must have noticed. "The Elks Club is delivering the rental chairs and tables."

Part of Emma's prewedding duties, and the reason she arrived early, was to help prepare the ranch house for the event.

"Give me a shout if you need a hand," Leonard offered.

"We'll be fine. You go ahead and ride out with Nick."

"If you're sure."

She patted his cheek. "You know you want to."

He chuckled and covered her hand with his big, burly one.

"What time are we meeting for the Walk of Lights tonight?" Nick had polished off an impressive two sandwiches and two heaping servings of macaroni salad.

"Seven." Emma's mother rose and retrieved a covered tray from the cooler. "Dessert, anyone?"

Holly selected a cookie decorated to resemble a wreath. "It must be weird for you two, being in the wedding together." She stared pointedly at Emma as she broke the cookie in half. "How long ago was it you left our Nick at the altar?"

Emma tensed.

"Six years," Nick said, answering for them both. "And we're over it."

"Really?" Holly arched her brows. "Because I think having your bride walk out on you an hour before your wedding is something you never get over."

Emma didn't know why, but Holly was purposely goading them. She was convinced of it.

"Then again," Holly continued, "Emma had her reasons. That pregnant woman did show up at the church claiming you were her baby's father."

Emma's mother inhaled sharply.

"That's enough, Holly." The reprimand, gently issued, came from her father.

She huffed, as if put upon. "I just figured we should stop ignoring the elephant in the room."

"There's no elephant." Emma turned to Leonard. "Let me wash the dishes. It's only fair since you cooked."

This conversation, she thought as she cleared the table, and people like Holly, were the reasons Emma refused to move back to Mistletoe.

NICK MET THE wedding party at the gazebo for the Walk of Lights rather than drive from the ranch with Leonard and the rest of the family. Lunch had been difficult enough. Nick wasn't in the mood for a round two. Also, this way, he could leave at any time with a legitimate excuse—a very early morning. The cattle wouldn't move themselves to the home pastures.

Emma had handled herself well at lunch. Kudos for that. Holly's obvious attempts to get a rise out of her had mostly failed. They'd succeeded, however, with Nick, but he'd held his temper rather than make things worse by losing it.

"There you are." Leonard hailed Nick over. "I was just about to send out a search party."

"Sorry I'm late." After a long afternoon in the saddle, Nick had thought it best to shower and change into clean clothes.

He bent and kissed Candy on the cheek. From the corner of his eye, he saw Emma shy away. *Fine. Be that way.*

More hellos, hugs and handshakes were exchanged as Nick greeted the rest of the group. Besides Leonard's entire family, including his two grandkids, there was his best friend and best man, Carl. Carl's family. Gladys Givens and her large brood. Several of Candy's coworkers and an abundance of friends. They weren't just a group, they bordered on being a mob.

Wasn't that what weddings were about? A gathering of family and friends? Nick automatically sought out Emma. They'd had a similar prewedding get-together at the Fall Hoedown.

"How 'bout we get started?" Leonard took Candy's arm and led the way.

The group fell naturally into place, forming a long line of two and sometimes three abreast. Nick eventually found himself strolling alongside Emma. Okay, maybe he'd planned it that way. Not from the start. Only after she attempted to avoid him.

"People are staring at us," she said under her breath.

"Let them."

She rolled her eyes.

Every few minutes, the group paused to take in a particularly extravagant or unusual window display. The café had outdone itself with strings of multicolored lights that blinked on and off in synchronization with recorded music. The feed store had put out a life-size plastic horse pulling a sleigh filled with presents. The clothing boutique sold sweatshirts with mistletoe printed on the front.

With each stop, the minimob bunched together. Getting close to Emma was inevitable and unavoidable. It was also enjoyable. More enjoyable than it should be. Nick would be lying if he said he didn't find her as attractive as ever.

"You're doing that on purpose," she said when he brushed up against her for the umpteenth time.

"I was going to accuse you of the same thing."

Her eyes narrowed. "Not funny."

"What has you on edge?" he asked. "Holly's laser stare burning holes into the backs of our heads?"

"Really! What's with her?" Emma frowned with displeasure. "Mom told me she isn't happy about the marriage."

"It's hard when a parent remarries."

"Not for me."

"Your mother didn't recently die from cancer."

"You're right. That wasn't fair."

"She and her mom were close. Then, after her mother died, Holly took over. At home and at the ranch office. She probably feels her place is being usurped by another woman."

"I understand that," Emma agreed. "Only Mom isn't interested in working at the ranch office."

"But she will run the household."

"You'd think Holly would want her father to be happy and not live the rest of his life alone."

"She's still grieving and feels like Leonard is betraying her mom's memory."

"You didn't have a hard time when your mother started dating."

Nick reached into his jacket pockets and pulled out his gloves. He tried not to think about warming his right hand by holding Emma's left. "I didn't live and

work with her, either. Plus, she waited five years before dating."

"Exactly. Your mother waited. My mom and Leonard are charging full steam ahead."

"There's no right or wrong timetable, Emma. Folks
get married when they're ready."

She rubbed her brow with her mittened hand. It did
nothing to erase the deep creases. "I'd hate for Holly
to ruin the wedding."

"She'll behave."

Another stop, this time in front of Frozen Delights
with its signature holiday ice cream. Leonard's young
grandkids jumped up and down, pleading for cones.

"Pralines and cream still your favorite flavor?" Nick
asked Emma.

She shot him a decidedly less hostile look. In fact,
her expression verged on sentimental. "We came here
for our first date."

"I remember." They both stared through the lit window into the shop. "You probably don't want to hear
this," Nick said, "but those six months we spent together
were the happiest of my life."

He couldn't say why he suddenly felt compelled to
tell her that. For some reason, it seemed important.

When she answered him, her voice was no more than
a whisper. "I don't mind."

"The memories, they're not all bad, Emma. Actually, they're almost all good."

"Except for the very last one."

The group moved on, chatting and laughing. Carolers
dressed in Victorian period costumes strolled the sidewalk on the opposite side of the street, singing, "Deck

the Halls." An elderly couple kissed beneath one of the many mistletoe sprigs.

Nick and Emma stayed where they were in front of the Frozen Delights window.

"I didn't lie to you," he said. "When I told you I hadn't dated anyone for a year before we met, it was true."

"Right. That gal was just a weekend fling."

"I was young and stupid. I made a mistake. What matters most is the baby wasn't mine."

Doubting the woman's claim, Nick had insisted on DNA testing immediately following the baby's birth. The results were negative.

"But it might have been yours." Emma sniffed. From the cold or from prodding old wounds?

"If you had stayed in Mistletoe and not left—"

"How could I stay? *Everyone* knew. I was so embarrassed. One hour before my wedding, a pregnant woman shows up at the church, swearing my fiancé is her baby's father. I was convinced she'd lost her mind. But then you said it was possible. That you'd slept with her."

"Two months before I met you."

"Excuse me for being shocked and hurt enough to not want to see you again." She turned away from the window. Away from him.

"You could have come back, Emma. Once the DNA test was done."

She sniffed again. "I already had a new job and an apartment with a lease."

"Those are excuses. Not reasons."

"I wasn't ready." She faltered. "I didn't trust you."

That was closer to the truth, though it didn't explain why she'd remained scarce for six years.

Part of him wanted to say, "You're here now," but their complicated past stopped him. She'd hurt him, too. Walked out on him, on them, without a backward glance. As if their love had meant nothing.

"What do you want from me, Nick?"

"Only for us to get along, at least through the wedding. After that, we can go our separate ways." Now he was the one being less than totally honest.

What he wanted most was to get over Emma Sturlacky once and for all. Move on. Stop comparing every woman he met to her and deciding they came up short. Nick was tired of being alone. He craved what he'd almost had with Emma and what his boss had found with her mother. A wife and family to call his own.

Standing close, brushing up against her, wasn't the way to put her and their former relationship behind him. Distance served his purpose much better.

"We'd better go." Without waiting for her, he started up the sidewalk. "Or Leonard really will send out a search party."

CHAPTER THREE

NICK AND EMMA joined the rest of their group at the hot chocolate stand, a fund-raiser hosted by the local Girl Scout troops. Dropping a ten-dollar bill in the donation jar, he grabbed two foam cups and sought out Emma. She was holding her hands to her mouth and blowing warm air into them.

"Here." He passed her a cup. "This will help."

"Thanks." Her tone was reserved. No surprise after their conversation in front of Frozen Delights.

Leonard strolled over. "Kind of like old times, seeing you two together."

Emma jerked back as if struck. "There's nothing between us," she stammered, and hurried away, her hot chocolate sloshing over the sides of her cup.

Leonard stared after her, his expression stricken. "Guess I put my foot in my mouth with that one."

Nick tried to make light of the situation. "Might be best if you didn't bring up our former relationship. Not until after your wedding, at least."

"Maybe I should talk to her. Or ask Candy to."

"I'll go." The words were hardly out and Nick was in motion.

Emma's back greeted him. She was standing on the edge of the group near the street corner, isolating herself from family and friends. Exactly what she'd been doing these past six years.

"Don't blame Leonard." Nick downed his hot chocolate. "He has his head in the clouds, what with the wedding in a few days."

Emma's squared her shoulders before facing him. "I doubt he's the only one thinking or gossiping about me."

Anger surged inside Nick, and he spoke more gruffly than he intended. "You think you were the only one who was hurt and embarrassed?"

She blinked. "Of course not."

"Right. Because you left. While I stayed and got to listen to all the condescending remarks, all the empty platitudes and all the jokes." He tossed his empty cup in a nearby trash receptacle. "You had it hard? News flash. It was a living hell for me, so don't expect my sympathy."

"And whose fault is that?" she demanded.

"Be honest with yourself, if not with me. How much of a difference would it have made if I'd told you beforehand I'd had a two-day fling with a woman I met in a bar? Would you have gone through with the wedding after she showed up?"

"I guess we'll never know."

"Speak for yourself."

Her eyes flashed with indignation. A defense, Nick was sure, because he'd called her out. She would have left anyway, and they both knew it.

"The one difference," he continued, "is you'd have to take full responsibility for walking out and not blame me."

Wrong thing to say if he had any hope of getting along with her until after the wedding. She instantly stiffened and might have issued a comeback if not for Gladys Givens's appearance.

"Aren't you going to kiss her?" She looked expectantly at Nick. When he didn't respond, she stated the obvious. "You two are standing under mistletoe."

Both Nick and Emma raised their gazes. There, dangling from the street sign, a foot above their heads, was a mistletoe sprig tied with a red ribbon. Great.

Emma froze.

"Can't defy tradition." Gladys beamed at them. "It's bad luck."

Nick could feel the many stares on them. Hear the slight intake of breaths. He contemplated how best to make a clean getaway and came up blank. They had only one choice.

As if reading his mind, Emma shook her head. "No. Don't you dare."

That did it. He was like a kid confronted with a freshly baked cake, unable to resist swiping his finger along the side and stealing a glob of frosting. Taking hold of her upper arms, he hauled her onto her tiptoes.

Her eyes went wide. She didn't, however, pull away.

Here goes nothing, Nick thought and dipped his head, aiming for her cheek. She gasped in anticipation, her lips parting slightly. The sight was too much to resist, and he changed his mind. Instead of a chaste peck, his mouth settled possessively on hers.

The kiss was so much like the one after their first date at Frozen Delights. Soft. Sweet. Tender. Slightly hesitant but full of promise. He hadn't been able to stop then, and the same held true tonight. Ignoring her murmured protest, he deepened the kiss.

Wham! Heat shot though him like a fireball with a

mile-long tail. Old desires, never fully banished, returned with a vengeance, and Nick's carefully maintained control slipped.

His hand moved from her arm to cradle the side of her face and angle her head just so, allowing him to part her lips farther. She resisted—for a moment longer. Then she melted into his embrace. Unclenching her hands, she laid them flat on the front of his jacket. As the kiss went on, they traveled slowly toward his neck.

Crazy as it was, Nick willed her to wrap her arms around him. Apparently, his powers of telepathy were lacking because she stopped there. And like that, the kiss ended.

He didn't let her go, not right away. He was too captivated by the look in her brown eyes. In that moment, she was the old Emma. The one who loved him and wanted to be his wife despite their young age and uncertain future. The one he believed wouldn't leave him under any circumstances or for any reason.

The next instant, the look vanished. She was the new Emma once more, the one who hadn't forgiven him for what she saw as a betrayal.

"Don't do that again," she said through clenched teeth.

"Might be hard. There is mistletoe everywhere."

"Find a way."

She charged off and was immediately swallowed up by the group. Nick couldn't be sure how he felt. He was still reeling from the one-two punch of their kiss.

A small commotion caught his attention and refocused it. There, at the center of the group, stood Holly, Leonard and Candy. Holly appeared on the verge of tears.

"I just don't understand."

"Holly, sweetie." Leonard put an arm around his daughter's waist. "I know this is hard for you."

"You obviously don't know, or you wouldn't be marrying her. You wouldn't be marrying *anyone*."

Holly ran off then. The crowd parted to let her by. Poor Candy looked ready to cry herself.

"I'm sorry," Leonard announced. "She still misses her mother."

Clearly the wrong thing to say, for Candy left then, too. In the opposite direction. Leonard hesitated, as if unsure of which woman to follow. He picked Holly. That probably wouldn't go over well with Candy, either. A moment later, Emma went after her mother.

Hushed conversations ensued. Nick didn't want to listen to them. Convinced no one would miss him, he started off toward the parking lot and his truck. Two vehicles over from his, he spotted Emma with her mother.

Not stopping, he climbed into his truck. The problem with Holly was between Leonard and Candy. Not his place to intercede.

Nor was it Emma's. Unfortunately, from the look on her face and the rate of speed at which her mouth was moving, she was likely doing precisely that.

EMMA'S MOTHER THREW open the front door. Cole stood on the stoop, tall, broad shouldered and grinning from ear to ear. At his feet sat a small suitcase. "Hey, Mom."

She launched herself at him. "Cole, honey. It's wonderful to see you!"

Emma waited, wanting to hug her brother, too, but giving her mother first chance. Behind them, through the open door, she saw Nick's truck back out of the driveway and head down the street. He'd picked Cole up at the airport and driven him here, a three-hour round trip. The least he deserved was a heartfelt thanks.

Yet he'd left without even getting out of his pickup. Did she really expect to see him after last night? Was she hoping for another kiss?

Absolutely not! How she'd allowed things to go as far as they had was beyond her. Temporary insanity, obviously. The only plausible explanation. What she needed to do, what they *both* did, was to forget the kiss ever happened. Also, to avoid mistletoe at all costs.

"How was your trip?" Emma's mother finally released Cole. "Any problems? And where did Nick go in such an all-fire hurry?"

"The trip was great. No problems. Nick took the back roads so we missed traffic. Said he had work to do." Cole opened his arms to Emma. "How's my baby sis?"

She squeezed him tight, a lump forming in her throat. "I've missed you." Between her brief visits to Mistletoe and Cole moving to New Orleans a few years ago, they saw each other infrequently.

"You look great. I dig the short hair." He held her away from him, then dropped his arms in order to put one around their mother. "But not as good as the bride-to-be. She's stunning."

"Oh, Cole." Emma's mother blushed, then closed the front door behind him. "Come in and get settled. I hate to rush you, but we have an appointment at I Now Pronounce You Wedding Attire in an hour for fittings."

At some point, Cole's old room had been turned into a TV den.

Emma's mother waited in the doorway, fretting. "Sorry about the lack of accommodations."

He dumped his suitcase on the couch with its hide-away bed. "I can sleep anywhere."

They were ready to leave in less than an hour. Emma drove, Cole rode shotgun and their mother chatted non-stop from the rear seat.

"Your tux isn't the same as Leonard's, Carl's and Nick's. I hope you're okay with the style I picked."

"Anything you want, Mom." Cole smiled, showing his dimples.

Emma wondered how it was possible no woman had yet snatched him up.

Gladys Givens waited outside I Now Pronounce You Wedding Attire. The moment they entered the shop, the owner seated them in circle of comfy chairs near the fitting rooms. Next, he brought out a tray with champagne flutes and a plate of chocolate-covered strawberries. An assistant carried a silver bucket with a bottle of champagne submerged in ice.

Gesturing expansively, the shop owner popped the cork on the champagne and poured four glasses. "Enjoy."

Emma's mother giggled. "Drinking at two o'clock in the afternoon. It's practically immoral."

"It's heavenly." Gladys sipped at her glass, then rubbed her nose as if the bubbles tickled. "Try the strawberries."

Emma attempted to participate in the good times and enjoy the camaraderie, knowing how important it was to her mother. In truth, she just wasn't in the mood. Even the champagne, something she usually loved, tasted bland. Taking only a few sips, she set her glass aside.

It had to be their surroundings. There was only one wedding-attire shop in town. Six years ago, she'd pur-

chased her bridal gown and Nick had rented his tux at
I Now Pronounce You. They'd sat in these same chairs
while sipping champagne and feeding each other strawberries.

Two days after their failed nuptials, Emma had returned the wedding dress to the shop with instructions
to forward the refund money to her mother. It had been
her final task before leaving town.

"Can I please have some water?" she asked the shop
owner, her throat suddenly burning.

"Of course. And I'll bring more champagne."

"None for me," Emma insisted. Another glass and
she'd probably break down in tears.

Damn Nick. Why had he kissed her last night? Why
had she kissed him back? Her emotions were already
a tangled mess where he was concerned. All this close
contact on top of everything else wasn't making it easier.

"Would the young lady like to go first, or the gentle-
man?" The shop owner smiled broadly. He'd been joined
by a petite woman wearing elf ears and a Santa hat and
carrying a small seamstress's box. Emma presumed she
was there to help with her gown fitting.

Before Emma could volunteer, Cole sprang up from
his chair. "Let's get this show started."

The seamstress faded into the background as the
shop owner led Cole to the men's fitting room.

"How fun is this?" Gladys's cheeks had taken on a
rosy glow thanks to the champagne.

Talk centered on wedding preparations. Emma's
mother consulted her ever-present list. After the fitting, she and Emma were heading to Merrick's Mistle-

toe Farm to finalize the selections of floral decorations. Cole was visiting an old friend.

"I don't suppose I can monopolize all his time," Emma's mother lamented, her lower lip protruding.

Cole emerged a short while later, wearing the black tux their mother had chosen for him to lead her down the aisle. The sleeves were a bit too short and the pants too long. Still, he looked great.

"Honey." Emma's mother rose, then, putting a hand to her mouth, and started to cry. "Sorry, I'm really emotional lately." She glanced at Gladys. "My boy's all grown up, isn't he?"

"You can say that again."

Emma couldn't speak. She was having her own reaction. In her mind, she was seeing a younger version of her brother wearing a similar tux. One he'd selected for her wedding. He'd looked great then, too. Except once Emma saw Nick waiting for her at the altar, she had eyes only for him.

This, she decided, was going to be a very long day. Harder to get through than lunch at the Yule Tide Ranch yesterday.

While the shop owner stole Cole away for more measurements, the three women continued chatting. Well, Emma's mother and Gladys chatted. Emma nursed her champagne and tried to act happy.

"Between Cole and Nick," Gladys observed, "the single women in this town will go gaga."

Emma snapped to attention. Just how many single women were attending her mother's wedding anyway? The next instant, she tamped down her emotions. She wasn't jealous. Not one bit.

"Oh, to be twenty years younger and seven sizes

smaller." Gladys fanned herself with her hand. "I'd give those two young men a run for their money."

"Gladys!" Emma's mother pretended to be shocked. "That's my son we're talking about."

"All right. Just Nick, then. It's not as if he hasn't been on the prowl these past couple years."

"Now, now. *Prowl* is a strong word."

"I swear he's dated every available woman under thirty-five this town has to offer."

Nick dated a lot? The last Emma had heard, and admittedly, her mother was the source, he'd practically sworn off women altogether. Emma hadn't entirely believed her mother, but Nick a player? That didn't sound like him.

"Since when?" Emma was surprised to hear the question pop out of her mouth.

Gladys peered at Emma over the rim of her glass. "It's no secret he's in the market for a wife and looking to settle down. Hasn't found anyone yet, but it's only a matter of time. He's quite the catch. The *Mistletoe Herald* ran a feature on him last Valentine's Day. The town's most eligible bachelor."

Emma's mother shot Gladys a warning look. "Maybe Emma doesn't want to hear about this."

"I'm fine," she said. "Really. It's not like I don't date, either."

She did, now and again, though none of her relationships had lasted particularly long. Nick had swept Emma off her feet, their romance straight from the pages of a fairy tale. When he'd proposed after a mere four months, she couldn't think of anything she wanted more than to become Mrs. Hayes.

Convinced their impulsiveness was what had ultimately led to disaster, she insisted on taking things slow with any new guy she met. Very slow. So slow, in fact, that the guy usually tired of waiting and moved on. Emma had yet to care. None of the men she'd dated came remotely close to evoking in her the same feelings Nick did.

Had, she corrected herself. As in, the past. He most certainly did nothing for her now.

What did she care that he'd dated scores of women?

The seamstress reappeared, sewing box in tow. "Are you ready now, miss?"

"Absolutely." Emma all but ran to the fitting room.

The gown her mother had chosen was deep maroon and went well with Emma's hair color and complexion. The slim-fitting bodice and flared skirt showed off her figure to its best advantage. The cap sleeves gave her a dainty, feminine appearance. Emma reminded herself to compliment her mother on her good taste.

The seamstress measured this, pinned that and marked there. "You look lovely." She smiled with satisfaction.

Emma emerged from the fitting room, feeling the best she had all day. She quite enjoyed the sensual swishing sound the silky fabric made when she walked.

She stepped out to gasps of delight from her mother and Gladys and a low wolf whistle from her brother.

"Goodness gracious," Gladys gushed.

"You're an absolute vision!" Her mother clasped her hands together. "Isn't she?"

"Yes, indeed." The deep male voice didn't belong to Cole.

Emma looked up to find Nick staring at her, an unreadable expression on her face.

"What are you doing here?" she sputtered.

"Same as you. Getting fitted."

Duh! He stood before her, dressed in a Western-cut tux that looked like it was custom-made for him. The only thing missing was a black dress Stetson.

The floor of the shop seemed to tilt at a sharp angle, hurling Emma six years into the past. She breathed deeply, desperately attempting to regain her balance. This wasn't her wedding. Nick wasn't the groom. They could barely stand each other.

"You're beautiful."

Did he have to say that? With a low, husky voice that sent tingles cascading down her spine?

"Thank you," she murmured and brushed self-consciously at her hair. "You look nice, too."

Nice? He was her every fantasy come true.

"My, my, my." Gladys sighed expansively. "How lucky am I to be paired with you?"

Of course, Emma thought. As maid of honor, she'd be paired with best man Carl. Thank goodness for one small favor.

"When will the alterations be done?" Emma's mother asked the shop owner.

"We'll deliver the tuxes and gown the morning of the wedding."

"That's cutting it close, but it will have to do, I suppose."

The seamstress, evidently not knowing that Nick and Emma weren't paired in the wedding party, took them by their hands, pulled them to the large triple mirror and positioned them side by side. "Aren't you stunning together."

At that moment, Cole came out of the fitting room,

wearing his regular clothes. Catching sight of them, he stopped in his tracks. "Whoa! That takes me back."

"Doesn't it though?" Gladys agreed.

Emma and Nick's expressions stared at them from the mirror. Hers was stricken. His was guarded.

The seamstress beamed and pointed to the mistletoe hanging from the suspended light fixture directly above their heads. "You must kiss."

Emma tensed. She couldn't take a repeat of last night. "It's okay," she insisted. "We don't have to."

The seamstress's mouth fell open in shock. "But it's bad luck not to kiss."

If Emma ever found out who started the stupid bad-luck-not-to-kiss tradition, she'd give them a kick in the you-know-what.

Before she could voice another protest, Nick turned, swooped her up into his arms and planted his mouth firmly on hers. The floor tilted again, this time for an entirely different reason.

Emma promptly panicked.

No, no, no! This had happened to her before, and not just today or last night when Nick had kissed her beneath the street sign. He'd always had this uncontrollable effect on her. Always had and probably always would, whether he intended to or not. It was how she'd lost her heart to him in the first place.

Pushing against his chest, she disengaged herself from his embrace. Not caring what the others thought, she lifted the hem of her dress and hurried into the fitting room. *Please, please,* she silently begged. *Don't let anyone follow me.*

Thankfully, her wish was granted. Emma was able to change out of the gown without assistance. Five minutes later, her hands were still shaking. A knock on the dressing room door had her jumping out of her skin.

"Emma?" her mother said.

"Be out in a second." Arranging the dress inside the garment bag, she zipped it up.

"Are you okay?"

"Fine."

Only she was far from fine. As Nick had kissed her there in the store, Emma had experienced a startling and most unwelcome revelation.

She was still in love with him. Heart, body and soul.

CHAPTER FOUR

"I WANT TO make a stop before we go to Merrick's."

Emma thought her mother's suggestion was a good idea—and not just because she needed to walk off those few sips of champagne she'd drunk. Realizing she still loved Nick had sobered her faster than being hit in the face with a bucket of ice water.

"Where?" she asked.

They stood outside I Now Pronounce You, buttoning their coats and winding wool scarves around their necks. Gladys had already left, and Cole's old high school buddy had swung by the shop to pick him up.

Nick was still inside. Emma hadn't been able to escape the shop fast enough.

"Mistletoe Magic." Emma's mother linked arms with her, and they started out. In broad daylight, the lights and decorations along Main Street paled in comparison to the ones they'd viewed the other night.

"You need something for the wedding?" Emma asked.

"In a manner of speaking."

The new age shop wasn't far. Two blocks away. The icy air penetrated the fabric of Emma's heavy coat, chilling her to the bone. That, or her recent encounter with Nick had left her feeling utterly exposed. Had he read the emotions reflected in her eyes and realized she still loved him? Good grief, she hoped not. She'd never be able to face him.

A jingle bell announced their arrival at Mistletoe Magic, which occupied the entire first floor of a converted Victorian-style house. Smells assaulted them the moment they entered, sweet and a little exotic. A nontraditional version of "Jingle Bells" played in the background.

The only other customer in the store was leaving, her arms laden with shopping bags. Emma and her mother smiled and exchanged a cheery "Merry Christmas" with the customer.

"Hi, Mrs. Sturlacky." The shop owner came out from behind the counter, her expression warm and welcoming. "It's Emma, right?"

"You have a good memory." Emma's recollections of Finley were vague, mostly from when she worked part-time at Merrick's and the McCarthy family visited the farm store.

"How can I help you today?"

"I need two things," her mother said. "My friend Gladys mentioned a lotion you carry."

"Body or hand?"

"Body. My friend says the scent is supposed to… well, make a woman more attractive to the opposite sex and make him more…more…interested in her."

Emma bit back a laugh. Was her mother looking to purchase an aphrodisiac? Did they even sell those things? Suddenly serious, she glanced around the shop.

"Ah." Finley lit up. "I know the one you're talking about. Very effective," she emphasized with a knowing nod. "Right this way."

They navigated the aisles, their shelves brimming

with products. Emma had never been in the shop before and was admittedly intrigued by the many offerings, some of them quite curious and out of the ordinary.

"Mom, why do you need a lotion to attract men? You're getting married in two days. I'd say whatever you've been doing has worked pretty well."

"For the honeymoon."

Emma recalled all the small and endearing ways Leonard paid attention to her mother. "I don't think you have anything to worry about."

"I want the night to be special."

There was a wistfulness to her mother's voice and a hint of shyness. Was she nervous? If so, why? Hadn't she and Leonard done the deed already? Emma grimaced, not wanting to think about the intimate details of her mother and Leonard's private life.

"Here it is." Finley removed a test bottle from a display and squirted a dab onto Emma's mother's hands. "Would you like to try it?" She held the bottle out to Emma, who automatically opened her palm.

Rubbing the lotion in, she and her mother brought their hands to their noses for a whiff.

Her mother's eyes went wide. "Smells delightful, doesn't it, Emma?"

"Very nice."

There was indeed something about the lotion that went straight to Emma's head. She blinked and took another strong sniff. Would Nick like it? Would he find her irresistible and forget about all the other women he'd been dating?

Enough! She had to stop thinking about him. What did she care if he dated?

"I'll take a bottle." Her mother snatched one off the

shelf, then, after a moment's hesitation, went back for a second. "No, two."

"You won't be disappointed," Finley assured her. "My customers report excellent results."

Emma clamped a hand to her forehead. She didn't want to know.

"What else can I help you with?" Finley inquired of Emma's mother.

"I'd like one of those mistletoe lucky charms you sell."

"Absolutely. They're by the register."

A lucky charm? Emma refrained from rolling her eyes. Who was this woman claiming to be her mother? Certainly not the conservative and straitlaced individual who'd raised her. Besides, her mother obviously had all the luck she needed. She was marrying a great guy who adored her.

Emma browsed the displays near the register while her mother paid for her purchases. One item that had her looking twice was a magic potion aimed at children. According to the sign, a few drops placed on a pillow Christmas Eve night would result in the person's fondest wish coming true on Christmas Day.

What would Emma wish for? She didn't need to think twice, and reached for a small vial of the potion. The next instant, she replaced the bottle and withdrew her hand. This was insanity. She didn't believe in potions and charms any more than she believed in Santa Claus and elves. No silly superstition would help her get over Nick. For that, she had only to harden her heart.

"Happy holidays," Finley called after Emma and her mother as they left. "Come back again."

"Wait." Emma's mother stopped on the sidewalk

outside the store. Opening the sack containing her purchases, she reached in and withdrew the mistletoe charm. "Here. I bought this for you."

"Why?"

"Take it. The charm has special magic. The luck isn't in the having, but the giving."

"I don't understand."

She wiggled the charm, which danced on the end of a red velvet ribbon. "The person who receives it gets the luck." Tears abruptly filled Emma's mother's eyes. "I want you to be happy, sweetie. I don't care if it's a new job or a man in your life or even a pet dog. Just as long as you find that niche you were talking about." She opened Emma's fingers and deposited the charm, then covered Emma's hand with her own. "Keep this. For me. Make your mother happy."

Emma stared at the charm, sprigs of mistletoe poking through her fingers. Glitter was already falling off and adhering to her skin. She shook her head. No trinket this inconsequential could possibly turn her life around. But rather than hurt her mother's feelings, she dropped the charm in her coat pocket.

"Sure, Mom. Thank you."

On impulse, she hugged her mother, which made her feel a tiny bit better. Maybe there was something to the charm's magic after all.

The moment they arrived at Merrick's roadside farm store, Mrs. Merrick—Karen, Emma had to remember that—shuffled them to the workroom in the back of the store.

"What do you think?" Karen waved an arm toward the long table. "I was up till midnight last night."

Festive centerpieces, fragrant hangings for the

church pews and one especially large arrangement stretched from one end of the table to the other. Most were made from a variety of evergreen boughs, and all included gold-and-silver ribbons, miniature jingle bells and, of course, mistletoe.

"What about the lilies?" Emma's mother asked.

"They're arriving tomorrow morning. We want them to be as fresh as possible." Mrs. Merrick peered out the window, her brow creased with worry. "As long as the storm holds off and the highways aren't shut down."

As planned, the large centerpiece, designated for the bride and groom's table at the reception, would also contain white lilies. Having once worked in the farm store, Emma knew the importance of flowers at their freshest.

"Ooh." Emma's mother laid a hand over her heart, her expression melting. "Everything is absolutely beautiful. I couldn't be happier."

They spent several minutes inspecting Mrs. Merrick's handiwork and discussing details. Emma's mother requested only a few teeny-tiny changes. Times were decided on for delivering the centerpieces and large arrangement to the ranch for the reception and the pew hangings to the church for the ceremony.

"And last but not least." With a flourish, Mrs. Merrick presented Emma's mother with a bouquet fit for a bride, its long gold-and-silver ribbons almost reaching to the floor. "I'll add the lilies tomorrow. Here are the ones for Emma and Gladys." She indicated two smaller bouquets.

"This is really happening." Emma's mother started to cry softly. "It's not a dream."

Her joy was incredibly touching, and Emma felt tears prick her own eyes. Not only because she shared in her mother's happiness but also because it made Emma's empty, wandering, here-and-there life feel even more lonely.

Mrs. Merrick escorted them to the car. After giving Emma's mother a hug, she cornered Emma. "Maybe the day after the wedding you can come back and talk to me about that job opening we have. Our office manager is leaving in a few weeks. Her husband was transferred to San Jose, of all places."

"Thank you, Mrs. Merrick. Karen," Emma amended when the other woman wagged a finger at her. "But I'm not moving back to Mistletoe."

"Why? We miss you. And you love it here."

She did. Which was why she'd never truly been content elsewhere, continually changing jobs, apartments and towns. Nothing compared. Only she couldn't come home.

Forget being the talk of the town. Nick was right; that would die down eventually—as long as they didn't keep kissing each other in public. But the truth was, Emma refused to stand by and watch him date other women, knowing her heart still belonged to him.

Nick was searching for a wife and ready to settle down. The kisses they shared, while wonderful for her, had meant nothing to him and happened only because he'd been goaded into it. His lackluster reaction testified to that.

"I do appreciate the offer," she said before climbing in behind the steering wheel.

"I'm not giving up on you," Mrs. Merrick said, then waved goodbye.

Emma pulled out of the farm store parking lot, more determined than before to fall out of love with Nick. In order to accomplish that, she'd have to continue searching for a place that felt as much like Mistletoe as possible.

Slipping her left hand in her coat pocket, she fingered the charm. Her imagination must be really running wild, for she swore it gave off a warm, tingling sensation.

"WHAT ABOUT THIS?" Emma stood back, affording her mother a better view of the card table.

Scrunching her mouth in concentration, her mother walked over slowly. "Good, I think. But we need something to spruce it up a bit."

They were debating on where in the large dining room to put the table, which would hold the wedding cake. Emma's mother liked the wall with the scenic oil painting. Emma liked the wall with the picture window. They were compromising on left of the door. That way, the line of guests waiting for a piece of cake could wrap around the room.

"I agree," Emma said. One white linen cloth didn't quite hide the card table's worn condition and wobbly legs. "Got any ideas?"

"What about…" Emma's mother sorted through the boxes of accessories and decorations she'd brought with them and came up with a red silk table runner trimmed in gold. "This?" She draped the runner over the tablecloth.

"Better." Emma studied their combined efforts. "But it's still missing that right touch of pizzazz."

"We could wrap these strands of gold garland down the table legs."

"Too Christmassy."

Emma's mother laughed. "Well, Christmas is the theme of my wedding."

Since breakfast six hours earlier, they'd been readying the Yule Tide Ranch house for the reception. Over two hundred guests were expected. Having a sit-down dinner was impossible. Instead Emma's mother and Leonard had opted for a buffet of pulled chicken and beef, homemade rolls and an assortment of sides. Nothing resembling a traditional Christmas dinner. Emma's mother didn't want to interfere with anyone's menu for the next day.

Together, she and Emma tested the garland idea by wrapping a glittering strand down one table leg. Emma and her mother concurred that it didn't look half-bad, so they tackled the remaining three legs.

"You two have been busy!" Leonard's booming voice hailed them from the doorway.

Emma's mother instantly brightened. "What do you think?"

"It's great." He went over and gave her an affectionate hug while flashing Emma a smile.

She knew her mother's secret worry. She didn't want this wedding to resemble either her or Leonard's first ones in any way whatsoever. That was one of the reasons they'd picked Christmas Eve for the ceremony and the ranch house for the reception.

"How's the family room coming along?" her mother asked.

"Nick and Toby will be here any minute. Two pairs of strong arms, as promised."

Emma silently cursed her sudden intake of breath. If simply hearing Nick's name caused her to react, what would *seeing* him do? She hoped her mother and Leonard had eyes only for each other and didn't notice Emma chewing her lower lip as she rubbed her hands along the legs of her jeans.

"Have the guys finished moving all the cattle to the home pastures?" her mother asked.

"All but a few strays. Nick swears they'll have those rounded up by tomorrow morning."

"I feel bad, taking them away from their work just to set up folding tables and chairs."

"Nick insists," Leonard assured her. "And if he didn't, I would."

The two of them continued, jumping from one topic to the next. Last-minute changes with the caterer. Their recent consultation with the photographer. Music selections for the keyboardist and singer they'd hired. Emma busied herself by going through the boxes of decorations, on the lookout for any sudden inspiration. It didn't keep her mind off Nick as she'd hoped.

Her phone rang, interrupting her while also giving her a good excuse to leave her mother and Leonard alone.

"I'll take this in the other room." Grabbing her phone off the dining table, she hurried out. The number on the display was familiar, but she couldn't immediately place it. "Hello?"

"Hi," a pleasant female voice responded. "I'm calling for Emma Sturlacky."

"Speaking." Emma switched the phone to her other ear.

"Oh, good. This is Amanda Miller with Enterprise Investments."

The company Emma had interviewed with last week for an administrative assistant position. When she hadn't heard, she'd assumed they weren't interested in her.

Failing to pay attention to where she was going, she nearly collided with the broad expanse of Nick's chest before pulling herself up short. "Oops!"

"Excuse me?" the woman on the line said.

Emma's glance rose to meet Nick's. An amused twinkle shone in his dark eyes. A sensuous thrill wound through her. *Really? Now?*

"I'm sorry," she said to the caller. Darting away from Nick, she took refuge on the other side of the family room. "That's what I get for walking and talking at the same time."

"Did I catch you at a bad time?"

"Not at all."

"Well, the reason for my call is we'd like to bring you in for a second interview. Are you still available?"

"Great!" Emma found herself responding positively despite the fact that she'd left the initial interview unsure if the job was a good fit for her. "And yes, I'm still available."

"I know it's short notice, but can you come in tomorrow?"

"I'm sorry, I'm out of town for the holidays and my mother's wedding. I'll be back on Saturday. Is Monday too late?"

"No problem. It's always difficult to schedule interviews around the holidays. Monday's fine. Shall we say one o'clock?"

Emma felt Nick's stare from across the room. He and Toby were carrying in the rental tables and chairs from the garage where the Elks Club members had stored them. "One o'clock is perfect," she said.

"Plan for at least two hours. We'd like you to shadow one of the other assistants for a little while after the interview."

That sounded promising. Emma must have made a better impression on them than she'd originally thought.

"Thank you so much, Amanda. I'm looking forward to the interview."

After a few more pleasantries, they disconnected. Emma remained rooted in place, staring at the phone in her hand as if it would provide the answer to her lack of enthusiasm. The job opportunity was a good one, especially considering her less-than-desirable track record of job-hopping.

"Have an interview?" Nick appeared in her line of vision.

She quickly pocketed her phone and pasted a smile on her face. "Yes. On Monday."

"Congratulations. Where is it this time? Austin, or are you moving out of Texas?"

His tone rankled her. Mostly because seconds earlier she'd been chastising herself for almost the same thing. "Austin. Not that it's any of your business."

She instantly regretted her churlishness. What was she, six?

No, but she understood enough about herself to realize she was letting Nick get to her. Then again, he always could, and not just by annoying her. He could also make her melt on the spot or laugh till she thought her sides might split.

Noticing where Toby was placing the folding chairs he'd carried in, she left Nick and hurried over. "Not there. Mom wants the chairs in small groupings, facing each other." She demonstrated with her hands.

"Yes, ma'am." The young man promptly did as she instructed.

"Thank you."

He reminded her a little of Nick when he was that age, all arms and legs and lanky awkwardness. The only quality missing was the endearing charm Nick possessed, then and now. Except these days, he mostly kept that charm behind a shield.

She stared at his back as he went out the door, presumably to the garage for more chairs. Had she hurt him that badly when she'd left that he'd felt the need to close off the most appealing part of his personality?

Apparently so. Where she was concerned, at least. According to Gladys, not so much with the other ladies in town.

CHAPTER FIVE

NICK GROUND HIS teeth together before opening the front door of Saving Grace Community Church. He didn't immediately enter. He couldn't. The memories were like a ten-foot wall blocking him.

Four different churches in Mistletoe, and his boss had to choose this one. The same church where Nick and Emma had planned to marry. He hadn't been within a hundred yards of the place since then. The last time, he'd chased after Emma as she was sprinting across the parking lot, the voluminous folds of her dress clutched in her hands.

He'd caught up with her at the end of the lot. She was furious at him and refused to listen, her pain-ravaged features delivering the ultimatum: he'd betrayed her, and she would never forgive him.

Candy had gathered Emma up after that and taken her home. Other than from a distance, Nick hadn't seen her again until four days ago in the town square. The emotions he'd struggled to keep buried for six years surged to the surface, stronger than ever.

Shit. He was in trouble. And getting through this evening was only the half of it.

Tonight, tomorrow and the next day, he told himself. Then it was over. Emma would leave Mistletoe soon after the wedding, and Nick could resume his life. His shallow, empty, lonely life.

He strode into the church atrium and headed toward the sanctuary where the rehearsal would take place. Emma had already arrived, and he spotted her immediately, drawn to her like a magnet with an irresistible pull.

She waited near the altar with her mother, Cole, Leonard, Carl and Gladys. The minister and a woman Nick recognized as the church secretary were also with them. Leonard's oldest daughter, Megan, ran herd on her two rambunctious children, who weren't taking their flower girl and ring bearer duties seriously. Another woman sat at the piano leafing through sheet music.

No organ? Okay, one tiny difference from Nick and Emma's wedding. That didn't make any of this easier on him. With each step he took down the aisle, the invisible weight in his chest grew heavier.

"Oh, good," Reverend Sands announced upon spotting Nick. "We're all here now."

Naturally, everyone turned to look at him. Did they see the sweat lining his forehead? He resisted wiping it away with the back of his hand.

"Hi," he muttered. "Am I late?"

"Not at all."

The reverend was being kind. Nick had kept everyone waiting a good seven minutes—exactly how long he'd sat outside in his truck, gathering his courage.

Leonard gently reminded them of the time. "We have dinner reservations for six-thirty."

"Let's get started, shall we?" Reverend Sands and the secretary began instructing people on where to stand

and at what point in the music they were to commence their walk down the aisle.

Thankfully, Nick didn't have to escort Emma to the altar. He couldn't handle that. Watching her with Carl was hard enough.

She might be taking that new job in Austin. Not returning to Mistletoe. He should be glad. Relieved. The sparks were still there. Two scorching kisses had proved that. But the fact was, they wouldn't, couldn't get back together. He didn't trust her not to bail at the first sign of trouble. No way could he put himself through another heartache.

"Nick," Gladys hissed. "That's our cue."

"Yeah, sorry." Offering her his arm, he started forward.

"Not so fast. We aren't in a race with Emma and Carl."

"Okay. Got it."

He'd been through this before. In a manner of speaking. During *that* rehearsal, he'd stood at the altar, right where Leonard was now, and watched his groomsmen and Emma's bridesmaids make this same age-old promenade.

Was she also remembering? Hard to tell. She still waited at the back of the church. Just as Nick took his place at Leonard's left, Emma emerged on Carl's arm, her glance riveted on the altar as if she were using it to guide her. When her mother and Cole appeared and the music swelled, all eyes were on them.

Suddenly, Emma looked at Nick, and he knew for certain she was remembering. Misery shone in her eyes, and the weight inside Nick's chest grew heavier.

He made it through the rest of the rehearsal. How,

he wasn't sure. Carl and Cole left for the restaurant, dispatched by Leonard to alert the staff that they were on their way. Gladys helped Megan with her offspring. Holly hadn't attended the rehearsal, but she and several close family friends were meeting them at the restaurant.

"Nick," Leonard called. "Reverend Sands asked to confer with me and Candy for a few minutes. Can you keep Emma company till we're done?"

"Sure." Why had Nick agreed? Emma was perfectly capable of waiting by herself.

Unless… Could Leonard be playing matchmaker and setting them up? No, he knew better. His boss had tried that on him once before. Last year, with Holly. She'd been thrilled. Nick, less so. Oh, Holly was fun to be with when her nose wasn't out of joint. But his feelings for her went only as far as friendship. Leonard had taken the eventual breakup harder than Holly.

Nick located Emma in the atrium. She was arranging the guest book, complete with white-feathered pen, on a small lectern by the door to the sanctuary.

"You doing okay?" Stupid question. He regretted it the instant the words were out of his mouth.

"Just getting a jump on tomorrow."

At the sight of her, his heart lurched. Her mascara had run, leaving dark smudges beneath her eyes.

"Are you crying?"

"Not at all."

"I wouldn't blame you," he said. "It was kind of rough in there. For me, too."

"We don't need to talk about this." Her glance darted to the east door. The same door an eight-months-pregnant Laurel Linkletter had waltzed though an hour before Nick and Emma were to exchange vows.

"I didn't remember her name."

"What?" Emma blinked in confusion. "Whose name?"

"Laurel's. She had to tell me who she was. I didn't even recognize her."

Emma frowned. "That doesn't say much about you. Sleep with someone and then forget she ever existed."

"It says a lot. Once I met you, every other woman faded into the background."

Tears filled her eyes. "There's no point in rehashing the past."

"I think there is."

"Nick—"

"Neither of us has moved on. You go from job to job, town to town. I…"

"Go from conquest to conquest? Gladys was quite informative about your dating history. Mistletoe's most eligible bachelor."

"Okay. I've dated more than my share of women in the past couple of years. But none for long, none of them seriously."

"Am I supposed to think that's because you're still hung up on me?"

"Just saying, some closure might help both of us. And that would require we talk about what happened."

"You lied to me."

"I failed to mention a weekend hookup."

"Why? I would have understood."

"Like you said before, it didn't make me look good. And at the time, I was trying my hardest to impress you."

"She remembered *your* name. She came in here hollering it at the top of her lungs."

Nick grimaced at the recollection. "It wasn't as if I abandoned her. She kicked me to the curb the morning after our weekend together without so much as a 'nice knowing you.' No one could have been more surprised than me when she showed up that day."

"Oh, trust me, I was pretty surprised."

"You blew the whole thing out of proportion."

She gaped at him. "A pregnant woman crashes my wedding, and you think I blew things out of proportion?"

"Fine. I was a jerk. Guilty as charged. I had a meaningless fling and failed to mention it. But you deserted me. Without even giving me a chance to explain or apologize. If we're going to make comparisons, I think you committed the bigger mistake."

Emma drew herself up. "She claimed you were the baby's father."

"I didn't know she was pregnant. She never told me. I may not have been innocent, but I was ignorant."

That gave Emma pause.

"We were about to be married," he continued. "You owed me ten lousy minutes to explain."

She wiped at her damp eyes. "You're right."

Her admission gave *him* pause.

When he spoke, his hoarse voice betrayed him. "I couldn't believe you threw everything away like you did."

"I loved you so much, but I couldn't go through with the wedding. Not with that woman in the church and everyone talking about her. Talking about us."

"I understand that. It's the leaving town I can't get over." *Can't forgive,* he mentally added.

Her demeanor softened. "I'd change things if I could."

He studied her intently and asked the question that had haunted too many of his nights. "Is that your only regret?"

"What does it matter?" She shook her head. "We can't go back. We can only move forward, which includes getting through the wedding and reception."

At that moment, Leonard, Candy and the reverend entered the atrium from the hall.

"Good news," Leonard announced. "Reverend Sands and his wife will be joining us for dinner. Nick, can you drive them?"

"Absolutely." He forced a smile. He'd wanted to continue his conversation with Emma, but it wasn't to be. Not tonight anyway.

During the drive to the Roundup Steak House, Reverend Sands entertained them with stories of his more amusing wedding services. Nick tried to listen. Instead he kept thinking about Emma and her admission that, given the chance, she wouldn't have left town quite so quickly after Laurel's appearance.

Against his better judgment, a small spark of hope ignited inside him.

NICK HAD SEEN right through Emma. Then again, he always could. The rehearsal had been difficult on her. Their exchange in the atrium afterward, devastating. The dinner wasn't going any better. Not for her anyway. While the restaurant was different—she and Nick had hosted their considerably less lavish rehearsal dinner at the Mistletoe Café—there were still too many similarities not to tug at her heartstrings.

She remembered sitting at the table beside Nick, gazing at his handsome profile and thinking she was the luckiest bride in the world. How right she'd been. Emma hadn't been truly happy since the day of her *almost* wedding.

Not to say there weren't moments of contentment. Now, for instance, sitting with her mother and Leonard, so obviously in love, Emma experienced a rush of pleasure. Not, however, genuine happiness. It was as if that part of her emotional psyche was forever damaged.

"What can I get for you?" The waitress had finally made her way down the long row of connected tables to Emma.

"Um…" She peered at the menu, realizing all the time she'd been holding it, she hadn't so much as glanced at the selections.

"I can recommend the prime rib." The young woman held her pencil in midair above her pad.

Emma had no appetite, not after her conversation with Nick. "Do you have a Caesar salad?"

The waitress's features collapsed. Apparently diners who frequented a steak house didn't order salads for their main entrée. "It comes with a grilled chicken breast."

"Perfect. Thank you."

Emma nursed her wine, not in the mood for alcohol, either. Leonard had insisted on celebrating and ordered several bottles for the table. Emma assumed a toast would be made at some point. A minute later, Gladys dinged her fork against her wineglass, pushed back her chair and stood.

"It's customary for the best man to make a speech at the reception. And I promise not to steal your thunder." She grinned down at Carl. "But I couldn't let the evening pass without saying here's to family and friends." She raised her glass. "Thank you all for coming and for making Leonard and Candy's special day even more special. It wouldn't be complete without you sharing in their joy."

A chorus of, "Hear, hear," followed as the group clinked glasses. Emma's brother leaned over and gave their mother a loud, smacking kiss on the cheek.

"Love ya, Mom."

Emma noticed several pairs of eyes, including her mother's, dart in her direction. Did she appear that fragile? Apparently.

Nick wasn't one of those casting her surreptitious glances. He sat at the other end of the table, near the reverend and his wife, and didn't seem to be having any trouble with his appetite.

"Are you packed yet?" Gladys asked Emma's mother.

"Not quite. Imagine, going to the beach in December. Finding clothes to take hasn't been easy."

Leonard was flying them to Florida for their honeymoon. One mention of "I've always wanted to see Miami," sealed the deal. Leonard had arranged the entire trip, and they were leaving the Monday after Christmas. That was also the day Emma would return to Austin. Especially now that she had a job interview waiting for her.

"All that sun and sand." Gladys sighed wistfully. "While we're stuck in the snow."

"Speaking of which, has anyone seen the latest weather report?" the reverend asked.

Leonard's brow furrowed with concern. "They're predicting a blizzard. The kind that only comes around once in ten years."

"But not till Christmas."

Several of the guests assured Emma's mother the blizzard wouldn't dare disrupt her wedding.

Dinner continued, with the conversations loud and lively. No one seemed to notice Emma's lack of participation, and the glances in her direction tapered off. After another hour, the guests wound down. She grabbed her purse, swiped some ChapStick across her lips and waited for her mother and Leonard, who were delayed with all the goodbyes and well wishes.

Nick came up beside her. "I'll drive you home."

"It's okay." What in the world had possessed him to offer her a ride? "I'm going with Mom and Leonard."

"No room. They're taking Carl, Megan and her kids home."

"Why?"

"I didn't ask, Emma. But I can march over there and demand an explanation from Leonard if that will satisfy you."

"I'm not being difficult." Yet that was how he'd made her feel. "Simply curious."

"Holly could drive you."

Emma actually debated which was worse and settled on the lesser of two evils. "Let's get this over with."

"It's a ride home. Fifteen minutes. Not a death sentence."

Once more, he was making her feel like a petulant child. That, or the slim chance she was acting like one.

"I'm sorry if I put you on the spot earlier," he said. "Or made you uncomfortable."

They drove slowly down Main Street. The magnificent array of lights was almost blinding from the passenger seat of Nick's truck.

"You're not really going to bring that up again." She gazed out the window, her face so close, her breath fogged the glass.

"I guess once a day is enough."

There it was again, that hint of amusement in his voice. Did he have to pick now to lower his guard? That charm was why she'd fallen so hard for him in the first place. The reason she hadn't gotten over him or found anyone else.

Her phone chimed. Emma read the text and slumped in her seat.

"Problem?" Nick asked.

"It's Mom. She's staying at the ranch tonight." Emma didn't tell him the rest of the message, that this was her mother's last chance to spend time with Leonard before the wedding. Like many people, she believed it was bad luck for the groom to see the bride the day of the wedding until the chords of "Here Comes the Bride" played.

That left Emma and her brother home alone. No, wait. He was going out with Carl and some friends, then staying at his buddy's again. Closing her eyes, she let her hand slide into the pocket of her coat. The mistletoe charm was still there. She'd all but forgotten about it. Another of her mother's superstitions. Would it bring Emma luck? Maybe this new job would be the one that clicked. And when she left Mistletoe after the wedding, she'd finally be able to leave Nick behind for good.

Her glance darted to his profile, unreadable in the

dark. Nope. Not even the most powerful magic would help her get over him. She'd have to manage that feat on her own.

At her mother's house, Nick stepped out of his truck.

"What are you doing?" Emma demanded.

"Escorting you inside."

"You have got to be kidding." She grabbed her purse off the seat and slammed the passenger door shut. "This isn't a date."

"Just seeing you home safely, Emma."

She dug the spare key her mother had lent her from the side pocket of her purse. "I'm safe. Obviously."

He persisted and accompanied her up the walkway. *Drats.* Why hadn't her mother left the porch light on? It was pitch black on the stoop. She fumbled with the key, which once inserted, didn't turn.

"Let me," Nick offered. He stood calmly behind her, his hands at his sides.

"I've got it." Only she didn't. After another awkward thirty seconds, she moved aside. "You win."

He jiggled the key once and the lock opened. She cursed silently.

"Just takes the right touch."

"I could easily hate you," she grumbled.

"We both know you don't."

His tone took on a low, husky quality that sent a zing coursing through her. Emma steeled her defenses.

"I guess I'll see you tomorrow," she said, more shakily than she'd have liked. There were still a ton of last-minute preparations for the reception.

"Probably."

Why didn't he leave? Why didn't she go inside? She

put her hand on the doorknob and twisted, only her feet remained rooted in place.

"Nick. We… You…" She lifted her gaze to his.

Huge mistake. The hunger burning in his eyes struck her full force and rendered her weak-kneed. He may not love her anymore, but he desired her. That much was obvious.

He gripped her upper arms hard, his fingers digging into her flesh through the fabric of her coat.

"What are you doing?" she demanded.

"Kiss me."

"No. Are you crazy?"

"Without a doubt."

Nothing could be gained by this, and so much could be lost. She considered wrenching herself free of his hold.

Considered? She was actually thinking about of letting him kiss her?

"There's no mistletoe."

He lowered his head. "I don't need any."

"You don't even like me."

"Where did you get that idea?"

Oh, that voice. It stirred something inside her impossible to resist or ignore. Just like when they were younger. Only now Emma was well aware of how Nick was able to back up those sexy promises with actions— and how deeply he could wound her.

Realization dawned. The real reason she'd stayed away all these years wasn't embarrassment or shame or pride. Her unwavering love for him left her vulnerable. And afraid.

She should run. Bolt inside and lock the door. Instead she stood on tiptoes, the force of her feelings for him too powerful to resist. This, she told herself, would definitely, positively be the last time she kissed him.

"I don't suppose you'll leave until I relent."

His answer was to cover her lips with his.

CHAPTER SIX

WHAT HAPPENED NEXT was a blur. One second, Emma and Nick were kissing. The next, he was opening the front door—using only one hand—and the two of them tumbled inside. A small light atop the piano she'd played as a little girl provided the only illumination.

He found her mouth again and, lifting her in his arms, carried her across the living room to the couch. She tore frantically at his jacket with fumbling fingers. So much for exercising better judgment. At last, the stubborn snaps gave, and she attacked the buttons on his shirt.

Too long. That was her only coherent thought. Six years she'd waited. Not for something like this, for *exactly* this. Nick. Hard. Demanding. A release for the desperate need pent up inside her.

He laid her on the couch. More like dropped her in his haste. When he straightened, she cried out, "No! Stay."

It wasn't just the sex or a random physical connection. Emma needed Nick. In ways she wasn't ready to admit.

"Trust me, I'm not going anywhere." Shrugging out of his jacket, he tossed it aside. His cowboy hat was next. After that, he finished the job she'd started on his shirt. Peeling it off, he stood before her, wearing a white undershirt.

"Don't stop there," she insisted, watching with fascination and delight as he tugged the undershirt from his jeans.

His boots hit the floor with a thud. His socks landed soundlessly. Yanking on his belt, he undid the silver buckle. She smiled as he stepped out of his jeans, his erection evident through the fabric of his navy briefs. Whatever transpired between them, she just knew was going to be good.

"What are you doing?" she asked when he went down on his knees before her.

"Getting you naked."

She liked the sound of that, and toed off her shoes. "I'll help."

Nick had always been fearless and confident in bed, even when they were young and had little experience. In Emma's case, zero experience. He'd been her first. In more than one way. The first man she'd made love to and the first man she'd fallen in love with. To this day, the only man she'd ever loved.

If her feelings for him weren't still so strong, she wouldn't be here now, letting him slide her jeans down her legs. Drawing in a startled breath as he pushed her knees apart.

There would likely be regrets come morning, the worst being that this might only be temporary. She wasn't dwelling on those now. In fact, her mind emptied of everything save Nick and his fingertips skimming the bare skin of her belly.

She moaned softly and lifted her hips. Taking her

cue, he removed the thin wisp of material she dared to call panties, then went perfectly still.

"Cripes, Emma. You're beautiful."

The look he gave her went straight to her heart. "Touch me," she whispered, and arched beneath him, eagerly awaiting his next move.

A slow grin spread across his face. "I'm going to do a lot more than that."

THEY LAY TOGETHER on the narrow couch, exhausted and utterly sated. Memories of earlier, similar times returned, but Emma welcomed them rather than resisted them. In this moment, all was right with them. With the entire world. Were she just a little more sure of herself, she'd tell him.

Instead she said, "Mom isn't coming home tonight," as her fingers explored the familiar territory of his chest and stomach. "Or Cole."

"I'm not leaving. You're stuck with me for the rest of the night."

"I'm glad. But what if Leonard notices you don't come home?"

"Pretty unlikely. I don't live at the ranch. Haven't for a long while."

"Oh." He didn't? She'd assumed he stayed in the bunkhouse as when they were younger.

"I have my own place just outside of town. Three-bedroom house and small barn on some acreage."

"Sounds nice. I'd like to see it."

He pushed up onto his elbow to look at her, their faces inches apart. Despite the lack of light, she could discern every tiny detail of his attractive features. A small hint of doubt clouded his eyes.

"Are you serious?" he asked.

"Yeah, I am."

Emma couldn't be sure of her feelings at that moment. And she wasn't making any commitments past spending the night with him and seeing where he lived.

"For now, let's forget about the past and not worry about the future."

"All right." He smiled, and his features relaxed.

Emma fell a little more in love with him.

Eventually, they abandoned the couch in favor of the bed. They'd slept together before, but only during stolen moments. As they lay entwined in each other's arms, on the verge of sleep, happiness bloomed inside Emma. All her constant moving from job to job, place to place, she'd been searching for this. And here it was, the whole time, waiting for her.

FUNNY HOW QUICKLY one could fall into old habits. While showering together in the morning and getting dressed were new for Emma and Nick, their easy banter, laughing and teasing weren't. It gave Emma hope. Could this new, tentative relationship of theirs work? Was it too soon to tell?

"We're already late," she cautioned when he interrupted her brushing her hair to steal another kiss. "Leonard will definitely notice you're not at work."

"After last night's dinner, I bet he's sleeping in, too."

"Mom's expecting me."

Emma's job today, besides picking up her mother at the ranch and bringing her home later, was to oversee the many deliveries. Floral arrangements from Merrick's Mistletoe Farm. Gowns and tuxes from I Now Pronounce You Wedding Attire. Dishes, stemware and flatware from the caterer. She also needed to meet with the DJ and review the playlist, making sure it included her mother's favorite song for her and Leonard's first dance as husband and wife. Emma was already drained just thinking about everything.

Lack of sleep didn't help. She and Nick had awoken early, but then one thing had led to another. A brush of his lips. A silky caress. Shivers cascading along her skin as his mouth and tongue tasted every inch of her body. Yes, indeed, Nick was a talented lover.

"What are you doing for dinner tonight?" she asked, hoping he'd take the hint and suggest they eat out. Perhaps pick up where they were leaving off this morning.

"Not sure." He sat on the bed, tugging on his boots. "We're missing a few heifers. Probably hiding during the roundup. One of them is ready to deliver. Me and the boys are riding out today looking for them."

"Don't cows usually give birth in the spring?"

"She was already bred when we purchased her. Didn't know until this fall when she started showing."

Emma hid her disappointment. Work came first, and she respected that. Still, he could give her some reassurance their night together had meant something to him.

"There's always later. Call me when you get back."

He stood and gave her a quick, distracted hug. "Sure thing."

They didn't talk during the ride to the Yule Tide. At first, Emma assured herself that theirs was simply companionable silence. Halfway there, doubts crept in. Was Nick having regrets? Did he think they'd acted foolishly? He had been extremely noncommittal about dinner tonight.

She inched her hand across the console separating

them. When he finally noticed, he flashed her a grin
and squeezed her fingers, then withdrew his hand to
rest it in his lap.

Emma tried not to read anything into his actions. Her
insecurities won out, and she began creating scenarios
in her head, none of them ending well.

Once again, she'd jumped the gun with Nick. Why
had she kissed him last night at the front door? Maybe
she should have sent him home instead. But then they
wouldn't have made love. She didn't regret that.

At the ranch, Nick dropped Emma off in front of the
house. "See you later." This time when he kissed her,
his lips lingered.

See, Emma told herself. *Nothing to worry about.*
Watching his truck bump along the dirt drive to the
barn, her insecurities returned. He hadn't been entirely
honest with her once before. He could be holding back
again.

Opening the door to the ranch house, she stepped
inside.

"Morning, honey." Her mother stood in the center of
the living room, eyes red-rimmed and vivid splotches
marring her cheeks.

Not the picture of a woman about to be married.

"Sorry I'm late," Emma said.

"No problem." Her voice rang with artificial cheeri-
ness. "We just…just got started."

Emma hugged her mother, whose response was token
at best.

"Are you okay?"

"Of course."

It was then Emma spotted Holly on the other side of
the room, near one of the rental tables. Her future step-

sister held herself ramrod straight, and her narrowed gaze never left Emma's mother.

"Hey, Holly." Despite her rising alarm, Emma kept the greeting casual as she removed her coat. "Whatcha two doing?"

"Sorting gifts," her mother answered.

"Can I help?"

Holly erupted in bitter laughter.

"What's the matter with you?" Emma snapped. She didn't know what had put Holly in such a sour state, but she'd reached her limit.

"*This* is what's the matter with me."

The table beside Holly contained a pile of presents sent from long-distance friends and family members unable to attend the wedding. One package had been opened and the gift box removed. The lid sat askew, and white tissue paper spilled from the sides of the box.

Holly reached into the gift box and removed a blue-and-white heart-shaped condiment dish. It was quite pretty, very delicate and obviously expensive.

Emma turned to her mother. "I thought you were going to open these gifts at the reception."

"I am. Was." Her mother hesitated.

"I opened this one." Holly's features hardened.

"Why?" Emma didn't understand.

"It's from my dad's cousin. She lives in England."

"That doesn't give you the right to open a package not addressed to you."

"This is Wedgwood china." Holly raised the dish. For a split second, Emma thought Holly intended to smash the dish to the floor. "My dad's cousin has been sending my mother pieces for years. Every birthday and

Christmas. She had quite a collection. Now, evidently, there's one new piece to add."

"Uh-oh."

"Yeah, *uh-oh*," Holly mimicked.

"I have no interest in the china," Emma's mother insisted. "I told you that. I can't imagine why your father's cousin sent the dish. It was thoughtless on her part. And as far as I'm concerned, the entire collection, including that dish, belongs to you and your sister."

"You think I want this?" She waved the dish again.

Emma stepped between the two women. "I can see why you're upset, Holly. But this is hardly my mother's fault. She doesn't even know your dad's cousin."

"Well, she sure as heck is making herself part of the family. And the house. It doesn't look the same anymore. Pictures are missing. Furniture's rearranged."

"Holly." Emma's mother gasped. "That's not true. I've hardly moved a thing."

"Except your stuff into my dad's bedroom."

What Emma thought was jealousy on the part of Holly obviously went far deeper. She was still grieving her late mother and taking it out on everyone around her. Especially Emma's mother. Emma should be angry with Holly. Instead she felt sorry for the other woman. To be miserable all the time was no way to live.

That didn't, however, give her reason to ruin her father's wedding.

"Where's Leonard?" Emma asked her mother.

"With Nick, I think."

"I doubt it," Holly said. "Since Nick didn't get here until a few minutes ago. With you. I saw him drop you off."

Emma resisted rising to the bait. "Maybe we should find him. Your dad, that is."

"Don't pretend you and Nick didn't spend the night together."

Okay. Maybe Emma couldn't resist. "Frankly, what I do and who I'm with is none of your business."

"It is if the guy's my ex-boyfriend."

"Boyfriend?"

"Nick and I dated."

"I don't believe you."

"Last year. For four months. We were quite the couple."

Shock rendered Emma mute. Nick and Holly, boyfriend and girlfriend? No, impossible. He'd have told her. Or would he?

"My dad really wanted it to work out with us," Holly continued. "Still does. Ask Nick if you think I'm lying."

In a weird, terrible way, what Holly claimed made sense. By his own admission, Nick had dated extensively. And he had a proved history of not revealing the entire truth.

Emma swallowed, then inhaled deeply. Neither restored her equilibrium. She tried to think of what to say or do next and came up blank. In her mind, she was standing in the church dressing room, her mother behind her and arranging her veil. A loud commotion had sounded from another part of the church. All of a sudden, her maid of honor poked her head through the door. "Emma, you should come out here," she'd announced. "There's a problem."

After that, her entire world had imploded.

She shouldn't be hurt by this revelation about Holly and Nick. He and Emma weren't engaged. They weren't even dating. She had no ties to him. Yet she *was* hurt. Severely. The similarities between Holly and Laurel Linkletter were too striking not to affect her. Nick had purposely not told her about a past relationship. Would he also claim this time he was sparing her feelings?

Raised voices penetrated the haze surrounding Emma, and she blinked herself back to the present.

"Was that really necessary?" her mother demanded.

Holly shrugged one shoulder. "She has a right to know."

"But it wasn't *your* place to tell her."

"Well, then, you should have."

"You're stirring up trouble and targeting Emma for no good reason. It's me you're angry at."

Wait, Emma thought. Her mother knew about and Nick and Holly? Of course she did. Emma bit her lower lip. She would not fall apart. Not now.

Leave. That was best. She refused to give Holly more ammunition to use against her.

Wait. Was her car here? Emma couldn't remember where she'd left it last night. Yes. It was parked near the garage. She took a tentative step on legs too wobbly to support her.

The kitchen door opened. She knew this because her mother and Holly stared in the direction of boisterous male voices and heavy footsteps.

Nick and Leonard strode into the living room, only to come to an abrupt halt.

Leonard took one look at them and scowled. "What's wrong?"

What isn't wrong? Emma thought bitterly.

"Sweetheart?" He showed more sense than the other day and went to Emma's mother rather than Holly.

Nick stayed where he was, his jacket hanging open. He was wearing the same shirt from yesterday. Of course he was. He'd donned it this morning at her mother's house. Why was she even noticing his clothes?

Her glance traveled from Nick to Holly and back again. Such an unlikely pairing, though she could see why Leonard might favor the match. His single daughter and the ranch foreman he loved like a son.

By the way, Holly and I dated briefly last year. I thought you should know.

Two simple sentences. More than enough. Except Nick hadn't said them. Why?

Someone was crying. Emma looked around to see her mother in tears and Leonard comforting her.

"It's for the best," she said between sobs.

"Sweetheart, no. Please."

"Emma's right. We rushed into this and should have waited."

"For once, I agree with her," Holly bit out.

Emma forced herself to focus. "Mom? What's going on?"

"We're calling off the wedding."

"No," Leonard insisted.

"Postponing it, then. Holly is distraught, and I refuse to marry you unless the entire family is supportive. That's no way to start our lives together."

"We're getting married," Leonard insisted. "Tomorrow."

Emma felt the burn of Nick's stare and spun around. Their eyes locked, and she tensed. What did he have to be mad at? He wasn't he one who'd been lied to. Again.

"Leonard," her mother pleaded. "Be realistic."

"We're going to talk this out. I don't care if it takes all

day." He grasped her arm and, sending Holly a warning glare, led Emma's mother toward the hall and, Emma assumed, his bedroom.

"What have you done, Holly?" Nick said the second Leonard and Emma's mother were out of earshot.

"How is this my fault?"

"Your father loves Candy."

At that, Holly burst into tears.

Emma couldn't stay a moment longer. She had to get out of there. If only to escape a room suddenly void of oxygen.

Legs no longer wobbly, she bolted through the living room, to the kitchen and out the back door. There, she hesitated long enough to gain her bearings. Frigid wind cut through her, causing her teeth to chatter. Damn, she'd forgotten her coat. No matter, she wasn't going after it.

Hugging herself to ward off the cold, she set out in the direction of the garage. When had the weather worsened? A quick glance at the sky gave her the answer. Clouds had grown denser and darker since her and Nick's arrival.

"Emma!" Nick flew out the back door, calling her name.

She broke into a jog.

"Wait."

A quick glance over her shoulder confirmed he was gaining on her. Dammit. He was the last person she wanted to talk to right now.

CHAPTER SEVEN

NICK REACHED EMMA just as her fingers grasped the car door. "I don't understand why you're so angry at me."

Ignoring him, she wrenched open the door.

He had half a mind to let her go. At the last second, he blocked her way. Something was terribly wrong, and he needed to find out.

"What have I done? Because the last time I checked, which was thirty minutes ago, we were getting along great."

The glare she aimed at him would have a less determined man rethinking his decision. "You dated Holly."

"Ah."

"Ah! That's all you have to say?"

"We went out a few times. No big deal. She means nothing to me, other than she's the daughter of my boss and a friend."

"Four months, Nick. Hardly a few times."

"I've dated other women. You know that."

"Not her." Emma's voice cracked. "You should have told me."

"I didn't think about it. That's the truth."

"Kind of like you didn't think about your weekend fling with Laurel Linkletter?"

She *would* bring that up.

"Being with you does tend to make me forget about former relationships."

"Nice line, Nick. Use it on the next girl." She attempted to slip past him.

He stood his ground. "Look, my dating Holly didn't matter until last night. When exactly was I supposed to mention it? While we were making love? Or maybe this morning in the shower?"

"How about on the drive over?"

"If it had occurred to me, that would have been the right moment. But it didn't. Because my relationship with Holly is in the past. The forgotten past."

"You weren't honest with me."

"I wasn't dishonest. If you had asked me, I'd have told you about her."

"My mother is marrying her father."

"You haven't said one thing about previous boyfriends." He strived to maintain control. "And I haven't asked. For all I know, you have one tucked away in Austin."

Her eyes widened. "I would never have spent the night with you if I had a boyfriend."

"And I can say the same thing. I'm unattached, Emma. I don't care about Holly, other than as Leonard's daughter, and you shouldn't, either."

"She's going to be my stepsister. Every time I look at her, I'll be thinking she had you, too."

"We weren't involved like that." Nick's tone sharpened as his control weakened. "I never slept with her."

"Still, a little awkward. Wouldn't you agree?"

"Why do you constantly make everything about you? Your mom's called off her wedding, and all you can talk about is a previous, *meaningless* relationship I failed to mention."

"Why do *you* constantly dismiss my feelings as insignificant? I realize that my mom and Leonard are in crisis. Thanks to Holly." Her features hardened. "Quite a coincidence, isn't it? Their marriage is also interrupted at the last minute because of another woman."

"This isn't the same, Emma."

"Thank God. I'd hate for a pregnant woman to show up claiming Leonard was her child's father."

"Dammit, Emma. I get that you're still ticked at me, but do you have to keep bringing up Laurel?"

"Believe me, I'm done being ticked at you. Have been for a long time."

"Then why bend over backward to avoid me since then?"

"I was hurt."

"And I wasn't? You. Left. Me." He enunciated each word. "And you didn't come back or take my calls even after the DNA tests confirmed I wasn't the baby's father." That had hurt the worst.

"I didn't trust you anymore. And apparently with good reason. You haven't changed one lick."

Her not trust him? That was almost funny. He posed the same question he had that night outside Frozen Delights. "Would it have made any difference if I'd told you that Holly and I dated briefly? Would you feel less awkward or less insecure?"

"I'm not insecure."

That was debatable. Nonetheless, Nick reined in his temper. "I was trying to protect you. Both times."

"You keep justifying your lack of honesty." She shivered, and her teeth chattered. He'd take her in his arms if she'd let him. No chance of that. "When two people care for each other, they don't withhold important information, even if it might hurt the other person."

Nick was growing tired of arguing and tried a different approach. "We spent the night together, Emma. That's not something I do with just anybody."

"We hooked up for old time's sake."

If her intention was to wound him, she'd succeeded. "That's all it meant to you?"

"We have a lot of history. And I'm willing to admit the attraction hasn't died. But it's obvious you aren't serious."

"How can you say that?"

"You barely spoke to me on the drive here."

The past five minutes suddenly made sense. She was making less of her feelings in order to shield herself against heartache and disappointment.

"I was planning my day," he explained. "The blizzard's coming, and we have half a dozen missing heifers. My distraction had nothing to do with you or us."

"Right." Her voice dripped with sarcasm. "There I go again, making everything about me."

"Emma, please. Can we call a truce? At least until after the wedding."

She continued as if she hadn't heard him. "We were wrong to think we could pick up where we left off. There's too much damage. Too many unresolved issues."

"We've hardly tried." Twelve hours, by his count.

"Let's just get through the next two days. I'll go home and take that new job if they offer it to me. You can keep dating every available woman in town."

So much for controlling his temper. Nick exploded.

"Of course. Because that's what you always do. The second trouble hits, Emma heads for the hills. And you say you don't trust *me*."

"Not fair."

"Really? You aren't the only one allowed to throw punches. Has it occurred to you that the reason we have so many unresolved issues is because you don't stick around long enough to resolve them?"

Emma's mouth fell open, then snapped shut. "I'm leaving." She ducked under his arm.

"See you at the wedding tomorrow afternoon."

He shouldn't be so quick to blame her, he thought as he watched her drive away, his anger vented. She wasn't the only one using present circumstances to wage a battle rooted in the past. And there was a margin of truth to her statement that the two of them had spent the night together for old time's sake. Hadn't he used the flimsy excuse of mistletoe to kiss her the first time?

Putting their argument aside for the moment, Nick decided to see about Leonard and Candy. Hopefully they'd fared better at settling their differences than he and Emma.

Inside, Holly reported that her father and Candy were still sequestered in the bedroom. Nick took that as a good sign, though he wished Holly would find something else to do other than hang around like a vulture circling a carcass.

In the barn, he met with Toby and two of the other ranch hands before saddling his favorite horse. Each rider would each take a different section of the grazing range to search for the missing heifers.

Before leaving, Nick replaced the batteries in his walkie-talkie. With inclement weather in the forecast, now wasn't the time to be caught without reliable communication. Twenty minutes later he crossed the border into section number fifteen just as a few flakes of snow drifted lazily to the ground. Not exactly a blizzard as predicted, but that could change and probably would.

He rode along a steep and rocky ridge, periodically guiding the big gelding down into ravines or behind stands of trees where cattle typically liked to hide. Stopping on a rise, he took out his binoculars from his saddlebag and scanned the horizon. Swirling snow, however, impeded his view. Even so, Nick refused to give up. Fortunately, the gelding was young and strong and up to the task.

Finally, after another two hours—and a tip from one of the other wranglers out searching—Nick's efforts paid off. He located a heifer taking shelter in the bottom of a gully. At the sight of him, she gave a long, lusty low and scrambled up the incline, evidently more than ready to return to the home pastures where food, water and warm bodies to huddle next to waited.

Rather than start ahead, Nick tilted his head to one side and listened carefully over the roaring wind. Was that another heifer lowing in the distance? Maybe. Yes, definitely!

He herded the first heifer in the direction of the sound. Before long, he found the pregnant heifer he'd been worried about behind the decayed trunk of a long-ago felled pine tree. His relief was short-lived. She stood over the still body of what could only be her calf.

Swearing under his breath, Nick dismounted and tied his horse to a nearby branch. She'd picked a lousy time and place to deliver. The heifer snorted and shifted with unease as he neared her. Nick proceeded cautiously.

Mother cows had been known to be aggressive when protecting their young. Even their dead young.

He debated returning for the rope tied to his saddle. This girl may not want to leave and lassoing her could be his only option. Suddenly, a movement caught his eye. What in the...

The calf's right front leg twitched again.

"Well, I'll be," Nick muttered. The calf was still alive. Hard to believe, in this weather.

Wasting no time and disregarding his personal safety, Nick went to the calf, lifted it in his arms and carried it back to his horse. The poor thing was as cold as ice and hardly breathing.

Removing his spare rain poncho from the saddlebag, he wrapped the calf in the only protection he could offer and laid it across the horse's neck. Thankfully, the horse proved his worth and didn't spook.

With luck, Nick could get the calf, its mother and the other heifer back to safety before the storm hit. As he mounted, one hand on the weak calf to hold it steady, his glance darted to the sky. Not his imagination. Snow was falling harder. The blizzard might not wait till after the wedding.

"Hold on," he told the calf, and nudged his horse into a fast walk as he pushed the two heifers ahead of him and in the direction of home.

With all he had on his mind, and all the obstacles he faced, Nick was surprised to find himself thinking of Emma and their argument. Apparently once wasn't enough, and he'd required a second hard-hitting lesson before realizing they weren't meant to be together.

FEELING GUILTY FOR LEAVING, Emma phoned her mother the instant she pulled away from the Yule Tide Ranch.

On the one hand, the call was reassuring. Her mother and Leonard were still deep in conversation. Her mother's tearful tone, however, was troubling. Perhaps Emma should have stayed. Then again, Leonard had insisted on privacy.

Excuses, excuses. The truth was, Emma needed to escape. She and Nick hadn't conversed, privately or otherwise. They'd fought. But, dammit, she was right. He should have told her about dating Holly. Did he not think she'd find out eventually, or that it wouldn't hurt?

She swallowed a sob. History really was repeating itself. Would she have come back to Mistletoe if she'd known what would happen?

Yes, of course. For her mother, anything. But she'd have avoided Nick at all costs and definitely wouldn't have spent the night with him. Or kissed him. Or spoken to him unless absolutely necessary.

Her chest ached. Her throat burned. Her eyes stung. God willing, the drama was at an end. Regardless, Emma was leaving at the soonest possible opportunity.

Because that's what you always do. The second trouble hits, Emma heads for the hills.

Nick's voice reverberated inside her head. Was it true? Did she run away rather than deal with the consequences? Some might say her track record spoke for itself.

She slapped the steering wheel. Enough with the self-analysis. It accomplished nothing. Instead she phoned Cole, who was still at his buddy's house, and gave him the condensed version of their mother's altercation with Holly. The news that the wedding was on hold upset Cole, and he let Emma know in no uncertain terms.

"Well, I guess you got what you wanted."

"Wait a minute! I only—"

He didn't let her finish. "Swing by and pick me up."

Seeing him stumble from the door to her car, slightly hungover from the effects of last night, Emma did her own insisting and drove them straight to the Mistletoe Café for a late breakfast. The hearty food and gallon of coffee Cole drank revived him.

"Aren't you a little too old for partying all night?" she scolded as they neared the ranch. What they were going to do when they arrived she didn't know, but Cole would hear of nothing else. Their mother needed them.

Emma hoped Nick was still out searching for stray heifers. She couldn't handle another confrontation. Not today.

"Bachelor party." Cole closed his eyes and rubbed his temple. Apparently the three aspirin he'd downed hadn't kicked in yet.

"But Leonard wasn't there."

"Carl's idea. We decided to celebrate on Leonard's behalf."

"Stupid."

"I'm glad now he didn't come with us."

So was Emma.

"Poor Mom," Cole said. "She must be a basket case. I just hope they don't call off the wedding."

"I don't want them calling off the wedding, either. Though postponing it might not be a bad idea."

"They aren't you, Emma."

"I realize that," she snapped. Why was everyone, everyone being Nick and now Cole, giving her a hard time? "But Leonard isn't just Holly's father. He's her boss, too. The Yule Tide Ranch is also her home. They need to get along. If not, the business could suffer."

"Are you saying he should put his daughter before his own happiness?"

"I'm saying he shouldn't entirely dismiss her objections. And if that means giving her another six months to become more accustomed to the idea of a stepmother, then yeah, I'm in favor of it. That would also give Mom more time to show Holly she isn't a threat."

Emma commended herself for such a well-constructed and reasonably presented argument.

"Tell Mom that and I'll disown you."

"What?" She gaped at Cole.

"You need to be supporting her. Not complicating things."

"I'm not. I mean, I do support her. And I'm not complicating things."

"Really?" He sent her an arch look. "What about you and Nick? As if they didn't have enough to worry about. Now two members of their wedding party are at each other's throats."

Why had she mentioned her fight with Nick over breakfast? "I agree. We should have waited."

Waited to get married. Waited and not slept with each other this weekend. Waited to have their huge blowout until after the wedding. Their entire relationship, start to finish, was one continuous race.

"Fix this," Cole said. "Whatever it takes. You don't have to be friends. Just play nice during the wedding and reception."

"If there is one."

"Quit being such a pessimist."

Her brother's scolding, deserved or not, stung. Emma remained silent after that. At the ranch house, they knocked on the front door. To her surprise, Leonard answered and ushered them in. Had he and her mother finished *conversing?* Was the wedding back on?

Evidently not. When they entered the kitchen, her mother and Holly sat at the table, both hastily pulling themselves together. On closer inspection, Leonard also showed signs of strain.

Cole bent his head close to Emma's and whispered, "Follow my lead."

"What?"

"Divide and conquer. I'll take Holly."

Emma had no clue what her brother was up to and watched with curiosity as he went over and gave their mother a hug. "How you doing, Mom?"

"I'm fine." She leaned in to give his cheek a pat, only to cling desperately to him.

This was worse than Emma first thought. And, in her opinion, entirely preventable.

Holly stood and said tersely, "If you'll excuse me."

Leonard waylaid her. "Isn't there something you'd like to say to Emma before you go?"

Holly clenched her jaw and breathed deeply. "I'm sorry for the scene I caused earlier."

Just about the most insincere apology Emma had ever heard. Then again, Leonard had treated Holly as if she were a child. Under the same circumstances, Emma would have been annoyed at her father.

Glimpsing the hope on her mother's face and a warning look on Cole's, Emma accepted the lame apology with a much more heartfelt response. "I know it must have been hurtful, seeing that dish from your dad's cousin."

"It was." Holly turned to leave.

Cole's plan to divide and conquer became apparent

when he blocked Holly's exit. "Since this is my first time here, why don't you show me around the place?"

She stared at him suspiciously. "You want a tour?"

"Yeah." He grinned, his dimples in full force. "I've never seen a cattle operation before."

Holly's resolve visibly weakened. She was either susceptible to his obvious flirtations or jumping on any excuse to leave. "Okay. Let me grab my jacket. It's snowing outside."

Cole gave Emma a subtle nod, which she translated into, "Get Mom alone and talk some sense into her."

The problem was, Emma thought her mother was already being sensible.

"Glad that's settled," Leonard announced, and taking her mother's hand, hauled her to her feet. "Now, beautiful lady, we can get back to what counts. Namely, our wedding."

"Not so fast," her mother warned.

"But Holly—"

"She's being nice because you read her the riot act. She still isn't ready to accept me as your wife or her stepmother."

"I disagree. Besides, what we do isn't any of her concern."

"Emma has a point."

"Me?" Emma squeaked.

"About taking it slow," her mother reiterated.

"Now, just a gall darn minute." Leonard's patience was clearly used up.

"What difference will a few months make if Holly is more comfortable?"

That was exactly the point Emma had been trying to

make. Yet it didn't sound quite the same coming from her mother or in the face of Leonard's frustration.

"This isn't about Holly," he insisted.

"It's about all of us, if we ever expect to be a family."

Their debate escalated, becoming more and more personal until Emma felt like an intruder. She was also painfully reminded of her and Nick's earlier disagreement. Ignoring Cole's directive to talk sense into their mother, she slipped unnoticed through the back door.

On the stoop, she adjusted her wool scarf and secured the top button on her coat. No forgetting it this time. Though light, the snow was falling in earnest. She could only guess where Cole and Holly had gone off to and, frankly, didn't care. Joining them was last on her list of priorities.

Was Nick still searching for lost cows? She hoped not. As mad as she was at him, neither man nor beast deserved to be out in foul weather.

After a few minutes of aimless strolling, Emma tired of her own dreary company and was more than ready to return to the warmth of the house. Except, what if her mother and Leonard were still arguing?

Guilt ate at her. She wasn't responsible for this fiasco. Or the one with her and Nick. Not really. Okay, maybe a little. Perhaps.

Standing still, she squeezed her eyes shut and let the wind and snow flurries pummel her. This had turned into the worst day of her life. No, the second worst. And she had no one to blame but herself.

Hearing the sound of voices over the wind, she opened her eyes. Cole and Holly were walking across the large open area from the horse barn to the detached office. Unlike everyone else, they were getting along well. Splendidly, in fact. When the coast was clear, Emma started for the barn. While cold, at least the building provided cover from the elements.

Memories assailed her the moment she stepped through the wide doorway. She'd always loved visiting the Yule Tide's many horses, and Nick had frequently brought her here when they were dating. Teaching her to ride had been one of their favorite pastimes.

Nick. Did her every thought have to circle back to him?

She stopped at the stall of a small brown mare, who immediately came over and bumped her arm in a bid for attention.

"Aren't you a sweet girl." She continued her one-sided conversation while running her hand along the mare's sleek neck.

"What are you doing here?"

Startled, she gasped softly. Wind and cold had left Nick's entire face a bright crimson. Snow covered him from head to toe, freezing to ice on the shoulders of his heavy coat and the brim of his cowboy hat.

"Are you all right?"

Rather than answer, he brushed by her without stopping.

She hurried after him. "What's wrong?"

"I'm trying to save a life."

CHAPTER EIGHT

"I CAN HELP," Emma insisted.

It didn't take a genius to see that Nick wasn't happy about her accompanying him to a shed behind the barn. But after he'd told her about finding the mother cow and calf, which was at this moment clinging to life, Emma refused to leave.

"I don't need any help," he grumbled.

"Quit being so stubborn."

That earned her a disapproving scowl. All right, he wasn't the only one reluctant to compromise.

Emma watched him remove a jug from an old refrigerator in the corner. It contained a white substance, which he poured into a large plastic bottle and diluted with warm water from a laundry sink.

"What's that?" she asked.

"Colostrum."

Emma knew next to nothing about babies—human or cow—but she'd gleaned enough from TV and pregnant friends to understand that colostrum had something to do with mother's milk. The concoction Nick prepared must be a substitute.

He screwed an equally large nipple onto the bottle. With his free hand, he tugged a pile of old blankets off the shelf. Setting both down, he removed a tall lamp from the corner. It was unlike any lamp Emma had seen before, its bulb covered with metal mesh. Clean rags were added to the pile of blankets.

"You can't carry everything." Emma reached for the blankets and towels.

He made a disgruntled sound but didn't stop her.

While not heavy, the items were bulky. Emma stumbled more than once on their way to the empty horse stall where Nick had left the calf. At the sight of its still, pale form lying on the sawdust-covered floor, her heart broke.

"Where's the mother?" she asked.

"In the pasture. She'd only get in the way."

"In the way?" Emma was appalled. How could Nick be so cruel? "You'd separate her from her baby?"

"Her instincts are to protect her calf. She wouldn't understand we're trying to save it. She could be dangerous. Inadvertently injure me or her calf."

Emma's mistake. Nick wasn't being cruel at all—a fact that became more and more apparent as he gently but vigorously toweled the calf dry with the rags. His reward was a feeble bleating sound as the calf attempted to lift its head.

"Did you find all the missing heifers?" Emma hovered nearby.

"Toby's bringing in the last three. He radioed an hour ago."

"That's good."

Another disgruntled sound. After a moment, Nick said, "Would you plug in the heat lamp for me?"

Heat lamp. That explained the weird metal mesh covering the bulb.

"Sure." Steadying the lamp in the sawdust, she reached for the cord.

"The outlet's on the post outside the stall."

Two feet shy. If she pulled any harder, she'd topple the lamp. "The cord won't reach."

"There's an extension cord in the shed."

Her hurried trip to and from the shed startled the horses, who snorted and danced sideways. After plugging in the lamp, she flipped the switch. The bulb glowed a bright orange-red. For a relatively small device, it emitted a lot of heat. She aimed the cone-shaped shade toward the calf.

By then, Nick was sitting on the stall floor with the calf's head on his lap, attempting to feed it. The calf made a weak effort to mouth the nipple, then gave up with a pitiful sigh.

"Give him time," Emma encouraged. "Maybe he just needs to warm up a bit."

"We don't have time." He paused, studying the calf. "Go to the house. See if you can find a turkey baster."

Again, Emma did as Nick asked. She didn't remind him that he'd initially refused her assistance, only glad that she could provide it.

In the kitchen, she rummaged through drawers. Despite the racket she made, no one appeared. Finally, she found the baster. Next to the oven. She should have looked there first.

"How are Leonard and your mom doing?" Nick asked when she produced the baster.

"Not so great. Holly apologized to me earlier, but Mom's still worried she won't support the marriage."

"I'm sorry to hear that."

"I am, too."

"Really, Emma?" Unscrewing the nipple from the bottle, he filled the turkey baster with liquid.

"Of course I am. Mom obviously loves Leonard. I hate seeing her hurt."

"Yet you think she should have waited to get married."

"I don't want to argue about this now." *Or ever again,* she silently added.

Nick angled the calf's head and carefully pried open its mouth. He inserted the baster and squeezed the bulb. The calf drank several swallows. Emma went almost giddy with relief.

"He's eating!" she exclaimed.

"A little. We still have a long road ahead." After the calf accepted a few more mouthfuls from the baster, Nick tried the bottle. The calf suckled once, then dropped its head in Nick's lap, utterly exhausted. "That's enough for now. We'll try again later."

We? Did he realize he'd included her?

He pushed to his feet and covered the calf with a blanket. "I'm going inside for a few minutes. Get a cup of coffee and see if I can scrounge up a dry shirt."

"Good idea." Despite the warmth from the heat lamp, he was still soaked. "You don't want to get sick."

"Do you mind staying here and watching her?"

"Her? It's a girl?" Emma had called the calf a he.

"Yeah." Pausing at the stall door, he searched her face. "Thanks, Emma."

"Sure."

"And..."

"What, Nick?"

"I'm sorry about this morning. I shouldn't have argued with you. Not after last night."

He wasn't apologizing for what he'd said, only that

he'd chosen the wrong moment. Not what she wanted to hear.

"We're both stressed."

"Right." He walked away.

She stared after him. Had she not given the response he'd wanted to hear, either?

Emma focused her energies on the calf, which still lay on the stall floor, its eyes closed. The curious horse in the neighboring stall pressed its nose to the bars and snorted as if with disdain that a cow should be allowed in with the horses.

"You sleeping, little girl?" Emma went closer to the calf. After a moment, she knelt down beside it. "Poor, poor baby."

Extending a tentative hand, she stroked the calf's head. It didn't so much as flick an eyelash. Sitting back, she shoved her hands into her coat pockets—and encountered the mistletoe charm. Like the other day, it was oddly warm. But that was impossible.

The luck is in the giving. Wasn't that what her mother had said?

On impulse, Emma withdrew the charm and examined it. The leaves were still a bright, lush green, and the small white berries plump and round. How could that be?

Untying the red ribbon, she stretched it out, satisfied with the length. Gently easing her hand beneath the calf's head, she wound the ribbon around its neck and secured the charm with a knot. When she was done, she went back to stroking the calf.

Only then did she notice the tears streaming down her cheeks. She blinked them away, for all the good it did. More continued to fall.

Alone in the stall with the sleeping calf, Emma let herself cry. For her mother, for herself and for their thwarted weddings. Why hadn't they both waited? So much heartache could have been avoided.

Then again, what if Nick was right? Should she have married him anyway and faced their difficulties together, stronger as a couple? Emma had been so shocked and hurt at Laurel Linkletter's claim, she hadn't stopped to consider any option other than leaving. As if she'd needed to punish Nick for the pain he'd caused her.

Oh, God. She *had* been trying to punish him. And every day since then by staying away. Only in reality, she'd punished them both, preventing either of them from finding happiness.

Was it too late? For a while, last night and this morning, she'd thought not. Then she'd learned about Nick dating Holly and used it as an excuse to rehash the past.

A sudden pressure against her knee startled Emma, and she looked down. The calf was awake and stirring!

"Hey, little girl."

The next instant, the calf lifted its head and bleated.

"Well, well." Nick entered the stall.

He looked better than before. In fact, he looked incredible. Love for him filled her. She opened her mouth to tell him, then fell silent. Too risky. What if he didn't love her in return?

"I think she's better." Emma gazed hopefully at the calf, then at Nick.

In response, the calf kicked out with its front legs.

"You're right." He came over for a closer inspection. "Let's see if she can stand."

Bending at the waist, he grabbed the calf around the middle and lifted. The calf moved its legs in a swimming motion before planting all four hooves on the stall floor.

"She's standing," Emma exclaimed.

"Not quite yet."

The little calf's legs trembled uncontrollably for another minute, eventually easing to a mild shake.

"If you hold her," Nick said, "I'll get some fresh formula."

"What if I drop her?"

"You won't."

His assurance gave Emma the confidence she needed. When the calf leaned against her leg for support, she remained steady. "I've got her."

"Good girl."

Emma beamed. Nick used to say the same thing when she'd mastered a new skill during their riding lessons.

He wasn't gone long. When he returned with the bottle, he held it out to Emma. "You want to feed her?"

"Can I?"

"Go ahead."

Keeping one hand on the calf, she offered the bottle with the other one. The calf latched on and began drinking with gusto.

Emma laughed. "She's making a mess."

Indeed, some of the formula had dribbled from the calf's mouth and onto the stall floor.

"She's getting enough. Don't worry." Nick narrowed his gaze, then fingered the mistletoe. "What's this?"

"A lucky charm. My mom gave it to me the other day. I don't know why I put it on the calf."

"Seems to be working."

Emma had been so preoccupied, she'd failed to realize the calf had taken a step forward. Nick put his hand over hers and pulled the bottle from the calf's mouth. It immediately followed the bottle, taking another step.

"She's walking! We saved her. I mean, you saved her."

Nick grinned—at her, not the calf. "We'll share the credit."

Suddenly, all the broken pieces of her life mended, and her world became whole. Emma knew exactly what she needed to say, what she needed to do.

"Nick…I…"

"What?" His grin softened.

"Here." She handed him the bottle. "I have to go."

"Where?" He said it as if he didn't want her to leave.

"There's something I need to tell my mother."

"Just her?"

"Her first."

Impulsively, she hugged him, then hurried to the house. She threw open the back door. "Mom! Where are you?" she hollered.

Emma found not only her mother and Leonard in the family room, but Cole and Holly, as well. "Good. You're all here. I have something important to say."

"What's wrong?" Her mother started to rise from her chair.

"No, you stay there."

If anything, her mother's appearance had worsened. Had Holly said something else? Emma didn't waste a moment.

"Don't call off the wedding," she said. "Whatever you do."

"What's changed your mind?" The question came from Cole.

"I've come to my senses," Emma told him.

"Finally!"

"Now, Cole," their mother admonished.

"I was kidding." His tone conveyed otherwise.

"It's okay." Emma went over and sat in the chair adjacent to her mother. "I've been a fool. I shouldn't have left Nick at the church. And I sure shouldn't have left Mistletoe. Mom, don't make the same mistake as me."

"But we've already agreed. Leonard and I are going to wait. Probably till spring. And Holly's going to make more of an effort to accept me."

"Don't you dare postpone your wedding for her. She has no right to interfere. And you and Leonard are bigger fools than me if you let her."

Holly visibly bristled. "Now, wait a minute."

Cole reached across the couch where they sat together and placed a restraining hand on her arm. "Stay out of this."

"What!"

"I like you, Holly, even though you're pushy as hell. But if you don't keep quiet and give Emma a chance to finish, I'm going to drag you out of here, kicking and screaming if I have to."

She drew back, a stunned expression on her face. "You like me?"

Laughing, he hooked an arm around her neck and hauled her close. "Shut up, will you?

Holly did. Just like that.

"I was wrong, Mom." Emma thought she heard the back door open but ignored it. She was on a roll. "I should have stayed and given Nick a chance."

"You had good reason."

"I had a reason to be angry at him. He did lie to me.

His intentions, however, weren't malicious or manipulative. He didn't want to hurt me, and he never cheated on me. But I was too young and too pigheaded to see that at the time. Even after I'd calmed down. Just think." She clasped her mother's hand. "If I stayed, Nick and I would have talked things out. Even if the baby was his, we'd have come up with a plan." Her breath caught, and when she next spoke, her voice wavered. "I screwed up the best thing to ever happen to me."

"I'm sorry for what you went through, honey, but this situation is different. Waiting makes sense."

"No, it doesn't," Leonard interjected.

"He's right, Mom." Emma squared her shoulders. "And I'm going to see to it you marry him. Tomorrow."

Her mother smiled for the first time that day. "You can't force me."

"*Force* is a strong word. I prefer *convince*."

"I like the way she talks." Leonard came over and drew Emma's mother to her feet. "I love you, Candy. I didn't think I'd ever say that to another woman, or that I'd ever be happy again. Then I met you, and everything changed. I can't wait a day longer to begin our lives together."

"Oh, Leonard." Emma's mother brushed the silver hair at his temple with her fingertips, the gesture sweet and poignant. "I love you, too. And I'm sorry I've been so difficult."

"You're about to get married. You're allowed."

Tension evaporated from her face, leaving her looking years younger. "I really am, aren't I?"

"Wild horses won't stop us."

Leonard kissed Emma's mother with the enthusiasm of a man crazy in love. Emma approved.

Cole leaped up, dragging Holly with him. He gave his mother a warm hug once Leonard released her. Even Holly broke down when her father pulled her close.

"I'm sorry, Daddy."

"I love you, sugar pie. And I always will."

Emma let out a sigh. Disaster had been averted.

"Nice speech."

She whirled. Nick stood there, an expression in his eyes she hadn't seen for a long, long time. Her heart beat erratically.

"How much did you hear?" she asked.

"About everything."

"Oh." She waited, afraid to assume too much. Afraid to make the first move.

"Let's talk." He held out his hand.

Emma hesitated, then slid her fingers into his.

"Good luck, you guys," Cole called after them.

The second Emma and Nick were outside, she realized she'd forgotten her coat a second time. Not smart, what with the snow falling and temperature dropping. They stood on the back stoop, just under the roof's edge.

"Are you cold?" Nick asked.

"A little." She was freezing.

Before she quite knew what was happening, he had opened the front of his coat, pulled her close and wrapped her in his warm embrace.

"You aren't the only one who made a mistake." His warm breath caressed her hair. "I should have gone after you, Emma. I should have hunted you down, made you listen and insisted you come home with me."

"We were both young. And impulsive."

"Then, when I had the chance this morning to tell

you how I feel, I didn't. I got distracted by work instead."

Emma took a leap. The biggest one of her life. "How *do* you feel, Nick?"

"I love you. I've never stopped. That's why I haven't been able to date anyone seriously. The only reason Holly and I lasted four months was because of her father."

"I don't want to talk about Holly. She's done enough damage."

"It's not all her fault."

"Truthfully," Emma admitted, "hardly any of it is. Mom and I both had our doubts, and she played on them."

Nick lowered his head for a light kiss. "Don't go. Stay in Mistletoe. We deserve a second chance."

Emma started to object. She had a job to return to, one she didn't love. An apartment, such as it was. An interview on the following Monday for a position that didn't really interest her.

Leaving it all behind for a second chance with Nick? A no-brainer if she ever heard one.

"I need something from you first. A promise."

The twinkle she adored appeared in his eyes. "Name it."

"Love me and trust me enough to be completely honest. No exceptions. I can cope with any problem, big or small, as long as I'm not blindsided."

"Deal." He reached into his coat pocket and withdrew the mistletoe charm. He must have removed it from the calf's neck. "Marry me, Emma. Soon. Don't make me wait."

A thrill coursed through her. "Is Valentine's Day early enough?"

"How 'bout New Year's Eve instead?"

"A week? I can't possibly—"

He silenced her with a kiss that made the past six years of loneliness and heartache melt away. As his lips moved possessively over hers, Nick pressed the charm into Emma's hand.

She swore it gave off a mild warmth. But that was impossible...right?

EPILOGUE

EMMA WALKED SLOWLY down the aisle, careful to match her steps to the beat of the music. Cole smiled at her and patted the hand holding his arm.

"You're beautiful," he whispered, loud enough for only her to hear.

"Thank you." Emma felt herself blush. Then again, she was a bride.

One week earlier, she'd walked down this same aisle. Then, she'd been the maid of honor at her mother's wedding—a gorgeous event that went off without a hitch.

Her mother and Leonard had delayed leaving for their honeymoon until New Year's Day in order to serve as Emma and Nick's matron of honor and best man. Cole, too, had stayed on so he could give Emma away— and get to know Holly better. Emma hadn't seen that coming, but then again, the past two weeks had been one surprise after another.

Only a handful of guests attended her and Nick's New Year's Eve wedding, among them Karen Merrick and her husband. Emma had canceled her interview for last Monday, then given notice at her current job, moments after accepting the office manager position at Merrick's Mistletoe Farm. In a few weeks, she and Nick would travel to Austin in order to pack up her apartment and move her things to his house. This summer, they'd take a trip. Nick wanted to see the Grand Canyon. Emma, Lake Tahoe. Deciding would be fun.

Their small and intimate ceremony would be followed by a dinner at the Roundup Steak House. They'd insisted on keeping things simple—and speedy. Once again, Emma was rushing to the altar, arranging her wedding in less than a week. This time, however, there would be no interruptions. Regardless of who might walk through the church doors at the last second—it could be the Baby New Year himself as far as she was concerned—Emma was becoming Mrs. Nick Hayes.

He stood at the altar, wearing the same tux he had at her mother's wedding, just as she was wearing the same maroon gown, and looking like her every dream come true. Wait! He *was* all her dreams come true— and the love of her life.

Finally, Emma had found the place that felt like home. In Nick's arms and by his side, where she intended to stay for the rest of their lives.

* * * * *

MISTLETOE MAGIC

Marin Thomas

To single mothers everywhere
who go to great lengths to make Christmas special
for their children. Your love and devotion
is the real "magic" in their holiday.

CHAPTER ONE

NOT AGAIN.

Finley McCarthy swallowed an exasperated sigh Thursday afternoon when she spotted the familiar van parked in the handicapped space in front of her business. With Christmas two weeks away and the Mistletoe Magic crowded with customers searching for last-minute stocking stuffers, she didn't have time to deal with a geriatric shoplifter.

"Where's this potion all the kids in town are talking about?" The question echoed through the old Victorian.

When Finley had inherited the home after her grandmother died, she'd converted the second-story rooms into an apartment for her and her five-year-old twin sons, then turned the main floor into a new age store—the first of its kind in downtown Mistletoe, Texas.

She removed a miniature glass vial from the shelf behind the register and wove through the throng of bodies. "Here you are, Viola." She handed the item to the First Methodist Church children's-choir director. The church happened to be located next door to Finley's Victorian. Viola Keller's age was a mystery, but the streaks of gray running through her black hair and the wrinkles around her eyes hinted that she was in her mid- to late sixties. Viola had married right out of high school, but a year later her husband had run off with another woman. The ladies at the beauty shop claimed Viola's heart had been shattered, and that was the reason she'd never remarried.

"The store looks very festive, Finley."

"Thank you." When she'd first opened her business, only a handful of customers stopped by to browse the merchandise. As word spread that she sold herbs, healing stones, candles, incense and oils to promote health, harmony and happiness, her sales had increased. But those first months had hurt Finley's bottom line, and she needed to hit a home run with her Christmas sales to remain in the black. She'd invested all of her inheritance in the business. If it went bankrupt, she'd be forced to sell the Victorian—a home that had been in her grandmother's family since 1886.

"I don't believe in magic, but this silly potion is all my students talk about." The fusspot held the vial up to the light.

"It's harmless fun." In hopes of increasing her holiday profits, Finley had marketed a cute make-believe Christmas product geared toward children. Named after the store, Mistletoe Magick was a liquid of crushed mistletoe berries, lavender and peppermint. Children were supposed to sprinkle a few drops onto their pillow Christmas Eve and then they'd dream of the toys they'd find beneath the tree the next morning.

This past October her sons had taken a sample of the potion to school for show-and-tell and the very next day her phone rang off the hook with mothers placing advance orders for the product. Finley had worked long hours building her holiday inventory, and sales were holding steady.

"You don't get much for seven dollars," Viola said.

"You only need a few drops." Finley's gaze swung to the window across the room. Burt Hollis moved his power chair onto the lift attached to his van and lowered himself to the sidewalk. In less than five minutes he'd be inside her store. "Maybe you'd like a mistletoe charm instead." The charms were inexpensive and just as popular as the potion. "They're on sale for three dollars." She held one out. "Do you know how they work?"

"Not really."

"The recipient of the charm receives good luck," Finley said.

"And if I want the good luck for myself?"

"Someone has to give you the charm."

Viola's mouth puckered. "That will never happen."

Finley held out the charm. "Merry Christmas. Now you'll have good luck." *And hopefully a better attitude.*

Viola's eyes brightened. "For me?"

"Everyone deserves a present this time of year." Finley nodded to the vial. "How many children are in the choir?"

"Twelve."

"I'll gift wrap twelve Magick potions while you browse." Finley returned to the register and kept an eye on Burt, who steered his scooter up the handicapped ramp alongside the house. She had no clue why he'd picked her store to target.

"Thank you for the charm, Finley." Viola handed over her credit card.

"You're welcome. And don't forget to stop by after Christmas. Everything will be half off."

Viola signed the credit slip, but before she took her purchases the sleigh bells jingled on the door and Burt entered, his scooter knocking the table that held a rack of necklaces. The pieces of silver tumbled from their hooks, scattering across the red cloth.

Finley swallowed her frustration and forced a smile. "Hello, Burt."

"Ms. McCarthy." His bushy white mustache curved as he tipped his Stetson. If he weren't stealing from her, she'd find his manners charming.

"What can I help you with today that you didn't find—" *shoplift* "—yesterday?"

"Not sure. Think I'll mosey around a bit."

"Would you like a cup of hot cider?" Finley asked.

"Is that what I smell?"

She clasped her hands to keep from squeezing his neck. Burt knew darn well she served apple cider to her customers during the holidays.

"Guess I am a little thirsty."

"I'd be happy to fetch Mr. Hollis a glass of cider." Viola nodded to Burt, then made her way to the small kitchen at the back of the house.

"Do you know Mrs. Keller, Burt?"

He nodded. "Used to attend church services every Sunday until—" He waved a hand in front of his face. "Always enjoyed listening to the children sing."

"Here you are, Mr. Hollis." Viola held out a cup. "You haven't been to church in a long time." Evidently she'd kept track of Burt's attendance.

His gaze zeroed in on the choir director's bosom. "Reckon I should get back into the habit of going."

"Yes, you should." Viola's cheeks turned pink. "And bring that boy of yours with you." She nodded to Finley, then waltzed out the door.

A customer snagged Finley's attention, and by the time she'd helped the woman locate the holiday potpourri, Burt had disappeared. How he navigated from room to room in a scooter without making noise was a mystery.

"Excuse me. I'm looking for gold Christmas candles."

Chasing after Burt would have to wait. "Follow me." Finley led the lady to the candle display in the front hall, then went to help another customer. The afternoon flew by, and it wasn't until closing that she noticed Burt's van was no longer parked at the curb.

After ringing up her final sale, she flipped the sign to Closed in the front window and locked the doors, then climbed the staircase off the kitchen. She found the twins playing video games in the living room. "How's it going?"

"Good," her sons answered in unison.

"I'll be up after I straighten the store."

"Okay."

Feeling guilty for using TV and video games as a babysitter, she returned downstairs and stowed the leftover cider in the fridge, then bagged the garbage. Next she restocked the shelves and discovered a crystal necklace missing from her inventory. She'd begun the day with four but hadn't sold any. Now there were three. *Burt.*

Finley had priced most of her merchandise below twenty dollars, except the necklaces worn to promote spiritual harmony. She had to special order the crystals from Vermont, and sold them for $39.95.

Enough was enough. She intended to put a stop to Burt's shoplifting. She hollered upstairs. "Flint! Tuff! Turn off the TV and grab your coats. We're going for a ride."

The boys slid down the handrail and stumbled into the kitchen. She'd told them a thousand times that the house wasn't a playground, but she didn't have the heart to scold them when their faces glowed with excitement. Finley hated that she had to restrict her sons to the up-stairs apartment during business hours.

"If you're good," she said as they piled into her 2005 Subaru wagon, "we'll stop for ice cream on the way home." It was Christmas break—who cared if they ate dessert before dinner?

"Where are we going?" Flint asked.

"To visit a neighbor."

"Is it Burt?" Tuff asked.

"How do you know Mr. Hollis?" Finley turned onto Main Street and drove west out of town.

"Burt asked us what we wanted from Santa for Christmas," Flint said.

"It's *Mr. Hollis,* and when did you speak to him?"

"When we were playing in the backyard," Tuff said.

"He wanted to know where our dad was. We told him he lives on another planet." Flint giggled.

Finley had explained numerous times that Iceland was not another planet, but her sons had decided it was more exciting to tell people that the father they'd never met lived in a different solar system. Finley had no re-grets that things hadn't worked out between her and Alexander, but now that her grandmother was gone, she wished Alex would make an effort to get to know his sons. Besides, the boys needed a male role model in their lives, and Burt Hollis was not who she had in mind.

The Buckhorn Ranch was located five miles outside of town. Burt and his son, Cooper, raised South Texas whitetail deer, which were sold to ranchers looking to build their own herds. When she arrived at the house, Burt's van wasn't parked in the driveway. That didn't deter her—she'd speak with Cooper. "Wait in the car." She climbed the porch steps and rang the bell. No one answered, so she banged her fist on the door.

"Hold on, I'm coming!" The door swung open and Cooper Hollis glared down at her.

Finley's breath caught in her chest as she gazed into striking blue eyes. They'd never met in person. She'd only seen him from a distance. Up close he was drop-dead gorgeous. Short-cropped whiskers covered his chiseled jaw, reminding her of an outlaw from the Old West.

"May I help you?"

His question startled her. "I'm Finley McCarthy." She held out her hand. "I own the Mistletoe Magic in town." He shook her hand, his callused fingers sending a tingle up her arm. Her physical reaction to a near stranger confused Finley. Since the twins had been born, she'd lost interest in dating. Being a single mom took all her energy. By the end of the day the only thing she looked forward to was a hot bath and a good book. "I'm here about Burt."

"What happened? Is he all right?" Cooper grabbed his coat from a hook inside the door and shrugged it on.

"He's fine," Finley said, relieved Cooper was worried about his father. Surely he'd be concerned over Burt's stealing and would want to rectify the situation.

"Okay. Well, what is it you want?"

She'd rehearsed a speech during the drive to the ranch, but she'd forgotten every word and cursed her adolescent nervousness. Why was she tongue-tied all of a sudden? "Maybe I should come back when Burt's home."

"If you drove all the way out here from town, it must be important."

Finley wasn't a mean person, and even though Burt was in the wrong, tattling on him didn't sit well with her. Still…she couldn't afford to continue losing money. "For the past six months your father has been visiting my business and—"

"What business?"

If he'd forgotten already, then she hadn't made much of an impression on him. "Mistletoe Magic. The mint-green Victorian at the end of Main Street."

She ignored his blank stare. "Your father is stealing from my store."

Cooper's mouth sagged open and she rushed on. "Each time he visits, a piece of merchandise comes up missing."

"You're crazy if you believe my father's taking your magic tricks."

"I don't sell magic tricks, Mr. Hollis. My business promotes harmony and spiritual well-being. I sell herbs, healing stones, crystals—" his eyes glazed over "—and white sage or charcoal if you're looking to rid yourself of a ghost."

"Sounds like a bunch of hocus-pocus crap to me," he said. "What would an old man want with your rocks?"

She removed a crystal necklace from her coat pocket. "One of these went missing today after he came into the store."

Cooper stared at the piece of jewelry. "You're coming after the wrong person."

Finley's gut insisted Burt was the culprit. "I need your father to return all the items he's taken."

"You have a lot of nerve accusing a cripple of theft. Do you have surveillance video of him stashing things in his pockets?"

Finley didn't have the money to install a security camera in the Victorian. "No."

"Then we're done talking." The door shut in her face.

That went well. Hopefully, Cooper would warn Burt to steer clear of the store. When she got into the car, the backseat was empty. "Flint! Tuff!" Heart pounding, she raced into the barn. "Boys?"

"Here, Mom."

Finley followed Tuff's voice to the back of the structure, where the boys ogled a pair of baby fawns. "Oh, how sweet."

Flint pointed to the deer with antlers. "Is that one of Santa's?"

"Santa's reindeer live at the North Pole," she said. "C'mon. Let's go." She grabbed their hands and led them outside.

"Can we come back and see the reindeer?" Flint asked.

"I don't think so, honey." The next time she visited the Buckhorn Ranch she'd probably be greeted by a shotgun.

COOPER CHECKED HIS watch for the hundredth time. The ditzy blond businesswoman had left over an hour ago. Where the heck was his father?

Since they'd purchased the handicapped-accessible van, Burt hardly remained at home. Cooper didn't be-grudge the old man his freedom. He appreciated not having his day interrupted with doctor appointments and grocery shopping. The van had alleviated much of the stress in their relationship, but they still argued on occasion—the last quarrel having to do with not putting up a Christmas tree this year.

Cooper found it tough to get into the holiday spirit after his former fiancée had broken off their engagement last year on Christmas Eve. Denise had gotten cold feet because she hadn't wanted to be burdened with the responsibility of caring for his father, and he'd refused to put Burt in a retirement home.

By the time Cooper had finished his second cup of coffee, the van pulled into the driveway. He was out the door in a flash. "Are you stealing from that blonde's shop in town?"

"What are you talking about?" Burt moved his chair onto the lift, then lowered himself to the ground.

"She came by."

"Who?"

"Finley McCarthy."

Burt hit the key fob and the lift returned inside the van, then the door locked. Cooper followed his father up the ramp at the front of the house. "She said you've been visiting her store."

"I may have stopped in the Mistletoe Magic a time or two."

"Why in the heck would you shop at a store like that?" Cooper opened the front door and they faced off in the living room. "Have you been stealing from that woman?" His father wouldn't make eye contact. "Dad?"

Burt steered the scooter into the kitchen and rummaged through the refrigerator. Fed up with the silent treatment, Cooper went into Burt's bedroom. The place was a pigsty, but when he offered to clean, his father became defensive. He rummaged through the nightstand drawers and found a pair of scissors, nail clippers, pocket change, a Bible, three pens and a rock. *A rock?* Cooper examined the polished stone—his father hadn't found it in the yard, that was for sure.

The dresser drawers revealed bottles of scented oil and sticks of incense and miniature candles. *Unbelievable.* He gathered the evidence and dumped it on the kitchen table. "What have you got to say for yourself?"

"Since when do you have permission to go through my personal belongings?"

"Since that hippie woman appeared on our doorstep, accusing you of shoplifting." Burt's face glowed as red as the fake poinsettia on the kitchen table. "Dad, tell me you didn't steal from her."

Burt hit the power switch on the scooter and escaped to his bedroom, slamming the door behind him. Cooper wasn't letting him off that easy. He rapped his knuckles on the door.

"Go away."

"You have to return that stuff to her store."

Silence.

Burt had been acting odd lately. Maybe Cooper should have him evaluated by a geriatric physician. He might be suffering from the beginning stages of dementia. Heck, he might have even forgotten that he'd stolen the items.

Tomorrow Cooper would take the junk to the blonde's shop and apologize for his father. He'd look like a fool, but what did he care? A year ago he'd looked like the biggest fool ever in front of the whole town when his fiancée had given back his engagement ring on Christmas Eve.

Cooper closed his eyes, expecting Denise's face to materialize in his mind; instead it was Finley's blond hair, pretty brown eyes and petite frame.

Finley. What kind of a name was that for a woman? The little entrepreneur looked like a fairy—a sprite with white-gold hair and translucent skin. If he'd ventured into town more often, maybe they'd have met under different circumstances. And maybe he'd have asked her out on a date.

Who was he kidding? No sense thinking about his love life until he no longer had the responsibility of caring for his father. When that time finally came, he'd be an old man himself.

CHAPTER TWO

"HEY, MISTER."

Cooper paused before the front steps of the green Victorian on Main Street and glanced to his right, then to his left. He swore he'd heard someone speak.

"You're the reindeer man." Identical twin boys moved from behind the bushes and stared at him. They wore matching coats, scarves, mittens and hats. The temperature hovered near fifty degrees—hardly cold enough to be bundled up. Mistletoe didn't get a lot of snow in the winter, but weather forecasters were warning of a possible storm hitting the area by Christmas.

"I raise Texas whitetail deer," he said, trying to recall if he'd ever had a conversation about his livelihood with kids before.

"We saw 'em in your barn." The boy climbed onto the first step. "They look like Santa's reindeer." He glanced behind him. "Don't they, Flint?"

"Tuff thinks you're Santa's helper," the boy named Flint said.

He'd never heard of names like Flint and Tuff. "Sorry to disappoint you, but I don't work for Santa, and the animals in the barn can't fly."

"That's not what Burt says." Tuff spoke again.

"How do you know Burt?"

"When he visits my mom's store, he lets me push the buttons on his scooter."

Jeez, how long had his father been pestering Finley and her sons? "Burt likes to tell stories. They're not real reindeer." Cooper climbed the remaining steps. "Is your mother here?"

"She's always working." The barely audible comment had come from the quieter boy, Flint.

"Aren't you two supposed to be in school?" It was early in the afternoon on a Friday.

The brothers frowned. Then Tuff spoke. "It's Christmas break."

Cooper glanced up the street. He hadn't made a trip to town since before Thanksgiving and he'd barely noticed the holiday decorations. Lights blinked in store windows and plastic candy canes lined the sidewalks. Fake reindeer and sleighs sat on several rooftops and wreaths hung on all the doors, including Mistletoe Magic's entrance. Two blocks away, Santa's Village occupied the town square, surrounded by fake evergreen trees decorated with red bows. And last but not least, hanging from every lamppost along Main Street was a giant Texas star made from mistletoe. "I guess I forgot."

The boys' mouths dropped open. "You forgot about Christmas?"

Feeling chastised, Cooper asked, "How old are you guys?"

"Five," Tuff said.

"I'm thirty-five, and it's easy to forget about Santa when you're as old as I am." He reached for the door just as it opened and Finley stepped outside. Cooper removed his cowboy hat. As much as it stuck in his craw, he intended to beg the pretty shopkeeper for forgiveness.

"You weren't bothering Mr. Hollis, were you?" Finley looked at Cooper for confirmation.

"Not at all." He cleared his throat. "May I speak with you in private?"

"Of course."

He motioned for Finley to precede him. Inside the store, muted Christmas music echoed through the rooms and the smell of cinnamon and apples wafted in the air.

"I'll be with you in a moment." Finley walked off to help a customer.

Her words barely registered as he took in her outfit—a long black skirt and a red velvet blouse, which hugged her small frame. A body he had no business ogling.

While Finley was occupied, Cooper studied his surroundings. Twinkling white lights decorated miniature Christmas trees, which sat on tables covered in red fabric and fake snow. As he checked out the merchandise, he spotted several of the items his father had shoplifted.

"Thank you and merry Christmas." Finley locked the cash register, then walked in his direction. She wore an assortment of sparkly bangles on each wrist, and the delicate chain of silver bells hugging her hips chimed when she moved. The melodious sound should have annoyed him—instead it soothed the anxious knot in his stomach.

"What can I help you with, Mr. Hollis?"

The bright light from the crystal chandelier above their heads made Finley's blond hair appear almost white—a startling contrast to her brown eyes and dark lashes. "Um, what?"

"You wanted to speak to me about something."

"Right." Embarrassed that he'd been caught gawking, he emptied his coat pockets onto a table. "I came to return these."

Her eyes widened.

"I owe you an apology. My father took these from your store." Cooper waited for an "I told you so" but none came.

"Thank you." One by one she put the items in their proper places.

"I'd also like to apologize for my rudeness when you stopped by the ranch."

"No worries. We all have our bad days."

Maybe, but Cooper had been having a bad day ever since Denise had left him. "Burt's an old fool and he meant no harm. Is there anything I can do to keep you from pressing charges against him?"

"You must not think very highly of me, Mr. Hollis, if—"

"Cooper."

"Cooper...if you believe I'll report your father to the police."

The hurt that sparked in her eyes socked him in the gut. "You'd have every right to."

"I'm not going to, but..." She dropped her gaze to the stand marked Mistletoe Charms and played with one of the trinkets.

"But what?"

She jutted her chin. "I have to wonder if Burt's behavior is a cry for attention."

"What are you getting at?"

"Maybe your father feels as if he's being ignored at home."

Whoa. "You don't know a thing about our lives."

Cooper couldn't help it if he had to leave the house for hours at a time to take care of the deer and the ranch. He set his hat on his head and nodded. "You can expect an official apology from my father tomorrow." He left the store, skipping down the steps and past the twins riding their bikes in the driveway.

Who was she to accuse him of neglecting his father? He'd given up his own happiness for Burt. As much as her words had angered Cooper, he couldn't get the image of Finley and her halo of blond hair out of his mind.

"HOW COME YOU always gotta work?" Tuff asked early Saturday morning as Finley cleared the cereal bowls off the kitchen table.

Yesterday had been the first day of Christmas break and already the boys complained of boredom. At times like this she really missed her grandmother. The twins had minded Great Granny and enjoyed her company. It had been a shock when the eighty-year-old had passed away peacefully in her sleep.

"You guys know I work in the store on Saturdays." Saturday was the busiest day of the week. She couldn't afford to close the shop and miss out on any sales. "Why don't you play on the swing set in the backyard?"

"I hate swinging," Tuff said.

"I made your lunches." Ignoring their grumbling, Finley opened the fridge and pointed to the brown bags and juice boxes.

"I don't want a peanut-butter sandwich." Tuff crossed his arms over his chest. "I want macaroni 'n' cheese."

Guilt pricked Finley. Her sons deserved a hot lunch after eating cold sandwiches all week, but she didn't have time to cook for them. She checked the clock—eight forty-five. The store opened at nine. "I have to go." She pressed a kiss to the tops of their heads and breathed in the scent of bubble bath. "Tell you what. If you stay out of trouble today, I'll take you to Santa's Village tonight."

"I'll be good," Flint said.

"What about you, Tuff?" Finley eyed her son.

"Yeah, okay. I'll be good, too."

Holding their promises close to her heart, she went downstairs and filled a large kettle with apple cider, then placed it on the stove to simmer. Next she opened a package of cookies and arranged them on a plate before setting out napkins and cups. In the front room she put the money drawer in the cash register, then turned on the radio station that played nonstop Christmas carols. Satisfied all was in order, Finley flipped the sign in the front window and froze. Burt Hollis's van sat parked at the curb. When he saw her, he waved.

The day was not starting out well at all. She reached for her shawl on the hook behind the counter, then stepped outside, intending to send Burt on his way sooner rather than later.

He saw her coming, but instead of waiting for her to reach the van, he opened the side door and moved his chair onto the lift.

"There's no need to get out, Burt," she said. "Cooper mentioned that you might stop by."

"Came to apologize."

A group of ladies exited Molly's Antiques farther up the block and began walking toward the Victorian. "Apology accepted. I imagine you have things to do today."

"Not really." He rode the lift down to the sidewalk. "Cooper said I have to make amends for my poor judgment."

"Good morning, ladies." Finely spoke to the group. "There's cider warming on the stove in the kitchen. I'll be right in." When the women moved out of earshot, Finley said, "I'm awfully busy right now."

"If I go home and tell Cooper I didn't do anything for you, I'll have to listen to him bellyache at me."

This was ridiculous—standing in the cold arguing with Burt. "Fine. You can entertain the twins outside." The temperature was supposed to climb into the upper fifties—typical Texas winter, warm one day, freezing the next.

"Sure, I'll play with the tykes."

She hurried into the house while Burt locked the van. "Boys," she called up to the apartment. "Grab your coats. Burt's outside waiting for you."

Tuff and Flint raced into the kitchen, coats in hand. "Stay out of trouble, you hear?" she said as they ran out the door. The morning passed quickly, and Finley was pleased with the number of sales she rang up. At eleven-thirty she peeked out the kitchen window and discovered the twins sitting at the picnic table, sharing their lunches with Burt.

Her sons were doing all the talking—obviously they loved having Burt's undivided attention. When Great Granny died, the twins had taken her death in stride, probably because they hadn't understood all that was happening—the visitation, the church service and then the trip to the cemetery. Finley had chalked up their stoic demeanor to their young age, but as she watched them interact with Burt, she suspected they missed

Granny more than they led on. Maybe she should put up with Burt's visits if he helped fill the void in the boys' lives.

The bells on the front door jingled and Finley hurried into the main room, where she discovered the town mayor, Debbie Monahan, standing inside the front door. "What brings you by, Debbie?"

"I'm reminding all the merchants about the children's parade next Saturday. You'll need to have your float parked in the church lot next door by three in the afternoon."

Drat. Finley had forgotten she'd volunteered to provide a float for the parade. "Okay, sure."

Debbie laughed. "You haven't even started on it, have you?"

"No." Finley blushed. "But don't worry—I'll think of something."

"If you need help, Jim down at the hardware store offered his services."

Ugh. "Thanks for the warning." Jim Jenkins was several years older than Finley and had inherited his father's business after his parents retired to Florida. He'd set his sights on her after Granny died, and Finley had already turned down his invitation to several holiday activities. He wasn't her type, and she didn't care for the way he ignored the boys whenever they were present.

"The twins are having a good time with Burt Hollis over at the church."

The church? What were they doing at the church?

"See you next Saturday," Debbie said, then left.

Finley went into the dining room and peeked out the window just in time to see Burt set the twins on his lap, then steer the scooter down the handicapped ramp. Her sons laughed and pumped their fists in the air. Then suddenly the scooter drove off the side of the ramp and all three spilled onto the ground.

Finley gasped and sprinted outside but put the brakes on when she saw Viola Keller exit the church. Finley couldn't make out what the older woman yelled, but it was obvious Burt was getting a scolding.

Finley hurried across the property. "What in the world are you three up to?"

"No good, that's what," Viola said. "Burt's acting like an old fool."

Finley set the heavy power scooter upright. "I hope the battery isn't damaged."

Viola wagged her finger at Burt. "It would serve you right if you had to push yourself everywhere you went."

Together Finley and Viola lifted Burt off the ground and helped him back into his chair. Before Viola moved aside, Burt grabbed her wrist and tugged her onto his lap. "You're sure full of sass 'n' vinegar, Mrs. Keller."

Viola popped off his lap. "Someone needs to keep you in line, Burt."

"You up for the challenge, Viola?"

"You couldn't handle me."

"Is that so?"

Fearing the conversation was heading in the wrong direction, Finley asked, "Is anyone hurt?"

"No," the three males answered.

"That was awesome, Burt!" Tuff said.

"Yeah, that was cool." Flint high-fived Burt.

"Someone could have been seriously injured." Finley grasped Burt's shoulder and peered into his face. "Are you in any pain?"

"If I was, I wouldn't feel it."

Viola snorted. "You get along better than most men your age."

Burt narrowed his eyes. "How would you like to go for a ride in my van, Viola?"

"We'll go with you, Burt," Tuff said.

"There will be no rides in the van or on Burt's scooter." Finley stared pointedly at the boys. "Or I send Burt home."

"Okay," the twins answered.

Viola disappeared inside the church, probably embarrassed by Burt's flirting. "C'mon back to the house and let me take care of those scratches." Finley nodded to Burt's scraped knuckles.

"I'm fine."

"Hey, Mom," Flint said. "Can Burt come with us when we go to Santa's Village?"

Tuff set his hand on Burt's arm. "Did you tell Santa what you want for Christmas?"

Burt rubbed his mustache. "Don't think I did."

"Burt's gotta tell Santa what he wants, Mom," Tuff said.

She studied the trio of pleading faces. "Be ready to leave in two hours." She walked alongside the boys as Burt maneuvered his scooter across the yard. She'd suggest that Burt play video games with the twins but she had no way of helping him up the stairs. "Burt, would you like some warm cider?" The boys gaped at her as if she were trying to steal their playmate.

"No, thank you."

"You're not cold, are you?" she asked him.

"If I get cold, we'll sit in the van and warm up."

"Can we see your van, Burt?" Tuff asked.

"If your mom says it's okay." He winked. "I won't drive off with them."

She didn't have time to argue. Who knew how many customers had entered the store then left without buying anything because she'd been absent. "Fine. But you boys better mind Burt and do as he says. Understood?" The last thing she needed was one of her sons releasing the emergency brake and sending the van careening down Main Street, taking out Christmas decorations.

CHAPTER THREE

Tired, grumpy and sore after a day of clearing brush, Cooper headed to the house for a hot meal, a beer and a shower—not necessarily in that order. When he pulled into the ranch yard, he noticed Burt's van was missing. What was the old man up to now?

He removed his cell phone from his pocket and pressed the number two. No answer. He was dang tired of keeping tabs on his father. Now that Burt had transportation, he gallivanted all over the county without informing Cooper of his whereabouts. He shouldn't worry, but the thought of the van stuck in a ditch on the side of the road was enough to send Cooper searching for him.

He drove into town half hoping his father was making a nuisance of himself at Finley's shop. He'd thought twice about insisting his father apologize, but she deserved the consideration after agreeing not to press charges against Burt. When Cooper reached town, he turned onto Main Street and spotted the van in front of the green Victorian. He pulled into the driveway and parked behind Finley's station wagon.

Ignoring the closed sign, he climbed the porch steps, then rang the bell. After a minute he peered through the glass pane. He didn't see anyone inside, so he meandered along the candy cane–lined sidewalks in search of his father. A week ago Cooper had believed Christmas was overrated. People stuck gaudy decorations in their yards and spent too much money on presents that ended up at the bottoms of closets or regifted. But after meeting Finley, the holiday chaos didn't seem so crazy at all.

Cooper headed to Santa's Village in the town square. The line to see St. Nick wound around the block. Mistletoe drew a lot of visitors during the holiday season. Parents from all over the county brought their kids to visit the town and claim a kiss beneath its namesake. He peered around the crowd and caught sight of Burt's scooter near the front of the line. Had his father gone off the deep end? He made his way through the throng of people but before he reached Burt, Finley bumped into him, her sons trailing behind her.

"Look, Mom, it's the reindeer man," one of the twins said.

Cooper swore Finley's brown eyes sparked when their gazes clashed.

"What are you doing here?" Burt asked.

"I was about to ask you the same thing," Cooper said.

"Burt's holding our place in line." Finley handed Cooper's father a bag of roasted chestnuts.

He nudged Burt's arm. "You could have texted me your whereabouts so I wouldn't worry."

"Sorry, I forgot."

Yeah, sure.

A little hand tugged Cooper's coat. "Can we come visit your reindeer?"

"Flint, stop pestering Mr. Hollis," Finley said. "I told you those weren't reindeer in his barn." Tonight Finley wore a snow-white cape, concealing most of her body except for her angelic face.

He tore his gaze from her and studied the boys' pouting expressions. He remembered the excitement of visiting Santa as a kid. "What do you two want for Christmas this year?"

"I want a—"

"Let me talk—"

"No, you got to tell Burt about the basketball hoop and—"

Jeez, he hadn't meant his question to trigger an argument between the kids.

"Did not!"

"Did, too!"

"That's enough," Finley said. "It's not polite to shout in front of people."

They moved up a few feet in line. "How long have you been waiting?" he asked.

"Almost an hour," she said.

They had at least fifteen minutes before they arrived at Santa's stoop. "Dad, have you had anything to eat besides nuts?"

"I'm not hungry."

His father needed a decent meal if he was going to drive the van home later tonight. "After the boys visit Santa, why don't we all grab a bite to eat at the Mistletoe Café?"

"Yeah!" The twins jumped up and down.

"We don't want to intrude," Finley said.

"You won't be intruding." This wasn't how Cooper had envisioned his quick trip into town would end, but he wanted to repay Finley for being kind to his father. The least he could do was buy dinner for her and the twins.

"Finley!" Jim Jenkins, the hardware-store owner, made his way toward them.

"Hello, Jim. You know Cooper Hollis." Finley placed her hand on the back of the scooter. "And his father, Burt."

"Jim and I were in the same high school class," Cooper said. He didn't appreciate the way Jenkins's gaze roamed over Finley. The former football quarterback had slept his way through the cheerleading squad.

"Haven't seen you in town, Hollis." Jenkins inched closer to Finley. "Thought you'd moved away."

Like hell. When Jenkins touched Finley's arm, a surge of jealousy ripped through Cooper.

"How would you like to take a sleigh ride with me later tonight?" Jenkins asked Finley.

"She can't." The words were out of Cooper's mouth before he could stop them. Ignoring Finley's startled gaze, he said, "I'm taking her and the boys out to eat after they visit Santa." He stared, daring the man to object.

Jenkins turned to Finley. "I'll take a rain check on the sleigh ride. I heard you're participating in the children's parade next Saturday."

"Yes, but I haven't come up with an idea for a float yet," she said.

"I'll stop by the store and brainstorm ideas with you." Jenkins walked off. The schmuck hadn't even said hello to the twins.

"Who was that?" Flint slid his hand into Finley's.

"Just a friend, honey."

The line moved forward, and they reached the stoop of Santa's house.

"Is Burt your friend, too?" Tuff asked.

"He's our friend." She glanced up. "And so is Mr. Cooper."

Cooper wasn't sure what to make of Finley's statement or the warm feeling squeezing his chest.

"Are you ready to talk to Santa?" she asked. "You're next."

Flint motioned for Cooper to bend down. "I know he's not the real Santa. That's Mr. Walker."

Roger Walker was married to the owner of the Mistletoe Café. His big belly and gray hair won him the role of Santa each year.

Cooper whispered in Flint's ear. "When I was a kid, Mr. Pumpernickel pretended to be Santa."

"Who's that?"

"Mr. Pumpernickel died years ago." The former Harley-Davidson motorcycle club member had owned a rough-and-tumble bar on the outskirts of Mistletoe and usually arrived at Santa's Village each night inebriated.

"Flint, it's your turn." Finley guided her son forward. Tuff had already taken a seat on one of Santa's knees.

"You boys sure are getting big," Santa bellowed. "Ho, ho, ho."

Cooper tapped his father's shoulder and motioned for him to move his scooter aside so the child next in line could watch the twins.

Tuff wiggled on Santa's lap. "I want a Yo Baby Kick Flipper."

"What the…?" Santa cleared his throat. "I've never heard of that."

"It's a skateboard," Tuff said.

"I want a Stomp Rocket. You jump on the pad and the rocket shoots into the air." Flint raised his arms above his head and made a whooshing sound.

"I'll be sure to tell my elves to make those toys." Santa handed the twins a candy cane. "Stay on my nice list. You don't want a chunk of coal in your stocking."

"We'll be good," the boys echoed in unison, then slid off Santa's lap.

Finley reached for their hands but Tuff pulled free and patted Santa's knee. "And if your elves can't make my Yo Baby Kick Flipper, then can you let Burt be our grandpa?"

Santa gaped at Finley.

"C'mon, boys. It's time to eat." She led the twins through the crowd.

Cooper walked next to his father's scooter. "What was that all about?" he asked when Finley and her sons were out of earshot.

"Haven't any idea."

"Did you tell the twins you wanted to be their grandfather?" Cooper should check into senior day care in their area—Burt needed to socialize with people his own age, not five-year-olds.

Finley and the boys crossed the street, but when Cooper and his father arrived at the corner, the light turned yellow. "Wait, Dad."

"We can make it." Burt shot onto the crosswalk and Cooper raced after him. If he didn't know better, he'd think the scooter was powered by rocket fuel and not a battery.

"HERE THEY COME!" Flint stood on the booth seat and pointed at the café door.

Finley glanced over her shoulder and watched Burt and Cooper enter the restaurant. She didn't know what to make of Cooper's reaction to Jim Jenkins. The dark tone in his voice when he'd informed Jim that she and the boys were eating supper with him had left no doubt in her mind that he objected to Jim's interest in her. But how could that be when she and Cooper barely knew each other?

Maybe Cooper senses you're attracted to him.

Finley couldn't argue with the voice in her head. Cooper had occupied her every other thought since she'd paid him a visit at his ranch. Then yesterday when he'd stopped by the store to give her the items Burt had taken, there'd been no denying the awkwardness between them that Finley was certain stemmed from their attraction to one another.

Burt arrived at the booth and parked his scooter on the end while Cooper sat with Tuff across from her and Flint.

"Well, this is a surprise." Suzie Walker, the owner of Mistletoe Café, stopped at their booth. "How do you all know each other?"

Burt's face glowed red and Finley rescued him. "Burt kept the boys occupied today while I was busy with the store."

Suzie laughed. "Ever since Cooper bought you that van, Burt, you've been tooling around town like a teenager looking for a hot date."

Cooper sent Burt an exasperated look and Finley hid a smile behind the menu.

"Did you boys visit Santa?" Suzie asked.

The twins nodded. Then Flint said, "Mom's gonna take us again next week."

"Can't hurt to remind Santa what you want for Christmas." Suzie pulled a pencil from her curly red hair. "What can I get you folks?"

Finley ordered chicken-tender baskets for the boys and a deli sandwich for herself. Burt said he'd eat what the twins were having and Cooper asked for the meat loaf special.

"This on one ticket?" Suzie asked.

Cooper nodded. "And milk shakes for everyone."

Milk shakes were expensive. Finley opened her mouth to protest, but Cooper held up a hand. "My treat."

The boys chose chocolate, she picked vanilla and Cooper and Burt both ordered strawberry. While they waited for their food, the twins carried the conversation, telling Cooper about their adventures with Burt. When they got to the part where the scooter drove off the church ramp, Finley entered the conversation.

"I didn't realize what they were doing until I looked out the window and saw all three of them sprawled on the ground," she said.

"Mrs. Keller got mad at Burt." Tuff grinned.

"Mrs. Keller has a crush on me." Burt winked at the boys.

"Is that so?" Cooper scowled at his father.

"What's a crush?" Tuff asked.

Finley ignored her son's question and said, "Viola came out of the church when she heard the commotion."

Flint said, "Burt was gonna take Mrs. Keller for a ride in his van but she said no."

Cooper's laugh caught Finley by surprise. She didn't know if it was his deep, sexy chuckle or his bold smile and white teeth that made her breath catch. She and Cooper had gotten off on the wrong foot, but she sensed a subtle softening in him compared to his stiff demeanor when they'd first met. She couldn't deny that she wanted to get to know him better. His good looks aside, he intrigued her, and she wouldn't be a female if she weren't curious about why his fiancée had broken off their engagement last Christmas.

"Food will be up in a few minutes." Suzie set the shakes on the table.

"Mr. Cooper," Flint said, "can me and Tuff play with your reindeer tomorrow?"

Finley intervened. "Not tomorrow. We need to figure out what kind of float we're making for the parade."

"Burt can help us," Tuff said.

"Mr. Jenkins offered to help," Finley said. "I'll call him—"

"Bring the boys out to the ranch," Burt said. "We got stuff in the barn you can use to build a float."

"I appreciate the offer, but we don't want to interfere with your day."

"Ouch!" Cooper glared at Burt. "Dad, could you get your wheel off my foot?"

"I don't like Mr. Jenkins," Flint said.

"Yeah." Tuff licked the glob of milk shake hanging off the bottom of his straw. "He never talks to us."

"I'm sure he'll speak to you when we work on the float," Finley said.

"Burt's right." Cooper cleared his throat. "There's got to be something in the barn that would make a good float."

Finley sensed the invitation had been given reluctantly. "Thanks, but—"

"It's the least I can do for all the trouble—" Cooper nodded at Burt "—someone caused."

He'd offered to help only because he wished to make amends for his father's shoplifting. Even knowing that, she couldn't deny Cooper intrigued her, and she was hard-pressed to reject the invitation.

"Please, Mom," Tuff begged. "Can we go to Mr. Cooper's ranch and see the reindeer again?"

"Yeah." Flint joined his brother's campaign. "Mr. Jenkins has bad breath."

Burt chuckled.

"Okay, we'll visit the ranch tomorrow after church." Finley's gaze connected with Cooper's across the table and the corner of his mouth curved upward. Suddenly tomorrow couldn't come soon enough.

CHAPTER FOUR

"STARING OUT THE window won't make them arrive any sooner," Cooper said.

His father powered the scooter across the room and stopped short of the kitchen, where Cooper loaded lunch dishes into the dishwasher. Most days he didn't care if the dishes piled up in the sink—then again, a woman hadn't entered their house since Denise had left him.

"You should ask Finley out on a date."

"Are you smoking weed again?" Cooper had found a toke in the pocket of his father's jeans several weeks ago when he'd done laundry. He'd threatened that if he ever found another joint in the house, he'd take the keys to the van and that would be the end of Burt's freedom.

"What's wrong with asking the young filly out on a date?"

"Finley isn't a horse." She was a hot-blooded woman.

"She's pretty."

"Yes, she is." And last night when he'd gone to sleep, he'd imagined what it would feel like to hold her in his arms. Then Burt's shout for help getting out of bed this morning had reminded Cooper why he couldn't get involved with Finley.

"Ask her out before that butthead Jenkins gets to her first."

Cooper agreed that Jenkins was a butthead, but dating Finley was out of the question. No way would he risk his heart to another woman, then have her leave him high and dry when she realized Burt and Cooper were a package deal. "What happened to the twins' father?"

"Suzie at the café said Finley never married the guy and he isn't involved in the boys' lives."

"That's too bad." And Cooper meant it. He loved his father and they'd always had a close relationship despite their bickering. He had fond memories of Burt teaching him how to hunt and fish. Flint and Tuff were missing out on all those father-son adventures. After Burt had been thrown from a horse and broke his back, leaving him paralyzed from the waist down, they'd switched roles and Cooper had become more of a father, taking care of Burt's basic needs.

"What's up with the twins' names? I've never heard of Flint or Tuff."

"The boys said their mom named them after rocks because their father's a geologist."

"I know what flint is, but I've never heard of tuff," Cooper said.

"I searched it online. Tuff is a rock formed from volcanic ash."

Cooper wondered if the boys' father even appreciated that Finley had thought of him when she'd named his sons. "They're cute kids." He and Denise had talked about starting a family right away when they married, but after their breakup, he'd let go of that dream. "What's going on between you and Viola Keller?"

"Nothing."

"You offered to take her for a drive. That sounds like something," Cooper said.

"If anyone needs to worry about their love life, it's you."

A car engine echoed outside, and Burt went to open the door.

The twins were the first to rush into the house, their eyes wide as they took in their surroundings. Then Finley arrived, and Cooper felt a zap shoot through his chest. When she spotted him in the kitchen, her smile widened. "I didn't know cowboys did dishes."

Wow, she was pretty when she smiled. He dried his hands on a towel, then joined the group in the living room. "Glad you could make it."

"Hey, boys," Burt said. "It'll take a while for your mom and Cooper to figure out what they're gonna use for the float. How 'bout you stay inside with me and bake cookies?"

"What kind of cookies?" Tuff asked.

"Any kind you want."

"I wanna make cookies," Flint said.

"Are you sure, Burt?" Finley frowned. "The twins will make a mess."

Burt waved a hand. "We'll be fine." He scooted into the kitchen and searched the pantry. "Tuff, climb on that stool and hand me the bag of flour on the top shelf."

Cooper knew exactly what his father was doing—making sure his son had time alone with Finley. He grabbed his jacket from the hook by the door and shrugged it on. "After you." As they cut across the driveway to the barn, a gust of wind carried Finley's scent past Cooper's nose—she smelled like spring.

When they entered the barn, he broke the silence. "I was thinking about the twins believing the whitetails are reindeer."

"I tried to explain that the deer don't belong to Santa." She approached the pen at the back of the barn. "Why are these little guys in here?"

"They weren't eating enough. I'm fattening them up before putting them back with the herd."

Cooper couldn't drag his eyes from the soft expression on her face when the fawns nuzzled her jacket. "Here." He gave her a scoop of feed. "If you don't mind the slobber, they'll eat right out of your hand."

Finley fed the babies and giggled. "Their tongues tickle."

One of the fawns licked the inside of the scoop. "This one reminds me of Tuff. He's greedy."

"It must be difficult raising twins by yourself," he said.

"I don't know how my grandmother did it."

"What do you mean?"

"She watched the boys after they were born while I went back to school to finish my business degree."

"Do they miss their grandmother?"

She nodded. "I think that's why they've taken such a liking to Burt."

"I'm not sure what's wrong with my father," Cooper said. "He's been acting strange for a while now."

"How so?"

"He drives all over without telling me where he's going. And stealing from your store…" Cooper shook his head. "He's never done anything like that before."

"I told you he wants attention."

Cooper stiffened.

"I'm guilty of the same thing," she said. "Tuff and Flint have been rebelling lately, and it's because I spend so much time in the store and they're left to entertain themselves."

He didn't feel bad now that she'd pointed out her own flaws.

She brushed a strand of hair from her eyes. "I knew it would be challenging starting a business, but I didn't expect it to be this time-consuming."

Ask her out before that butthead Jenkins gets to her first.

Finley didn't have time to date. And why start something when it couldn't go anywhere as long as Cooper had Burt to look after? "What about the boys' father? Can he help you?"

"He lives in Iceland."

Iceland was a long ways away. Cooper suspected Finley felt as alone as he did—they were both shouldering all the responsibility for their loved ones.

"With my busy schedule I shouldn't have volunteered to do a float, but I thought it would give the boys something to look forward to."

"I'll put them to work in a little bit. Come check this out." He walked behind the barn, where an old buckboard sat. "We don't use it anymore, but it's in decent shape. The boys and I can paint it red and hang Christmas lights on it. I thought we could pile hay in the back and use one of the fawns as Rudolph."

"That's a great idea." Finley's eyes sparkled. "The twins can wear their elf costumes from the school Christmas play."

"I'll hitch two of our horses to the wagon and you and Burt can drive the buckboard down Main Street."

"You don't want to drive?"

The sun bounced off Finley's hair, creating a ring of

light above her head. He wished he could run his fingers through the locks and decide for himself if it was as soft as it looked. "I think Burt would really enjoy being part of the parade."

"I love the idea. But are you sure you want the boys to help you paint?"

"If you keep Burt busy this afternoon, I can handle them."

Her smile tugged at his gut. "You've got yourself a deal." She offered her hand. When he grasped her fingers, his gaze zeroed in on her mouth. Tiny puffs of warm air escaped from between her lips and feathered across his chin. Then her pupils darkened until her brown eyes appeared black.

A powerful yearning spread through his chest, across his shoulders and down his spine. He brushed his fingertip over her cheek and a shudder shook her body. The groan he'd been holding hostage in his throat escaped as she tilted her face toward his.

"Mom! Where are you?"

Finley jumped away from Cooper. "I'd better check on the boys."

Cooper rummaged through the paint cans in the barn's storage room while he waited for his body to cool down. He'd almost kissed Finley. What the heck had gotten into him? He grabbed the paint, a tarp and a couple of old dress shirts he used as polishing rags. When he flipped off the lights, he almost bumped into the twins hovering in the doorway.

"My mom said you're gonna let us paint," Tuff said.

"Follow me."

The boys trailed after him. "Is that gonna be our

float?" Flint asked when Cooper stopped next to the buckboard.

"We'll turn this into Santa's Christmas wagon." Cooper spread the tarp beneath the front end.

"Who's going to be Santa?"

"No Santa, but your mom said you two can wear your elf costumes."

The twins groaned.

"I'll bring one of the fawns and we'll pretend he's Rudolph."

"Do we get to ride in the back with the reindeer?" Tuff asked.

Cooper nodded. "Put on the shirts so you don't get paint on your clothes." He helped the boys button the smocks before handing over the brushes. "Have you two ever painted before?"

They shook their heads.

"It's easy. After you dip the brush into the paint, scrape the sides against the edge of the can like this. That way we don't waste paint and it doesn't drip on you or the ground."

"Where do we start?" Flint asked.

"You paint the seat." Cooper lifted Flint and set him in the front of the buckboard, then placed a can of paint next to him. "Tuff, you work on the side of the wagon." Cooper confiscated two stools from inside the barn. "Stand on this one, Tuff, and I'll set the can on the stool next to you."

"This is fun," Flint said, slopping red color all over the seat.

"I'll do the tailgate." Cooper poured paint into a plastic bowl and retreated to the back of the wagon.

"Mr. Cooper?" Tuff asked.

"What?"

"How come you and Burt have so many deer?"

"We raise them so other ranchers can start their own herds."

"Do you like deer?" Flint asked.

Cooper hadn't really thought much about liking deer. "What I like most about raising deer is getting to work outdoors." Ever since his father put him on a horse, Cooper had loved riding. Even now he preferred to ride on horseback to check the herd and used his truck only when it was cold or rainy.

"My mom says our dad works outside."

"Oh?" Cooper didn't want to push the boys into talking about their father, but he couldn't deny he was interested in learning more about the man who'd attracted Finley's interest.

"He likes rocks," Tuff said.

"How often do you see your dad?"

The boys exchanged puzzled glances. Then Tuff said, "We don't see him."

"Never?" Cooper had a difficult time believing a man wouldn't want to visit his own flesh and blood.

"Mom says he lives too far away."

Iceland was far away. A plane ticket probably cost a small fortune.

"Mr. Cooper?"

"Yeah?"

"How come you're not a dad?"

"I'm not married."

"Our mom's not married and she's a mom," Tuff said. "Don't you like kids?"

"Sure, I like kids," he said.

"Do you like us?" Flint squinted over the seat.

The conversation grew trickier by the minute. "Of course I like you guys."

"What did you ask Santa to bring you for Christmas?" Tuff changed the subject and Cooper breathed a sigh of relief.

"I haven't decided what I want." If he thought Santa would come through for him, he'd ask for one night alone with Finley.

"I want a train set like Jacob's," Flint said.

"What kind of train does Jacob have?" Cooper asked.

"It doesn't have any controls," Tuff said. "You have to push the trains with your hands."

Cooper and his father could make the boys a train set. "What are you two getting your mother for Christmas?"

The twins shrugged. Then Flint said, "We don't have any money."

"You could make her something."

"Like what?" Tuff asked.

"What sort of things does your mother talk about all the time?" He wanted to know what captivated Finley's interest.

"Mom likes chocolate," Flint said.

"And birds," Tuff added.

"What about building your mom a birdhouse?"

"We don't know how to make a birdhouse," Tuff said.

"I'll help you. You can come out to the ranch next week and we'll work on it."

"But we can't tell Mom what we're doing," Flint said.

"Yeah, we gotta keep it a secret," Tuff added.

"It'll be our secret." Cooper set aside his paint bowl and checked on the boys' progress. "You're doing a good job, Flint." The kid beamed at the praise. Then Cooper spoke to Tuff. "You, too. Lookin' good."

He predicted it would take at least a couple of hours to paint the wagon. Hopefully, Finley could put up with Burt for that long.

"THOSE COOKIES SMELL GOOD," Burt said. He sat in his scooter in front of the family room window.

"Would you like a few?" Finley asked.

"Yes, ma'am."

She placed two chocolate-chip cookies and an oat-meal one on a plate, then poured a glass of milk. "Here you go." She peered outside. "How far do you think they've gotten?" Finley worried that the boys would grow bored, but to her amazement neither of them had called it quits.

"I bet they're almost done. I saw Cooper throw one of the paint cans in the garbage." Burt bit into his cookie. "You sure can bake, Finley."

"Granny taught me."

"Never knew your grandmother, but when I drove through town, she was always on her knees in the flower bed at the front of the house."

"Granny loved her rosebushes." Finley wished she had more time to work in her grandmother's garden, but she was lucky if she could keep up with the weeds.

"Tell me, young lady. Are you and Jenkins all cozy now?"

Finley retreated to the kitchen to clean up. "We're not cozy anything, Burt. He's just a friend." Not really even a friend.

"You think he'll be mad when he finds out Cooper helped you with the float?"

"No." Jim's ego was too big to allow him to be jealous of other men. Cooper, on the other hand… She recalled the determined set of his jaw when he'd insisted on helping with the float—a definite sign he was jealous of Jenkins. But now wasn't the right time to become involved with a man. She had her hands full managing her and the boys' lives—adding a significant other to her list of things that needed her attention was crazy.

Can't you be friends? She admitted the idea appealed to her.

"How come you aren't married?"

"Are you always this nosy, Burt?"

"Yes, ma'am." He finished the cookies. "You got two young boys out there that need a father."

"They have a father."

"Any man who abandons his kids isn't worth the dirt he walks on."

"It's complicated, but our split was amicable. And the boys are doing fine." Except that her sons were missing out on all the things little boys and their dads did together—camping, sports and…painting buckboards.

"You should set your sights on a man and marry."

"I don't have time to date." Besides, there wasn't a man in town who interested her. Cooper's face flashed before her eyes—their almost kiss behind the barn called her a liar. Even now the image of his mouth inching toward hers made her pulse race.

Good thing the boys had interrupted them, because she feared one kiss from Cooper would never be enough.

CHAPTER FIVE

"FINLEY?"

"Right here." Finley entered the parlor room on the first floor of the Victorian and found Viola Keller browsing the display of scented pillow sachets and assorted body lotions and sprays. "I didn't see you come in."

The children's-choir director avoided eye contact with Finley. "I can't make heads or tails out of all these products." She motioned to the bottles and jars. "What's the difference between a body butter and body glitz?"

"The butter is a thicker cream and the glitz is a spray that contains glitter."

"Glitter? Good Lord."

"Younger girls like to sparkle."

"What about scents? I'm looking for something…" Viola blushed.

Finley took pity on her. "Special?" She reached for the tester bottle of Summer Sandalwood, which contained man-magnet pheromones. "Try this." She pressed a drop of the lotion onto her palm.

"Smells nice."

"Can I ask you a personal question, Viola?"

The woman's eyes rounded. "I suppose."

"Are you interested in Burt?"

Viola gasped.

Christmas was a magical time of year. Even though Finley didn't have a husband or boyfriend to celebrate the holiday with, she wanted others to be happy. Maybe Viola needed a little nudge in Burt's direction. "I saw the way you stared at him the other day, and it's obvious he likes you since he offered to take you for a drive."

"Nonsense. He doesn't even know I exist."

He will if you use that lotion. "Burt's always glancing out the window toward the church when he's in the store."

"Really?"

Finley nodded.

"I haven't had much luck with men."

"The next time you think you might run into Burt, use this lotion. I guarantee he'll notice you." She crossed the room and selected two candles. "If you find the courage to invite him over to your place for dinner one night, light these an hour before he arrives."

"Why?"

"The scent relaxes and soothes. You'll feel comfortable with each other in no time." Finley plucked a swag of mistletoe from the tree in the corner. "If Burt sees this hanging in one of your doorways, I bet he'll kiss you."

Viola inched closer. "You won't tell anyone I bought these things, will you?"

"Absolutely not." She bagged Viola's purchases and sent her off with a smile, hoping the older woman found the courage to pursue Burt. While Finley straightened inventory, every few minutes her eyes strayed to her iPhone on the counter.

Call him.

She wanted to see Cooper again, but there was no

reason to visit his ranch after he'd promised to put the finishing touches on the buckboard and deliver it in time for the children's parade.

The front door banged open, ending her daydream. Jim Jenkins stepped inside. "Hi, Finley."

"Hello, Jim."

He shoved his hands inside his coat pockets and rocked back on his heels.

"Are you shopping for someone today?" she asked.

He glanced over his shoulder at the two ladies chatting in the dining room. "About the other night."

"Other night?"

"When I ran into you and Cooper Hollis in the town square."

"What about it?"

Jim's gaze narrowed. "Are you dating Hollis?"

I wish. "No."

"Good." He expelled a long breath. "Would you like to join me for dinner tonight?"

Finley's insides cringed. She wasn't attracted to Jim—all she could think about was Cooper. "I'm sorry, but I have plans."

"You do?"

As she searched for an excuse, her gaze landed on a stack of brochures advertising the town's Christmas events. "I'm taking a sleigh ride." *Oops.* She'd forgotten he'd asked her to go on one the other night.

"With who?"

"Cooper Hollis."

"I thought you weren't seeing each other."

"We aren't. We're...friends."

Jim shook his head. "Maybe next time."

"Sure." The slamming door drowned out her answer.

She reached for her phone, hoping Cooper would agree to join her on the sleigh ride—otherwise she'd be caught in a lie of her own making. Burt answered on the second ring.

"Burt, it's Finley. Would you and Cooper like to go for a sleigh ride with me and the boys tonight?"

BURT DROVE HIS scooter into the barn Monday afternoon. "You didn't come in for lunch after you checked on the herd. What's got you too busy to eat?"

Cooper set aside the piece of wood he'd measured. "I'm making a train set for the boys."

"Tuff and Flint?"

"What other boys do we know?"

"Smart-ass." Burt parked his scooter in front of the workbench.

"I could use your help painting the cars," Cooper said.

"Sure. You gonna paint the track, too?"

"Thought I'd stain it."

"Good idea. Why are you doing this?"

"The twins said their friend's dad built a train set and—" he shrugged "—since the twins' father is out of the picture…"

"You making anything for Finley?"

"Why would I make something for her?"

"Because you like her."

"Don't get any matchmaking ideas in your head. Finley's a nice woman, but I'm not interested in starting a relationship with anyone."

"You ought to be thinking about starting something with someone before you're too old."

"Leave it alone, Dad." Cooper and his father had

had this conversation before, and each time it ended in slamming doors. He didn't have the heart to tell the truth—that he couldn't pursue a woman until after Burt wasn't in the picture.

"Did you give Seth Anderson a call?"

"Yeah. He wants to hold off picking up his deer until after Christmas." Cooper turned on the table saw, then cut out the caboose. "Here." He handed the piece of wood to his father along with a square of sandpaper. "Make yourself useful."

"The Weather Channel is forecasting snow for our area. Lots of it." Burt said.

"When?"

"Christmas."

"I'll believe it when I see it." The weathermen liked promoting ominous conditions to improve their station's ratings.

"Might be a good idea to bring the herd in closer. Put 'em in the pasture behind the house."

The acreage in back of the ranch house was heavily wooded, which provided shelter from the hot summer sun and cold winter winds. "Wouldn't hurt to move them later in the week and put out extra feed."

"I'll get the barn ready for the mamas and their babies," Burt said.

"Let's wait and see if the storm hits before you go to all that trouble."

"I can help out a lot more than you let me, you know."

His father meant well, but most of the time his *assistance* made more work for Cooper. Besides, Burt admitted he didn't enjoy doing chores anymore. Too bad Finley didn't need a babysitter. Burt was a pro at goofing off with the twins.

"You got plans for tonight?" Burt rubbed the sandpaper back and forth against the rough edges of the caboose.

"Nope." Cooper never had plans.

"Good, 'cause we're going on a sleigh ride."

What? "Since when have you wanted to take a sleigh ride?"

"Since Finley invited us along with her and the boys."

"Finley called?" Cooper ignored the leap his heart took inside his chest.

"She wants us to meet at her house at seven."

Cooper checked his watch. He had four hours to work on the train, eat, shower and drive into town. "Then quit bugging me so I can finish my work."

Burt chuckled, then set the caboose on the workbench and motored out of the barn.

Cooper's blood pumped faster through his veins as he thought about the kiss he and Finley had almost shared the other day. With the boys and Burt in the sleigh, there'd be no hanky-panky between them. Maybe it was best they had chaperones. He had a feeling once he got a taste of Finley, she'd become addicting, and she was a habit he couldn't afford to get hooked on.

"THEY'RE HERE! THEY'RE HERE!" Flint tugged on Finley's coat sleeve, pulling her out of the rocking chair on the front porch of the Victorian.

"Slow down!" she called as she hurried after the twins. Cooper hopped out of the passenger side of the van and gave high fives to the boys. The butterflies in her stomach beat their wings, and she pressed her hand to her midriff to squelch the fluttering. Cooper glanced her way and smiled—the first true smile he'd given her since they'd met. Holy smokes, the man was handsome.

She stopped in front of him. His short-cropped beard reminded her of a dangerous outlaw. If there was ever a man who looked right at home in Texas, it was Cooper Hollis. While the boys watched Burt position his chair on the lift, Finley's eyes remained glued to Cooper. What was it about this man that tugged at her soul?

"I hope you and Burt didn't have other plans." That was a stupid thing to say—if they'd had plans, they wouldn't have accepted her invite.

"Nothing other than watching TV." He removed his cowboy hat and shoved his fingers through his thick dark hair. She suspected he was as nervous as she was tonight.

As Burt stowed the chair lift in the van, Tuff spoke. "I don't want to go on the sleigh ride."

"Yeah, can we go to Santa's Village instead?" Flint asked.

"But you both wanted to take a ride earlier," she said.

"Well, now, I have to say I'm not too enthusiastic about getting in a sleigh and riding down the block." Burt's gaze focused on the church next door, where Viola Keller chatted with a group of ladies.

"C'mon, boys." Burt spun his chair. "Let's visit Santa."

"Stay right by Burt! Don't wander off!" Finley stared dumbfounded as Burt led the way up the block, stopping in front of the church to wave to Viola. The older woman excused herself and walked over to Burt and the boys. A moment later the group continued on together. Evidently, Viola wanted to visit Santa, too. "Burt did that on purpose, didn't he?"

"Yep."

Finley had trouble meeting Cooper's gaze. "We don't have to go if you don't want to."

"Have you changed your mind?"

She wished things weren't so awkward between them. "Not really. I hate letting coupons go to waste."

"Coupons?"

She looked both ways, waiting for an opportunity to dash across the street. When an opening in traffic appeared, she grabbed Cooper's hand and they hurried to the other side. After reaching the sidewalk, she reluctantly released his hand and removed the flyer from her coat pocket. "Two for the price of one."

"Save that and take the boys for a ride another day. I'll treat tonight."

"I asked you—" She caught herself before she said *out*. She didn't want him to believe this was a date, even though technically it was. Sort of.

They walked side by side, hips bumping once, but once was all it took to warm her blood. The town owned the sleighs used for the Christmas rides and local ranchers supplied the horses. The drivers worked for free and donated their tips to a fund set up to buy presents for needy families in the community. Texans were prideful people, but there was something about a child not receiving a toy from Santa that made even the most stubborn parents accept a gift for their son or daughter.

There were two couples standing in line, and all four loaded into the sleigh. The driver nodded to Cooper. "The next one is five minutes out." He flicked the reins and the horses trotted off.

"How's the store doing this holiday season?" Cooper asked.

"Holding steady." She smiled. "How's the deer business?"

"I'll have to keep an eye on the herd. Burt said the weathermen are calling for snow on Christmas."

Finley searched for something else to talk about. "Thank you for letting the boys paint the buckboard with you. They haven't stopped talking about the fun they had."

"They're good kids."

Silence stretched between them. "Have you ever taken a sleigh ride before?" she asked.

"Once." He stared down the sidewalk as if something had caught his attention. Before she could ask him about it, the next sleigh pulled around the corner.

"Good evening, folks."

"Hello, Sam." Finley introduced the men. "Sam, this is Cooper Hollis. He owns—"

"Buckhorn Ranch," Sam said. "My father-in-law, Ben Dunkin, bought several deer from you not too long ago."

"He sure did." Cooper shook Sam's hand.

"Ben isn't too happy that I married his daughter and moved her down the road to Buffalo Gap."

"Sam runs his own plumbing business," Finley said, accepting Cooper's help into the sleigh.

"I try to get back into Ben's good graces once a year by volunteering to drive the Christmas sleighs." He glanced over his shoulder. "There's a blanket beneath the seat if you get chilly." He clicked his tongue and the horses moved forward.

After a block, Cooper whispered, "Are you cold?"

"A little."

He spread the blanket across their laps and Finley

slipped her hands beneath the warm cover. A moment later she felt Cooper's knuckles bump her thigh. She didn't think—she just grabbed his hand and threaded her fingers through his. His grip was warm, his skin calloused, and she shivered as she envisioned his hands caressing her naked body.

"You said you'd been on a sleigh ride once before?" she whispered.

"With Denise."

Drat. She hadn't meant to bring up painful memories tonight. "I'm sorry."

"It wasn't meant to be. What about you?" he asked. "What happened to the boys' father?"

"I met Alexander when I studied abroad in Greece." His olive skin and dark eyes had attracted her immediately, and he had swept her off her feet.

"How come you didn't marry?"

"I didn't discover I was pregnant until after I'd returned to the States. When I told Alex, he'd already been accepted into graduate school in Iceland." She shrugged. There was no sense making excuses for Alex. He cared more about his career than he did his sons. "He's working toward a doctorate degree in geology."

The sleigh hit a bump in the road and she almost landed in Cooper's lap.

"Sorry, folks. Couldn't avoid the pothole."

"Anyway, Alex stayed in Iceland, and to be honest, it was probably a good thing."

"Why do you say that?"

"Alex was old-world Greek, and if we'd married, I would have been expected to move to Greece and live with his family while he pursued his education." She smiled. "I wanted more out of life for myself. I love my sons and I love being a mother, but I also like running a business. I just wish the store didn't take up so much time. I worry the boys are getting shortchanged."

As Finley's words soaked into Cooper's brain, he released her hand and placed his own on top of the blanket—away from temptation. A busy woman like Finley barely had time for herself, let alone him or helping with Burt.

Who says you have to become a couple? Just enjoy spending time together when you can.

The desire to take a chance with Finley was strong, but an honorable man wouldn't pursue a woman with children unless he was prepared to make a commitment down the road, which Cooper wasn't.

Sam pulled the sleigh to the side of the street and sat as still as a statue without saying a word. Cooper checked over his shoulder, but there was no traffic on the road. He glanced at Finley, who pointed above their heads to the Texas star hanging from the streetlamp.

"You know what they say about mistletoe, don't you?" she asked.

A person didn't grow up in Mistletoe, Texas, and not learn that kissing a girl beneath the sprig of greenery could be interpreted as a promise to marry or a prediction of a long, happy life together.

It's a superstition. He'd kissed Denise beneath the mistletoe and she'd dumped him.

You know you want to kiss her. Cooper's heart lurched inside his chest when Finley smiled at him. An invisible magnet pulled his mouth down to hers. He kept his eyes open, wanting to see her beautiful face as they kissed. When their mouths touched, her brown lashes fluttered closed. A shiver rippled through his chest and a not-so-gentle tug gripped his groin when he snaked his fingers through her hair. She tasted like moonlight and magic. And her hair was as silky as he'd imagined.

She broke off the kiss too soon and glanced at the back of Sam's head. He'd forgotten they had a chaperone.

"You folks ready?"

"We are." Finley snuggled closer to Cooper and a powerful yearning caught him unawares—a need to care for someone and have them care back. And maybe even love.

Love?

No. He meant… Hell, he didn't know what he was thinking anymore. But if the feelings Finley inspired in him after one kiss were any indication of his growing attraction to her, then he was in trouble. Big trouble.

"It's going to be a busy week at the store," she said. "I'm getting ready for a huge sale Thursday."

"What kind of sale?"

"A pre-Christmas sale. I'm opening the store at eight and closing at nine."

"What are you going to do with the boys that day?"

"Pray they behave themselves. I bought a new Christmas DVD and I'm counting on them watching it over and over."

"I'll come get the boys that day." The words were out of his mouth before he realized he'd spoken them.

"Seriously?" Finley's eyes lit up with excitement. "They're a handful. Are you sure?"

"I'll give them a tour of the ranch and we'll feed the deer. If they get tired of hanging out with me, Burt can teach them how to play checkers." And they'd have a chance to make Finley's birdhouse.

She curled her arms around his neck and kissed his cheek. "Thank you, Cooper. That's the nicest Christmas present anyone has given me."

CHAPTER SIX

THE LAST THING Finley needed to do Wednesday evening was close the shop early and spend two hours at the hair salon, but she couldn't resist a little holiday pampering after the boys had been invited to a sleepover at a friend's house.

You just want to draw attention to yourself tomorrow when Cooper picks up the twins.

Okay, fine. She admitted that she wanted to look pretty for Cooper. After the kiss they'd shared during the sleigh ride, she was more certain than ever that she wanted to see where things might lead between them. She'd come to the conclusion that her life would always be busy and there would never be a perfect time for a relationship, so she might as well jump in with both feet and see what happened. Once her sons were back in school after the winter break, she intended to ask Cooper to join her for lunch in town. Keeping that positive thought in mind, Finley entered Mistletoe Locks Beauty Salon.

"Look whose ears must have been burning," Maybelline said. The salon owner took pride in the fact that her mother had named her after the famous makeup company.

Finley touched her ears and played along. "They feel a little warm. What are you saying about me?" She hung her jacket on the peg by the door, then sat in the waiting area. Dozens of miniature mistletoe bouquets hung from the salon ceiling. Maybelline went overboard with the mistletoe—who were you going to kiss in a beauty shop?

"I was telling Joyce—" Maybelline nodded to the stylist who rolled Mrs. Crandall's thinning gray hair. The older woman's daughter dropped her off once a week for a shampoo and style while she ran errands "—that it's about time you found yourself a man and a father for your boys."

Uh-oh. Evidently, a bystander had witnessed her and Cooper's kiss during the sleigh ride. She feigned innocence. "What are you talking about?"

Maybelline and Joyce exchanged grins. Then Joyce said, "If you don't want to be the talk of the town, then you shouldn't kiss cowboys in public."

Finley gasped.

"Everyone knows you and Cooper kissed during your sleigh ride Monday night."

"Sam should have kept what he saw to himself," Finley said.

"Sam told his wife, and you know Doreen—she reads all those romance novels and thinks everyone in the world deserves a happily ever after. She told Suzie down at the café and Suzie told Helen at the dental office and Helen—"

"I get it." Finley scowled. *Great.* The gossipmongers would scare Cooper off.

"You know," Maybelline said, "I think Patricia feels guilty that her daughter broke off her engagement to Cooper."

"It's too bad Cooper doesn't have any siblings to

help him care for Burt." Joyce sprayed Mrs. Crandall's curlers with styling gel before helping her to the dryers. "I don't know how he manages both the ranch and his father."

Maybelline stepped in front of Finley and played with a strand of her hair. "Did you want another conditioning treatment?"

"I thought I might try a new style."

The beautician's tattooed eyebrows arched into her hairline. "You haven't done more than trim an inch off the ends in years."

Joyce joined her boss's side and studied Finley. "It's because of Cooper, isn't it? You want a sexy look that will make him all hot and bothered."

Hot and bothered? "I thought it was time to update my hairstyle, that's all." She glanced between the women. "Maybe something a little more sophisticated."

Maybelline nodded. "A bob."

"With side-swept bangs," Joyce added. "You have beautiful eyes, and bangs will accentuate their color and size."

"We'd have to cut off at least four inches. Is that okay with you?" Maybelline asked.

Finley tapped her shoulder. "Maybe to here."

"A little shorter will look better." Joyce lifted Finley's hair. "An inch above your shoulder."

"Okay. If I don't like it, I'll let it grow."

Maybelline and Joyce fussed over Finley for the next hour until the cut was perfect, then faced her chair toward the mirror.

Finley hardly recognized herself. The bob made her appear more mature and confident. "I look like a businesswoman."

The bells on the door jingled and Mrs. Crandall's daughter entered. "Finley McCarthy, is that you?"

"It's me."

Phyllis smiled. "So it's true?"

"What's true?" Finley asked.

"You and Cooper Hollis are dating."

"We're friends." She ignored Maybelline's eye roll.

"That's what they all say." Phyllis glanced at her mother nodding off under the dryer.

"Give me five minutes and I'll have her hair combed out," Joyce said.

"Leave her be. I've got a few more errands to run." Phyllis paused at the door. "All men start out as friends, Finley. Until you get them into bed." She winked and left the salon.

"So?" Maybelline stared at Finley's reflection in the mirror.

"What?"

"Have you invited Cooper into your bed yet?"

"That's personal, Maybelline."

"She hasn't slept with him," Joyce said. "Too bad. I bet Cooper's good in the sack." She held up her hands. "I'm not interested in him. I'm perfectly happy with my big potbellied teddy bear, Gerald." She put away the blow-dryer. "He turns a blind eye to my gambling. What more could a girl ask for?" Everyone in town knew Joyce had a love affair with internet poker.

Finley rummaged in her purse for her wallet. "You two should drop by the store tomorrow and finish your Christmas shopping. Everything will be half off."

"I want to buy my niece and nephew a bottle of that Mistletoe Magick the kids in town are talking about,"

Maybelline said. "My sister thinks it's a waste of money, but Christmas is all about magic, right?"

"That's right." Finley signed her credit-card slip and gave both women a generous tip before leaving. She wondered what Cooper would think when he saw her. Maybe he'd like the style so much he'd kiss her again.

Cooper's kiss was definitely one of the most magical things that had happened to Finley this holiday season.

"How MANY DEER do you got?" Tuff asked as he and his brother trailed Cooper into the barn.

"About two hundred." Burt had fetched the boys from town so Cooper had time to work on the train.

"That's a lot of deer to feed," Tuff said.

Now that Cooper had been with the twins a few times, he could tell them apart. When Tuff smiled, his eyes sparkled with mischief and he talked a mile a minute. Flint was shy and didn't ask as many questions, but he listened carefully to what people said.

"I thought we'd work on the birdhouse for your mom before we fill the deer feeders." Cooper paused inside the storeroom and groped for the light switch.

"How come Burt's not gonna help us?" Tuff asked.

"He didn't sleep well last night. He'll feel better after he takes a nap." He hoped the boys wouldn't put up a stink about Burt staying in the house.

"We hate naps." Tuff poked his brother's shoulder. "Right?"

"Our mom sends us to our room when we get into trouble but we never fall asleep," Flint said.

Cooper placed several pieces of wood on the workbench. "Do you guys know what kind of house you want to make?"

They shook their heads.

"We could build a regular birdhouse or we could build something special."

Tuff climbed onto the stool next to the bench and surveyed the pieces of wood. "Something special."

Cooper opened the book he'd checked out from the library yesterday. "What do you think of this one?"

Flint joined his brother on the stool and the boys peered at the drawing. "It's a bird motel," Cooper said. "It has eight nesting rooms."

"What's a nesting room?" Flint asked.

"A place where the female bird lays her eggs." The boys stared at Cooper with blank looks on their faces. "Or we could build a smaller one like this." He flipped the page.

"I like the motel," Tuff said.

"Me, too." Flint hopped off the stool and peered inside an empty stall. "What happened to the baby deer?"

"They're with their mother in the pen behind the barn." Cooper figured the fawns would be a distraction and had moved them outside. The kids seemed preoccupied. "What's wrong?"

The brothers exchanged guilty looks. Then Tuff dug into his pocket and removed a black rock. "Santa left an early present in our stockings."

Cooper examined the stone. "Were you guys supposed to look in your stockings before Christmas?"

"No," they said. Then Flint spoke. "Is it a chunk of coal?"

Before Cooper had a chance to respond, Tuff asked, "Does that mean we're on Santa's naughty list and we're not gonna get any toys?"

Cooper was baffled. Why would Finley put rocks in

their stockings? Had she wanted to teach them a lesson? As a kid, he'd been a handful, but his parents had never threatened to put coal in his stocking. Maybe the stress of the holidays was taking a toll on Finley.

"Are you two being good?"

The twins nodded.

"Are you putting your toys away and picking up after yourselves?"

They shook their heads.

"What about making your beds and brushing your teeth?" he asked.

"No," they mumbled.

"I think Santa's giving you a warning, and there's still time to get back on his good list."

"How?" Flint asked.

"From now on pick up your toys and try not to make a mess in the house. And you probably shouldn't fight with each other."

"And we can put away our video games," Flint said.

Tuff nodded. "And hang up our coats."

"And if we make our mom a birdhouse, Santa will be happy, right?" Flint asked.

"Right." Cooper would have hoped the boys wanted to make a gift for their mother because they loved her and not because they thought it would help them get back into Santa's good graces. But hey, they were five-year-olds.

"Let's get started." Cooper handed each boy a block of wood and a piece of sandpaper, then showed them how to smooth the edges. Once all the pieces were sanded, he said, "It's time to cut out the holes."

"Can I do it?" Tuff asked.

Cooper expected the boys would want to operate the table saw, but he hesitated, concerned for their safety.

"We never get to do stuff like this, 'cause we only got a mom," Flint said. "Toby's dad lets him help mow the yard on the tractor."

"And Michael's dad let him put his handprint on the porch step before the cement dried."

Feeling sorry for the kids, Cooper said, "I'll let you help with the power tools as long as you don't goof around." He retrieved an extra pair of protective goggles and handed them to Flint. "You're up first." Once he aligned the wood with the blade, he covered Flint's hands with his own. "I'm going to help guide the wood through the saw. Don't push—just let me move it, okay?" Flint nodded and Cooper turned on the saw. Carefully he moved the piece through the twists and turns needed to create the hole, then shut off the power.

"That was cool." Flint jumped off the stool and Tuff took his place.

"I won't push the wood." Tuff put on the goggles. Then Cooper placed his hands over his and repeated the process. He alternated between the boys until eight holes were cut out.

"Since you two listened and followed directions, I'll let you use the nail gun."

"What's a nail gun?" Tuff asked.

"This gadget right here." Before Cooper plugged it in, he showed the boys how the nails were loaded and where they shot out of the gun. "You never, ever point this at anyone. Understood?"

The twins nodded. "Tuff gets to go first this time." Cooper lined up the pieces of wood and held them together with one hand, then helped Tuff position the nail gun. "Put your finger over mine and when I count to three, squeeze." Cooper counted, "One…two…three." A nail shot out of the gun and pierced the wood close to the area he'd targeted. "Good job."

"My turn." Flint and Tuff exchanged places and the process went on for five minutes until the walls were nailed together.

"It needs a roof," Cooper said.

"Those are small holes. How are the birds gonna fit?" Flint asked.

"It's a finch motel."

"What's a finch?" Tuff asked.

"A really small bird." Cooper flipped through the pages of the book. "That's a finch."

"It's tiny," Flint said.

"The birdhouse will protect them from predator birds."

"What's a predator bird?" Tuff asked.

"Falcons and hawks. They eat the smaller birds."

"What color are we gonna paint the house?" Flint asked.

"What's your mom's favorite color?"

"Yellow," Tuff answered.

"Mom says yellow is the color of sunshine and happiness," Flint said.

Cooper had never considered the meaning of colors, but after meeting Finley, he believed happiness and warmth was the color of her hair. "How about a pale yellow with blue trim?"

"Okay."

Making sure the saw and nail gun were unplugged, Cooper said, "We'll slap on the first coat of paint, then feed the deer while it dries." The boys tagged along to the storage room.

"Mr. Cooper?"

"Yes, Flint?"

"I wish you were my dad."

Cooper froze, the air in his lungs expanding until his chest threatened to burst.

"Yeah, you let us use your tools and you have reindeer." Tuff kicked the toe of his shoe against the door. "Mom says our dad collects rocks. That's dumb."

"No," Flint said. "He studies rocks."

"So?" Tuff glared at his brother. "It's stupid."

"We better get to work. The deer will be hungry soon." Cooper grabbed the cans of paint, then divided the colors between the boys and handed them the shirts they'd worn when they'd helped paint the buckboard. He spread newspaper over the workbench and placed the birdhouse between them. "Flint, you start with the front and, Tuff, you paint the back."

After he was sure the boys could handle the task, he said, "I'll be right back." Once he escaped the barn, he leaned against the side of the structure and rubbed his brow.

The twins wanted him to be their father.

All this time, he'd worried that if he and Finley carried on with each other, one of them would get hurt—why hadn't he considered that the boys might get hurt, too?

Not wanting to bruise the kids' feelings was all the motivation he needed to stop seeing Finley. If he was smart, he'd end things with her tonight when he took her sons home. But he couldn't say goodbye just yet—not during the holidays. For the first time since Denise had broken off her engagement to him and left town, Cooper admitted that Finley and the boys were helping him recapture the joy of the season.

CHAPTER SEVEN

FINLEY WATCHED COOPER'S truck turn into the driveway, her heart beating a little faster. She flipped the sign in the window and shut off the lights. When she entered the kitchen at the back of the house, the door crashed opened and the boys began talking at once.

"Hold on." She laughed, giving them each a hug. "One at a time."

"There's this big—" Tuff spread his arms wide "—daddy deer with antlers."

Flint patted his mother's hip. "Burt said he's the boss of all the deer."

Finley glanced up and smiled at Cooper, who stood inside the door, hat in hand. How was it that he grew more and more handsome each time she saw him? Today he wore a gold flannel shirt that made his blue eyes appear brighter. "It sounds like they had a great time at the ranch." She peered past Cooper's shoulder. "Did Burt come with you?"

"He's at home." Cooper's eyes narrowed. "You cut your hair."

"I needed a change."

"I like it." The husky note in his voice sent a shiver down Finley's back.

She ran her hand over her bob. "Thanks. I made a chicken-enchilada casserole. Will you stay for dinner?"

She guided the boys to the stairs. "Wash your hands before we eat."

Once her sons disappeared upstairs, Finley said, "My great idea to hold an after-Christmas sale before Christmas was a bust." She shouldn't complain, because she'd made over five hundred dollars, but it was nowhere near the two thousand she'd hoped to bring in. Twice during the day there had been no one in the store for almost an hour, so she'd used the time to prepare the casserole.

"I'm sorry," he said.

She didn't care to talk about her flagging sales. "Will you stay? A hot meal is the least I can do to thank you for taking the boys off my hands."

Cooper's gaze warmed as he stared at her body. "I'd like that." He pulled his cell phone from his pocket. "I'll text Burt that I won't be home right away."

Relieved he'd said yes, she waited for him to finish the text, then led the way upstairs. Once they reached the landing, she held out her arm. "I'll take your jacket." She laid it across the back of the couch.

"This is nice up here," he said.

"It's small, but the boys and I like it." She caught a whiff of his cologne and shivered.

"Cooper, come play 'Super Mario' with us!" Tuff shouted from his bedroom.

"I'll rescue you in ten minutes," she said.

Cooper's gaze shifted to the mistletoe hanging in the doorway above his head. She'd hung bunches throughout the apartment, and the boys had made a game out of trying to dodge her hugs and kisses. When Cooper's attention zeroed in on her face, she stopped breathing.

His mouth inched closer....

"C'mon, Cooper! Watch what I can make Mario do!"

Heart racing, Finley hurried into the kitchen and removed the casserole from the oven, then shoved a baking sheet of the boys' favorite crescent rolls inside before pouring glasses of water and milk. After adding salsa and sour cream to small serving bowls, she announced, "Dinner's ready."

She hurried into the bathroom and checked her reflection in the mirror. Her carefully styled bob was a mess from running her fingers through the strands all day, and she spotted a cider stain on her white blouse where Mrs. Gunderson had bumped into her while holding a glass. She didn't look like any man's dream date.

Back in the kitchen, she pulled the rolls from the oven, slid them into a bread basket, then grabbed the butter dish and delivered them to the table. "I'm going to start without you guys," she called out.

A second later the trio appeared. Cooper waited for Finley and the boys to take their seats before he sat across from her.

"Let Cooper say grace, Mom," Flint said.

A red stain spread across Cooper's cheeks, and she came to his rescue. "Mr. Cooper is our guest. Why don't you do the honors tonight?"

"Okay." Flint set his elbows on the table and folded his hands beneath his chin. Finley nudged Tuff, and he copied his brother. Then she clasped her hands in her lap and bowed her head.

"Dear God," Flint said. "Thanks for this food even though I don't like Mom's enchiladas."

Cooper made a sound in his throat but Finley was too chicken to open her eyes and look at him.

"And thank You for my mom and my brother and Cooper and Burt. And thank You for the bird— Ouch!"

Finley glanced between the boys.

"He kicked me," Flint said.

"Because you're stupid."

"Don't speak to your brother like that, young man."

Tuff sent a pleading gaze toward Cooper. "He almost blew our surprise."

"What surprise?" She noted Flint's worried expression.

"Maybe I should say grace," Cooper said. Everyone quieted. "Thank You for the world so sweet. Thank You for the food we eat. Thank You for the birds that sing. Thank You, God, for everything. Amen." The boys and Finley added their amens.

"I never heard that one before," Tuff said.

"My mother taught me that blessing." Cooper passed the rolls to Flint, who grabbed two.

"How come we didn't see your mom at the ranch?" Tuff asked.

"My mother died a long time ago."

Good grief. Finley hadn't invited Cooper to supper so he could sit through an inquisition.

"That's okay," Flint said. "We'll share our mom with you." Flint looked at Finley. "Right, Mom?"

Finley forced a smile. "Sure."

Flint nudged Cooper's arm. "You'll like our mom."

Cooper stared at Finley and smiled devilishly. "I already do."

Thank goodness the rest of the meal passed without any embarrassing discussions. Afterward, Finley insisted Cooper relax with the boys while she stowed the leftovers and cleaned the kitchen. Truth be told, she needed time to gather her composure. The more she got to know Cooper, the more she liked him.

Okay, so her feelings had grown beyond like. She admired him. Loved how kind and patient he was with the twins. How thoughtful he was toward her. How he looked after Burt. His former fiancée had been a fool to give him up. As Finley placed the last of the dirty dishes in the dishwasher, she realized that being with Cooper made her forget her troubles. No matter what happened with the store, she'd survive, and best of all, Cooper would still be here.

After she cleaned the kitchen, she joined the guys in the living room. "It's bath time." Even though it was Christmas break, she tried to keep the boys on a schedule because it'd be easier to get back into the swing of things when school began.

"I better get going." Cooper reached for his jacket.

As much as Finley would have loved for him to spend the evening with her, she had to organize the store after the boys went to bed.

"You guys be good for your mother," Cooper said.

Flint and Tuff glanced up from their video game and both spoke at once. "Bye."

"I'll walk you to the door." Finley led the way downstairs. They avoided eye contact while Cooper shrugged into his coat.

"Can I ask you something?" he said, twirling his Stetson in his hand.

"Sure."

"Why did you put a rock in the boys' stockings?"

Her eyes widened. "I didn't think they'd peek."

"I'm guessing they're a handful at times, but they're

good kids and they shouldn't be worried that Santa might not bring them any toys this Christmas."

Finley's heart melted at the protective note in his voice. "Let me guess. They think they've been put on Santa's naughty list."

Cooper nodded. "They assumed the rock was a chunk of coal."

"Those aren't ordinary rocks," she said. "They're from a volcano in Iceland where their father is doing research. He sent them a month ago and wanted me to save them for Christmas."

"Oh." Cooper rubbed a finger alongside his nose, obviously embarrassed he'd jumped to the wrong conclusion.

"I should have wrapped the rocks in Christmas paper." When he remained silent, she asked, "What did you tell them?"

"I said it was probably a warning from Santa to behave down the homestretch." He glanced toward the stairs. "And I suggested they pick up their toys and not fight with each other to get back into Santa's good graces."

Her eyes flicked to the mistletoe above Cooper's head. Would he try to kiss her now that they were alone?

"I guess Burt and I will see you on Saturday."

"The float has to be in the church lot by three and the parade starts at four."

"I'll make sure we're there."

Again her gaze strayed to the mistletoe. This time when they made eye contact, a tiny pulse of electricity zapped between them. Then Cooper put on his cowboy hat and held out his hand. Finley slid her fingers across his callused palm and he reeled her closer, until her hip bumped his thigh. She rolled onto her tiptoes and snuggled against him.

He lowered his head. "All I've thought about since our sleigh ride is kissing you again."

"Me too," she whispered. He nuzzled her mouth, nipping the corner. Then the tip of his tongue snuck inside. Without warning the kiss exploded with passion, and when he finally pulled away, he'd left no doubt in her mind that he wanted more from her than just a kiss.

"HOW WAS DINNER with Finley and the boys?" Burt asked as soon as Cooper stepped through the door.

"Fine."

"Just fine?"

"Yeah, why?" Cooper hung up his jacket and faced his grinning father. "What?"

"When did you start wearing pink lipstick?"

Cooper ran his tongue over his lip and tasted Finley's gloss. "Mind your own business."

Burt followed him into the kitchen and parked his chair next to the table. "We gonna see the boys tomorrow?"

"Not until Saturday at the parade."

"I worked on the train set while you were gone. All the pieces are painted."

"Thanks." He nodded to the TV. "Have you heard anything more about the winter storm?"

"Gonna be a doozy. High winds and a half foot of snow or more."

"When do they think it'll hit?"

"Now they're saying Christmas Eve day." Burt powered his scooter to the fridge and removed a Fudgsicle from the freezer. "We should invite Finley and the boys back here after the parade."

"What for?"

"Flint and Tuff can help me decorate the tree if you get it out of the barn."

Cooper felt a pang of remorse that they hadn't put up a tree this year. Denise had left *him* high and dry last Christmas, not his father, yet he was making Burt suffer because he hadn't wanted any reminders of Denise's betrayal. "I'll bring the tree inside tomorrow."

"Good. 'Bout time we had a little holiday spirit in this house."

"Think I'll call it a night." Cooper disappeared into his room and thought about the kiss he'd shared with Finley. He had no doubt they'd be dynamite in bed, but what he felt for her was a lot more than sexual attraction. Tonight at the supper table with Finley and her sons, Cooper had known what it would feel like to have his own family—him, Finley, Tuff and Flint.

A loud noise in the kitchen startled Cooper from his reverie. He took off his watch and tossed it onto the nightstand, where it slid across the surface and off the back side. When he reached between the wall and the table, his fingers brushed against a piece of paper. He pulled the note free and when he realized what he held in his hands, he collapsed onto the side of the bed.

Dear Cooper,

I'm sorry. I've known for a while that I can't marry you, but with Christmas coming and all, I didn't know how to tell you. It's not that I don't love you, because I do. I'm just not ready to take on the responsibility of helping you care for your

father. I didn't want him living with us. I just wanted it to be me and you. I'm sorry.
Denise

Cooper closed his eyes. Just when he'd begun to believe he was ready to move on with his life and take a chance finding happiness with Finley and the boys, the note reminded of his other responsibility—Burt.

The past few days, he'd witnessed Finley's crazy-busy life. It wouldn't be fair of him to ask her to take on him and Burt. His father wasn't getting any younger, and one of these days he'd no longer be able to drive.

Finley was kind and possessed a gentle, caring spirit. If he asked her, she'd gladly embrace the challenge of managing her responsibilities and helping with Burt, too. But it would be selfish of him to take advantage of her that way. He shoved the letter into the nightstand drawer.

Saturday would be the last time he did anything with Finley and the boys.

"HERE THEY COME, MOM!" Flint pointed to the far end of the church parking lot, where Cooper's pickup towed the buckboard on a flatbed trailer. Burt's van pulled a small horse trailer.

"I see them." She grabbed the boys' hands and wove through the floats, the bells on their pointy elf slippers tinkling in the wind.

"Would you look at that," Burt said when the van door opened and the ramp lowered. "Two elves escaped from the North Pole."

"We're not real elves," Tuff said.

"You're not? Well, you sure look like real ones."

Flint tugged on the collar of his elf jacket. "Mom made these for our Christmas play at school."

Burt winked at Finley. "They look real professional."

"Thank you." She hurried to Cooper's side as he lowered the ramp on the trailer. "Can I help?"

"No, thanks." Cooper didn't even glance at her.

Maybe he'd had trouble getting the buckboard to town and was in a grumpy mood. "I can't thank you enough for helping with the float." He continued working as if he hadn't heard her. Burt and the boys joined them and watched Cooper lower the buckboard to the pavement.

"Do you know what place you are in the procession?" Burt asked.

"No," Finley said. "I don't think they're that organized."

The boys climbed into the wagon. "There's hay in here," Tuff said.

"That'll help the fawn keep his balance," Burt said.

"You're taking the reins, Dad." Cooper nodded to Burt.

Finley's heart plummeted to her stomach. "All three of us can fit on the bench seat if the boys are in the back with the deer."

Cooper shook his head. "I'll sit this one out."

The mayor came over to check out the float. Her gaze swung between Finley and Cooper. "What's this? Santa's sleigh and elves?" Debbie asked.

"It's Santa's buckboard and elves." Finley forced a smile.

"Where's Rudolph?" Debbie asked.

"Right there!" Tuff pointed to Cooper removing the fawn from the livestock trailer behind the van.

"How cute." Debbie laughed.

Cooper set the deer in the wagon, then secured its harness to the sides.

Debbie tugged Finley aside. "I heard you were dating Cooper Hollis. How are things going?"

"We're just friends." She forced a smile.

"That's what they all say. I better check on the others." Debbie walked off.

"Will you keep an eye on the deer while I put Burt's chair away?" Cooper asked after he lifted Burt into the driver's seat.

"Sure." Finley was beginning to fear he regretted kissing her on Thursday. But why? Ten minutes later Cooper had the horses hitched to the front of the buckboard.

"Are you positive you don't want to ride with us?" Finley hoped Cooper would change his mind.

"You can sit with us, Cooper," Tuff said.

"I'll watch from the street." He spoke to Burt. "Make sure to set the brake if you have to stop."

"It's my legs that don't work, not my brain. I know what to do," Burt said, his attention focused on something behind Cooper. Finley glanced across the lot to see what had captured his interest. Viola Keller. The choir director had a knack for showing up when Burt was around.

Cooper held out his hand to Finley, and she accepted his help climbing onto the seat. She squeezed his fingers, but he yanked his hand free and a lump formed in her throat. Something was very wrong, but she had no idea what to do to make it right.

"He's been grumpy since he woke up this morning," Burt muttered when Cooper walked off to his truck.

Burt snapped the reins and pulled the wagon into the line of floats heading out of the parking lot. They circled behind the church and came out on Main Street in front of the town square. Finley reminded the boys to wave as they drove past the crowd.

"Hit that switch down there," Burt said.

She located the battery-operated contraption and turned it on. White lights blinked along the sides of the buckboard and around the wheels. The people lining the sidewalks clapped. When they passed by Viola, Burt tipped his hat to her and she blushed.

Finley shoved her worries about Cooper to the back of her mind and did her best to enjoy the moment. When the buckboard reached the Victorian, she noticed Cooper's somber expression, and tears stung her eyes. The boys called out to him and he waved, but the gesture was halfhearted and Finley feared he was waving goodbye to them.

For good.

CHAPTER EIGHT

"THE WEATHERMEN MIGHT be right this time," Cooper said when he entered the house late Thursday afternoon. His gaze swept past the Christmas tree that remained undecorated in the corner and landed on his father's grumpy face.

"The wind is picking up and I smell snow in the air." Cooper hung his jacket and hat by the door. "It would be helpful if the forecasters would reach a consensus on when the storm will arrive." Tomorrow was Christmas Eve and half the news stations claimed the snow would begin early morning, the others late afternoon.

Burt remained quiet. The old man had been moody all week, and Cooper hadn't wanted to get into an argument with him, so he hadn't asked him what was wrong. Instead he'd spent long hours working outdoors.

Four days had passed since he and Burt had gone into town for the parade. Saturday night when they'd returned to the ranch, Cooper had almost talked himself out of his decision to keep his distance from Finley and the boys. But in the end he'd stuck to his guns, believing it was best for everyone. Even though he exhausted himself with physical labor, each night he still fell into bed and dreamed of Finley.

"You gonna bring the boys back here so they can work on the birdhouse for their mother?" Burt asked.

"I've got too much to do to get ready for the storm."

"I'll watch the kiddos while you're outside."

"It's not a big deal, Dad. I put the finishing touches on the project." He'd drilled a few holes and attached a rope to hang the birdhouse from a tree branch. The boys had done all the painting and signed their names on the bottom. He reached into the fridge for a beer. "I thought you could deliver their gifts early in the morning before the weather gets bad."

"Why don't you take them?"

"I need to check on the herd before it snows."

"Something happen between you and Finley?"

"No."

"Don't lie to me, son."

"Lie about what?"

"I've seen the way you two look at each other. It wasn't that long ago that I looked at your mother the same way."

Cooper had to end this conversation. He didn't want his father to learn the reason he was distancing himself from Finley and the boys. No matter how much he wanted the three of them in his life, his first priority was taking care of his father. "Leave it alone, Dad."

"I won't leave it alone." Burt reached into his shirt pocket and withdrew a piece of paper, then shook it at Cooper. "*I'm* the reason you stopped seeing Finley."

The blood drained from Cooper's face. "What the hell were you doing snooping in my room?"

"I'm your father. I can snoop if I want."

"Give me that." Cooper reached for the letter, but Burt stuffed it into his pocket.

"A while back I was looking for the photo of your

mother I gave you right after she died and I found the letter," Burt said.

"How did it end up behind my nightstand?"

"The scooter hit the edge of the table and the note slid off."

"That's old news, Dad. It doesn't matter anymore."

"It sure in hell does matter if it concerns your future."

"Quit talking nonsense."

"Don't you belittle me, son. I may be stuck in this chair, but I'm still your father and deserve your respect."

Properly chastised, Cooper held his tongue.

"I'm the reason Denise cut out on you." Burt held up a hand when Cooper opened his mouth to protest. "When I ran into Finley and the boys one afternoon at the café, I decided I needed to make things right."

"So you started shoplifting from Finley's store?"

"It got you two together, didn't it?"

"Look, Dad. I appreciate your good intentions, but I don't want you to worry about me. I'm fine. And I'll always be here for you."

"I know. That's why I took matters into my own hands."

"What do you mean?"

"I met with them folks out there at the Shady Acres Retirement Estates."

"You did what?"

"Got an apartment for myself. I won't be a burden to you no more."

Horrified that his father believed he was a responsibility Cooper didn't want, he said, "You're not going anywhere." Had Cooper given his father the impression that he didn't want to take care of him?

"You're a good son. You've stood by me longer than most kids would take care of their parents."

"And I'll be right by your side until the end."

Burt shook his head. "I may be stuck in this damned chair, but that doesn't make me less of a father. And since you haven't experienced being a father, you couldn't know that what fulfills a man most is his children's happiness." Burt's eyes welled with tears. "I don't want to stand in your way if you've got a chance with Finley and the boys. I had a great life with your mother, God rest her soul. That kind of love comes along once in a lifetime. I didn't raise a fool for a son." He placed his fist against his chest. "If Finley's captured your heart, then go after her."

Cooper shoved his fingers through his hair. "You've been an important part of my life, Dad."

"And I'll still be a part of your life—just not every single day like we've been living these past years."

Cooper couldn't imagine waking up in the house and not being the one to help his father out of bed and into his chair. Burt loved this ranch and had built it into a successful business. No way in hell should he have to sit in a retirement home and stare at four walls when he had acres of outdoors and deer on his own property to gaze at.

"Son, I don't want you spending the rest of your years caring for me. By the time something happens to me and you're on your own, you'll have to use those little blue pills they advertise on TV in order to have any fun in the bedroom."

Cooper's chest ached with love for his father. Humbled by the lengths he was willing to go in order for his son to be happy, he realized that the least he could do was have the courage to reach for the future Burt wished for him. But there was one thing he knew for certain—he and Burt were a package deal. If Finley couldn't accept that, then she wasn't the woman he thought she was.

Knowing his father wouldn't drop the subject until he won, Cooper said, "I'll give it some thought, Dad."

If things worked out the way he hoped, Burt wouldn't have to move anywhere.

CHRISTMAS EVE DAY started out with sunshine, but by noon the clouds had rolled in and a blustery wind brought snow flurries. Cooper had one more feeding station to fill before showering. He'd told his father that they'd deliver the gifts to Finley and the boys this afternoon. And while Burt entertained the twins, Cooper intended to sneak downstairs with Finley, kiss her beneath the mistletoe, then ask her to marry him.

When he arrived at the feeder, the herd was huddled together to keep warm. The wind buffeted Cooper's coat when he got out of the truck, and he tossed his hat onto the seat rather than risk it blowing off his head. The temperature was dropping and snowflakes were sticking to the ground.

After filling the feeder, he checked on the fawns, glad to see they stayed close to their mothers. When the female deer finished eating, they'd lead the herd into the trees and take shelter until the storm passed. He hopped into his truck, turned up the heat, then drove along a back road to the house. Before he reached the driveway, the sky unzipped and thick snowflakes poured down like rain.

He parked next to the barn, then moved Burt's van

into the garage so he wouldn't have to clean off the windshield when they drove into town later. Inside the house, he was greeted by his father's grim expression. "What's the matter?"

"The weather-alert radio sounded. They're warning everyone to stay off the roads."

"It's snowing hard but—"

"They're calling for a foot of snow in town. And there's only one plow for the whole county."

"Don't worry. We'll make it into Mistletoe." And maybe if they got lucky, they'd become stranded at Finley's for the night. "I'll grab a quick shower. Then we'll take off."

The shower was fast, but getting on the road wasn't. When Cooper stepped from his bedroom, he heard a commotion in the kitchen and rushed down the hall.

"Damn pipe burst." Burt shoved a pot beneath the sink to catch the water streaming onto the floor.

Cooper raced outside. Ignoring the stinging snow pelting his face, he attempted to turn off the water valve to the house, but the knob was stuck. He hurried inside and threw on his jacket. "The valve's frozen. I'll grab a wrench from the barn and see if I can get it unstuck."

After ten minutes of wrestling, Cooper turned off the water supply, his fingers red and numb with cold. Burt had tossed towels onto the floor, so Cooper got on his hands and knees and mopped up the excess water. "This is my fault. I should have wrapped the pipes," he said.

"You've been busy taking care of the deer."

"What's done is done. Let's load up the Christmas gifts and get into town."

By the time Cooper got Burt into the van and the presents packed safely behind the seats, a half hour had passed. The wind buffeted the van as they drove toward the county road and the windshield wipers were no match for the blowing snow. Cooper hit the brakes at the end of the driveway. If it had been just him, he'd have made an attempt to drive into Mistletoe but he couldn't take the chance of becoming stranded or sliding off the road with his father along.

"Looks like we'll have to settle for visiting Finley and the boys tomorrow."

His father's chin trembled. "Take me back to the house, then go on by yourself."

"You're not spending Christmas Eve alone." He shifted into Reverse and turned the van around. This Christmas Eve would be no different than last year—he and Burt would watch old movies until bedtime. But with a little help from Santa, Christmas Day would be memorable.

"Are Cooper and Burt coming over tomorrow?" Tuff asked as he slid beneath his bedcovers.

"I'm not sure, honey." After the parade Finley had extended an invitation for the men to join her and the boys for Christmas dinner, but after the cold shoulder Cooper had given her that day, she wasn't counting on their presence.

"How come we haven't seen Burt?" Flint asked.

"I think he and Cooper had to make sure the deer were taken care of in the snowstorm."

Her sons exchanged a secret look. Then Flint spoke. "They gotta come tomorrow, 'cause we made you a gift and it's in Cooper's barn."

"A Christmas gift?" She smiled. "What is it?"

"We're not telling!" Tuff said.

Helping the boys make her a present didn't seem like the action of a man who'd suddenly gotten cold feet.

"Mom?"

"Yes, Tuff?"

"Can we put some Mistletoe Magick on our pillows tonight?"

"Did you change your mind about what you want Santa to bring you?" She hoped not, because she'd purchased the toys a month ago and they were safely hidden in her bedroom closet.

"I want to add another present," Tuff said.

Flint sat up in bed. "Me, too."

Finley fetched the vial from the boys' bookshelf and handed it to Tuff, who tipped the bottle over too quickly and spilled half the contents onto his pillow.

"Save some for me." Flint sprinkled the rest on his pillow.

"It looks like you both drooled on your sheets." She kissed each son on the forehead. "I love you lots."

Finley retreated to the kitchen and opened a bottle of wine, poured herself a glass, then went downstairs, where she stood at the front window, watching the snow fall—blanketing the ground and her heart in a heavy white shroud.

"DON'T SEE HOW we're gonna get the van out of the garage, let alone make it into town today."

Cooper looked at his father's forlorn face and smothered a smile behind his hand. The old coot pouted like a kid, wanting to be with the twins Christmas morning. Burt had woken at 5:00 a.m. shouting for help out of bed. He'd wanted Cooper to start shoveling so they could leave before noon.

Cooper could shovel the driveway in a half hour, but they'd be stuck at the ranch until the country road had been plowed. He checked his watch. It was only seven. "I bet the boys are still sleeping."

"You were up at the crack of dawn, sneaking into the living room to see what Santa left you under the tree." Burt smiled at the memory, and Cooper couldn't love his father any more than he did right now.

The years flashed through his mind as he recalled the times his father had taken him fishing. All the Christmas Eves the old man had stayed up late, putting toys together so Cooper could play with them first thing in the morning. It was Cooper's turn to make sure his father got *his* wish this Christmas. "I have an idea."

"What's that?"

"It'll take a little longer to get into town, but I'll hitch the horses to the buckboard and we'll—"

"Go the back way." Burt's eyes brightened with excitement. "Don't forget to throw extra hay in the wagon and a water bucket for the horses when we get to Finley's. And a shovel in case you gotta clear her driveway so she can move her station wagon out of the garage."

"I got it covered. You bring extra blankets and change into your winter boots." Cooper paused at the front door. "And didn't you buy a red Christmas cap a few years ago?"

"I'll find it."

Cooper headed to the barn. The snow had quit falling, but the weatherman warned there would be pockets of heavy snowfall later in the afternoon. If they were going to make a break for town, now was the time. After Cooper hitched the horses to the buckboard and loaded supplies and the presents into the wagon, he went into the house to fetch his father. He carried Burt to the wagon and set him in the back, where he'd spread a horse blanket on top of hay. "Stay down and you'll be protected from the wind."

The ten-minute drive by car into town took over an hour. When the horses reached Main Street, Cooper noticed all the Christmas lights were covered in snow and the candy canes that lined the sidewalks were no longer visible. Mistletoe, Texas, had become a winter wonderland. Face stiff from the cold, Cooper bent his head against the wind and urged the horses to go a little farther.

"THEY'RE HERE! THEY'RE HERE!" Flint shouted from the back bedroom.

Finley left the kitchen, where she'd just put the turkey into the oven. Her heart thudded heavily in her chest, afraid to hope. "Who's here?" She entered the bedroom and found the boys with their noses pressed against the cold window, fogging up the glass.

"Cooper's driving our parade float," Tuff said.

Flint wiped the window so he could see better. "Where's Burt?"

Finley peered over their heads. "Sitting in the wagon." When Cooper guided the horses into her driveway, she rushed into the bathroom and checked her appearance in the mirror. It was too late to put on makeup or change out of her Bugs Bunny pajamas, so she threw on her robe and hurried downstairs, where the boys already waited in their coats and boots by the back door.

"Hurry, Mom!" Tuff said.

Finley stuffed her sock feet into her rubber rain boots, then stepped outside, the boys right on her heels.

Cooper smiled—a genuine ear-to-ear grin—and her heart swelled with hope.

"Can we shelter the horses in your garage?" he shouted.

"Sure!" She used the shovel she'd left by the back door and quickly cleared the steps and the short walk to the driveway. She entered the garage through the side door and pressed the opener. When the door lifted, she shouted, "I think there's room for the horses without having to move the car."

Cooper unhitched the geldings and led them into the garage, then asked the boys to fill the bucket with water. The twins dashed into the house while Cooper spread hay on the ground for the animals to eat.

Cooper looked at Finley, and his loving gaze warmed her cold toes. "I'll carry Burt inside. Then I'll come back for the presents." Cooper helped Burt get settled on the upstairs couch, then went outside and removed the burlap bag he'd stowed beneath the buckboard seat.

"What's in there?" Finley asked, holding the back door open for him.

"A surprise." He winked. Cooper had never winked at Finley before and she laughed, her spirits soaring. She made a move toward the stairs, but he snagged her bathrobe and spun her toward him. His hands settled on her waist.

She gazed into his eyes. "I didn't think you were coming today."

"A snowstorm couldn't stop me from being with you and the boys."

"But last week…at the parade…"

"I'm sorry for that. I was working through an issue

with Burt. But it's all good now." He glanced above their heads. "Merry Christmas, Finley."

"Merry Christmas, Cooper."

"Hey, Burt, I think my mom's kissing Cooper." Tuff's voice echoed at the top of the stairs.

"Yuck!" Flint giggled.

"You two gonna smooch all morning or get up here with the presents?" Burt hollered.

Finley and Cooper joined the trio in the living room, and Cooper gave the boys their present from him and Burt.

"It's a train!" Flint shouted.

"Did you make this?" Tuff asked.

"Burt helped me," Cooper said.

Flint and Tuff hugged Cooper, then Burt. "It's better than Jacob's train," Tuff said.

"Yeah, waaay better." Flint helped his brother place the cars on the track.

"Don't you two want to give your mother her gift?" Cooper asked.

"Oh, yeah." Flint took the wrapped package Burt held out and delivered it to Finley.

"You're gonna love it, Mom," Tuff said.

"Am I?"

"Cooper helped us make it," Flint said.

Finley tore off the paper and gasped. "A birdhouse for the backyard!" She hugged her sons. "This is beautiful. What an amazing job you two did."

"Cooper said it's a motel for really small birds." Flint pointed to the round holes. "It's got lots of rooms."

"A finch motel. It's lovely, boys."

"And this is from me." Cooper handed Finley a wrapped present.

She ripped off the paper, then admired the wooden box with carved flowers on the lid. "It's beautiful, Cooper."

"It's a keepsake box."

"What's a keepsake box?" Flint asked.

"A place for special things." She opened the lid and discovered the inside lined with emerald-green velvet. "Thank you, Cooper."

"Aren't you gonna hug him, Mom?" Tuff asked.

"Yes, I am." Finley left her chair and hugged Cooper, who stood by the Christmas tree. His hands tightened around her, and right then she wished she could steal away with him somewhere private and thank him properly.

"I have something for you and Burt." Finley grabbed the black jewelry pouches from beneath the tree.

Burt opened his first. "Gold nuggets?"

The boys laughed. "They're copper stones," Flint said.

"What am I supposed to do with these?" Burt looked befuddled.

"Hold them in your hands before you fall asleep at night. The copper's healing powers will help with arthritis and rheumatism."

"Thank you, Finley. It would be nice not to have any aches and pains when I wake in the morning."

"Open yours, Cooper," Tuff said.

He looked inside his bag, then stared. "It's a pink stone."

Finley laughed. "It's mangano calcite. Otherwise known as the heart crystal." She stared into Cooper's eyes, hoping he'd see that she was entrusting him with her heart.

He cleared his throat. "I was going to wait until the right moment to ask but—" he glanced at the boys and Burt "—right now is the perfect time." He grasped Finley's hands and stared into her eyes. "We haven't known each other very long, but sometimes all it takes is a look or a smile for the heart to recognize its soul mate."

Finley's eyes watered. "Cooper, I'm wearing a bathrobe."

"And you couldn't look more beautiful than you do right now."

"What's going on?" Tuff asked.

"Shh!" Burt hushed. "Cooper's asking your mom to marry him."

Ignoring the others, Cooper said, "You're the magic that's been missing from my life all these years." He squeezed her fingers. "I love you, Finley. Will you marry me?"

"Say yes, Mom!" Flint shouted.

"If Cooper marries Mom, will he be our dad?" Tuff asked Burt.

"Yep. And I'll be your grandpa," Burt said.

Tuff pushed his brother aside and patted his mother's arm. "Say yes, Mom."

Finley's heart swelled inside her chest. "I need you more than you need me," she whispered. "You keep me sane and grounded in my chaotic world."

"Young lady," Burt said, "before you give my son an answer, I want you to know that I'll be moving down the road into that newfangled retirement community. You won't have me underfoot."

Finley gasped and glanced between Burt and Cooper. "If I have anything to say about it, you're not moving into that home. This family won't work without you, Burt."

Cooper pulled Finley close and nestled his face against her neck. "How did I get so lucky to find a woman with such a generous heart?"

Finley clasped Cooper's face between her hands and stared into his eyes, which were bright with tears. "We both got lucky, Cooper." She kissed him softly on the mouth, mindful of the boys watching.

"Are you guys gonna kiss all the time now?" Tuff asked.

Cooper chuckled. "Probably."

"Yuck," Flint said.

"You caught yourself a real Christmas angel, Cooper."

"We both caught ourselves an angel, Dad."

The boys launched themselves at Cooper, knocking him backward on the floor. "It worked! It worked!" Flint shouted.

Finley laughed at their antics. "What worked?"

"The Mistletoe Magick," Flint said. "We asked Santa to bring us a dad for Christmas and he did!"

Finley raised her gaze to the ceiling, sensing Granny was smiling down on them.

"Now, if you'll excuse your mother and me, we need a moment alone." Cooper took Finley by the hand and led her downstairs, where they had more privacy. He gathered her close beneath the mistletoe. "Thank you for opening your heart to Burt and allowing him to be in our lives."

"I wouldn't have it any other way. Burt is a part of what makes you so special. We're going to be a family that stays together through good and bad. That stays together forever."

"I love you, Finley."

"And I love you, Cooper."

His mouth drew closer to Finley's, but before his lips touched hers, a knock on the back door startled them.

"Viola?" Finley said when she opened the door.

The choir director smiled sheepishly. "I'm sorry I interrupted your..." She cleared her throat, then shoved a pie at Finley. "I made a peppermint pie for you and the boys."

Finley suspected the older woman was angling for an invitation to Christmas dinner so she could spend time with Burt. "Come in out of the cold. You'll join us for Christmas dinner, won't you?"

"I don't want to impose," Viola said as she unbuttoned her coat. "Hello, Cooper."

Cooper struggled not to smile. "Mrs. Keller."

"Where is the old troublemaker?" Viola asked.

"Upstairs with the boys," he said.

Viola marched right up stairs.

"Mrs. Keller, guess what!" Finley heard Flint shout. "My mom's gonna marry Cooper and he's gonna be our dad."

"Well, now, isn't that nice," Viola said. "Merry Christmas, Burt."

"Merry Christmas, Viola. You look real pretty in that purple dress."

Finley leaned against Cooper and smiled. "Your father may not be living with us much longer."

"I'm not sure Burt can handle a woman like Viola."

"When Viola sets her mind to something, there's no

deterring her." Finley recalled the lotion the choir director had purchased and smiled.

"Our family might grow even bigger," Cooper said.

"I hope so." Finley pointed to the mistletoe above their heads and whispered as his mouth drew closer, "Merry Christmas, Cooper."

"Merry Christmas, darlin'."

* * * * *